THE FAIR COP

Hanson was now lusting openly for Flynn's body, and Flynn was taking it all in. He was quite the knowing tempter. He feasted on Hanson's gaze, pushing his hand harder and harder down the front of his trousers. His cock wasn't perceptible beneath the corduroy, but the thought of its being there was enough, for Hanson. Flynn moved his hips in a slow-motion pastiche of a fuck. His other hand went inside his half-loosened shirt. With the precision of a stripper, he undid the few bottom buttons and lifted his vest, keeping what was under it a secret. He rubbed and scratched his stomach slowly, luxuriously. Hanson got a glimpse of his hairy belly for just a second and the sight sent his heart into his mouth.

THE FAIR COP

Philip Markham

First published in Great Britain in 1999 by
Idol
an imprint of Virgin Publishing Ltd
Thames Wharf Studios,
Rainville Road, London W6 9HA

ISBN 0 352 33445 2

Cover artwork by Trademark

Typeset by SetSystems Ltd, Saffron Walden, Essex
Printed and bound in Great Britain by
Mackays of Chatham PLC

For Tim (Tom Markham),
who got me into all this.

SAFER SEX GUIDELINES

We include safer sex guidelines in every Idol book. However, while our policy is always to show safer sex in contemporary stories, we don't insist on safer sex practices in stories with historical settings – as this would be anachronistic. These books are sexual fantasies – in real life, everyone needs to think about safe sex.

While there have been major advances in the drug treatments for people with HIV and AIDS, there is still no cure for AIDS or a vaccine against HIV. Safe sex is still the only way of being sure of avoiding HIV sexually.

HIV can only be transmitted through blood, come and vaginal fluids (but no other body fluids) passing from one person (with HIV) into another person's bloodstream. It cannot get through healthy, undamaged skin. The only real risk of HIV is through anal sex without a condom – this accounts for almost all HIV transmissions between men.

Being safe

Even if you don't come inside someone, there is still a risk to both partners from blood (tiny cuts in the arse) and pre-come. Using strong condoms and water-based lubricant greatly reduces the risk of HIV. However, condoms can break or slip off, so:

* Make sure that condoms are stored away from hot or damp places.
* Check the expiry date – condoms have a limited life.
* Gently squeeze the air out of the tip.
* Check the condom is put on the right way up and unroll it down the erect cock.
* Use plenty of water-based lubricant (lube), up the arse and on the condom.
* While fucking, check occasionally to see the condom is still in one piece (you could also add more lube).

* When you withdraw, hold the condom tight to your cock as you pull out.
* Never re-use a condom or use the same condom with more than one person.
* If you're not used to condoms you might practise putting them on.
* Sex toys like dildos and plugs are safe. But if you're sharing them use a new condom each time or wash the toys well.

For the safest sex, make sure you use the strongest condoms, such as Durex Ultra Strong, Mates Super Strong, HT Specials and Rubberstuffers packs. Condoms are free in many STD (Sexually Transmitted Disease) clinics (sometimes called GUM clinics) and from many gay bars. It's also essential to use lots of water-based lube such as KY, Wet Stuff, Slik or Liquid Silk. Never use come as a lubricant.

Oral sex
Compared with fucking, sucking someone's cock is far safer. Swallowing come does not necessarily mean that HIV gets absorbed into the bloodstream. While a tiny fraction of cases of HIV infection have been linked to sucking, we know the risk is minimal. But certain factors increase the risk:
* Letting someone come in your mouth
* Throat infections such as gonorrhoea
* If you have cuts, sores or infections in your mouth and throat

So what is safe?
There are so many things you can do which are absolutely safe: wanking each other; rubbing your cocks against one another; kissing, sucking and licking all over the body; rimming – to name but a few.

If you're finding safe sex difficult, call a helpline or speak to someone you feel you can trust for support. The Terrence Higgins Trust Helpline, which is open from noon to 10pm every day, can be reached on 0171 242 1010.

Or, if you're in the United States, you can ring the Center for Disease Control toll free on 1 800 458 5231.

One

He was completely naked. He had been chained up like a dog. A whip, or it could have been a cane, had left its many signatures across his back and the cheeks of his arse. His head was shrouded in a pillowcase which, when removed, revealed a handsome, bookish young man with a rope around his neck. His expression showed no fear. Contrary to the expectation of the guardians of law and order who now stood looking at his corpse, Gregory Stein had met his maker in a state of utter bliss.

The body had not been discovered in the stereotypical way. This was not how you'd imagine it happening if your experience came from the movies or the theatre. There was no tray-dropping maid and consequently no scream on the landing; no neighbour's dog had sniffed excitedly, inexplicably interested in what lay behind a locked door. Gregory Stein's corpse had been found very easily indeed. Someone had placed a telephone call to the cops, advising them to collect the body and dispose of it.

The jovial, obese pathologist sweated over the remains, his manner showing the relish of the real connoisseur.

'Good-looking kid,' he said, as if the deceased ought to have been flattered by his words. 'It's a shame.'

The 'shame' was nothing to do with the way Stein had expired: it referred to his sexual proclivities, which were all too evident. Detective Inspector Roach snorted, not to show his contempt but because he'd forgotten his handkerchief. He pointed out they didn't require a bloody expert to give opinions on the man's looks. The pathologist was used to Roach's vitriolic manner and so he ignored it.

'Clear skin, well groomed,' he went on, more to himself than anybody else. 'He's looked after himself.'

He straightened, his voice taking on the tone he employed when he'd arrived at a conclusion. 'But then, not all these sissy types look like they're about to wither in strong sunlight. He's been dead no longer than twenty-four hours and I would hazard a guess he died from strangulation. There are no signs of a struggle. So, if you don't need me to tell you he was good-looking, you won't need me to tell you what he was about prior to meeting his maker. Could well have been forced on him of course – and suicide's a possible. But, if you want my opinion – yeah, I know, you don't, but here it is anyway – I reckon it was some weird sex game that went too far.'

Roach brightened at that. 'You mean all this – he let it be done to him – *deliberately*?'

The pathologist nodded in a matter-of-fact way. 'I've seen it before. And not just fruits either. It's amazing what some people will do to get rid of a hard-on. Which, by the way, is something this one didn't manage to do. By that I mean, whatever crazy sex thing this was, the victim died before it was fully consummated – for him at least.'

Roach was predictable in his response. According to him, messy deaths were inevitable when perversion was sanctioned by everyone on the block. 'Everyone on the block' was personified for him by the demure, quietly dissenting figure of his wife (dinner with the Roaches was not a pleasant affair unless you had a thing for Senator McCarthy's ideas of reasoned debate). His loathing of her passivity went some way to explaining his, almost permanent, foul impatience.

In Roach's book, you were either pro-vice or anti. Being anti meant you said so – often and loud. Roach read the *New York Times*: he knew a thing or two about the opinions of the 'ordinary man about town' (a mythical paragon who was under threat from the commies, the queers and the wishy-washy liberals). Roach was prepared to be drafted to fight for what was right – Armageddon was just around the corner.

Mark Hanson, new on Roach's team, was feeling distinctly uncomfortable. Roach's bigotry was hard to take; it was bad enough, even if you weren't one of the people it was directed towards. Hanson was a liberal: racial prejudice made him sick to his stomach. He was also a queer: sexual prejudice got him worried.

The pathologist left along with Hanson's 'pair', who said he was off to do some paperwork but was more likely going back to the ball game on TV. Roach took notice of Hanson for the first time. Hanson was twenty-nine and anxious to make something of himself. Listening to Roach sometimes caused him to be less anxious than he might have been.

'If the fags are getting their rocks off by killing each other, at least they're doing good for the community. What I call a fucking shame is, we have to waste public money to find who's done us this favour. I hope to God it *is* one of them and not some decent guy who's had enough of all this shit and decided to do something about it. What do you say, fella?'

It was 1954. The menace of the homosexual mafia was a favourite subject for any prophet of doom worth his salt. McCarthy might be last week's news, but only just – and his legacy lived on. Everybody and anybody went about their business followed by rumours of communist sympathies, sexual misconduct or preferably both. The list of subversives was

3

endless: government men, screenwriters and movie stars (as if they hadn't had enough trouble already) and even high-ups in the FBI.

Hanson, who had his reasons for doing so, tried to point out that, though there was good reason to suspect Stein had been queer, there was no evidence to show he'd enjoyed being murdered as much as Roach seemed to imply. Roach was having none of it. He flicked his cigarette out of the window. Hanson knew for a fact he'd rather have used the floor, but Roach was a one for protocol, even in a homo's bedroom.

Roach did not like Hanson; he didn't like anyone who was young and enjoying it. In his own early twenties, he'd been cursed by a sallow complexion, the physique of a plum duff and spots to go with it. Hanson, on the other hand, was the picture of robust health. Young Roach would have had sand kicked in his face; Hanson had the Charles Atlas seal of approval.

Roach drew himself up to his full, squat five foot six inches, pushed his hat to the back of his head and strode towards the door – he'd wasted enough time.

'No evidence, huh? Then damn well find some! I don't care where it comes from – just get it! I'm not staying here. I feel sick to my stomach. I'll take a progress report tomorrow – a.m., first thing, my office.'

The door slammed behind him and there was a silence in the room for a full thirty seconds. The cop who'd been first on the scene and had now been assigned to baby-sit the corpse flashed Hanson a nervous smile.

Hanson didn't respond, mainly because his mind had suddenly been taken up with appreciating how handsome this officer was. He checked these lustful thoughts. The cop was hefty enough, but he was a subordinate colleague. Anyway, despite his impressive bulk, the cop was too young for someone Hanson's age to hope for. They say that when police start looking young it's time to worry. Hanson guessed this 'youngster' to be maybe twenty-two or three. OK, so at twenty-nine, he wasn't so much older himself, but the few years he had on the other man contained a lifetime of wisdom and experience. At least, that's the way it seemed to Hanson.

The officer appeared to take Hanson's blank face to mean he'd gone off-limits by smiling at a superior. He returned his face to a serious frown. Hanson would rather have had the smile, but the frown had its endearing qualities too, so it would do for now.

Hanson was now studying the younger man's face, supposedly for signs of insubordination. It was an even, symmetrical face with a satisfying ruggedness around the jawline. It was showing signs of discomfort now. There was a fleeting blush and a trickle of sweat on that broad, flat brow. Hanson thought this to be just fine. It confirmed his own superiority, which was satisfying, but it also made him feel protective. This feeling was not a million miles away from his original feeling of lust. (Hanson would have preferred to call it 'romance'. Hanson liked romance: he was in love with the idea of being in love).

He tried to stop speculating as to what kind of a power-packed chest was hidden under that smart, blue shirt and did his very best not to meet the cop's eye any more. This wasn't too easy – the man was quite a looker – but it had to be done. Drooling over colleagues was a definite 'no-no'. Cops weren't queer; getting the hots for one was plain stupid.

There was always the option of taking a junior colleague under his wing and looking after him – just buddies. Hanson could set this ball rolling by suggesting they have coffee together when they were done. There was every chance the officer might accept.

He might have a date with his girl of course – or, worse, bring her along with him. Hanson had already got this man down as a sucker for the gum-chewing broad with bigger breasts than she could walk straight with and no brains at all. This prejudice was not Hanson's fault: he had been raised in New Jersey, where the whole world was a cliché.

The two men were physical opposites. The younger guy was far more the brawny, rugged and square-jawed American than Hanson would ever be. Hanson was lithe and fit, not an ounce of wasted flesh on him. If they had been sportsmen, the young cop would have been a ball player and Hanson an athlete. Hanson wondered what he was like out of uniform. He looked as if his powerful body was bursting out of this one. For himself (he didn't wear uniform), Hanson was always careful in the way he dressed: trousers neatly pressed; shoes you could see your face in. He'd once been accused of sporting 'effeminate neckwear'. Hanson was no sissy, but he was clean-cut and he was particular.

He expected Henry Flynn (as the cop turned out to be called) to be a sloppy dresser and the thought appealed. Hanson liked the look of a man who hadn't bothered to shave.

In the normal run of things he wouldn't have even thought of sex at a time like this but sex was right there in the room with them. The pathologist and Roach were more than likely correct in their assumptions: Gregory Stein had died because of it. Lethal though it might turn out to be, sex could not be ignored.

Hanson looked around the room trying to appear as though he knew what he was about. In order to give this action its full effect, he lit a cigarette and stroked his chin thoughtfully. Officer Flynn might have been impressed, but if he was he didn't show it. He fixed his eyes on the ceiling so as to avoid another *faux pas*. Hanson risked patting him on the shoulder – a precursor to taking him under his wing. He had the impression of his being a trainer with some great, lumbering, handsome animal.

'Not the best,' he said in a tone that suggested vast experience. 'Is it your first stiff?'

'Sir!'

Hanson wasn't sure if this was a 'yes' or a 'no'. He didn't pursue it: despite his obvious physical strength, the poor guy was nervous enough. The after-work coffee was increasingly unlikely. A pity really – if they'd started off on a different footing, Stein's case would have provided a natural opener to a certain kind of conversation. It wouldn't have been too difficult to find out if Flynn was interested and maybe Hanson might have discovered what he had lurking in his Y-fronts.

Hanson stopped himself. He was doing it again. He must remember, thick-set muscle did not come wrapped in pink paper: cops were never fags.

The photographers had come in by this time. They were busy recording the brutal scene for posterity. As they clicked away Hanson took in the late Mr Stein's scholarly looks and mused on the injustice of things. Stein's aquiline features and large, dark eyes reminded Hanson of an ex-boyfriend from years ago. He thanked God the vile Inspector Roach had at least kept anti-Semitism out of his rantings. Presumably, he thought, Stein's sexual proclivities were an easier target for prejudiced assholes than his family background.

The other people present were not behaving any better than Roach had. Nobody seemed to think the case was worth investigating. They were performing their duties for the record, but dead homosexuals – of whatever race – were not anything for them to lose sleep over. Hanson tried to blank out their ribald comments and began searching through the mess that covered Stein's desk.

Stein had done his damnedest to be a novelist. If life had been kinder to him he might have made mediocre; as it was he had failed with a capital F. For some people afflicted with an artistic calling, living in a damp room over a diner would be an artistic thing. This said, there was 'artistic' and there was 'artistic' – and this place was a dump!

Under the desk there were several copies of Stein's one and only published work. It was a trashy novel in which the boy hero finds true happiness in his relationship with a Dalmatian dog. Hanson had only to glance at a paragraph or two to make his critical assessment. Had he not met his end in the way he had, it would not have been likely Hanson would ever have heard Gregory Stein's name. Still, the pile of unsold copies all bore the author's photograph and these pictures might prove useful later on.

There was a battered cardboard box under the bed. It was empty but for the torn back page of some sex magazine. There was a line drawing of a naked youth being buggered by a hefty-looking man in motorcycle leathers. Hanson whistled. This kind of stuff was definitely not legal. From the way this crumpled piece of paper was stuck to the bottom of the box, it looked like it was all that remained of a pile of magazines which someone had removed. Either Stein had a discreet friend who had taken away the incriminating evidence after his death, or, like lots of queers, he had got scared at some point and dumped the stuff himself.

Further into the room was Stein's desk. There was a page resting on top of the carriage of the typewriter. It was blank but Hanson was diligent enough to examine it anyway. Sure enough, there were indentations: the paper had been used to cushion the impact of the hammers against the roller.

Hanson was intrigued to find the familiar words of a nursery rhyme:

Peter, eter, um kin eater,
Ha a wife an coul n' kee her,
He ut her in a umkin shell,
   And there he ke t her very well.

His instant reaction was to assume the verse represented something sinister. Crime fiction had a lot to answer for where Hanson was concerned. It was possible, even probable, the verse meant nothing at all, but that wouldn't be half so interesting. He resisted the temptation to try to decode the gaps: it was obvious they represented nothing more than uneven typing. He searched through the desk drawer to see if there were any more cryptic messages. There was one: a note that read 'Call Boy Blue – Tuesday'.

He noticed that the cop – Flynn – was following his movements very closely. This made Hanson preen (at first): the guy obviously looked up to him. He may even be thinking Hanson was the sort he could emulate – an old hand he might be proud of having for a buddy. Then he came down to earth. It was bullshit: the cop was bored, he'd been standing around all day with no one but a corpse to talk to.

Hanson carried on with his work, but he was now playing a part for Flynn's benefit. He broke off briefly to say, 'You looked through all these things when you arrived on the scene, yes?'

Flynn denied this. He'd waited, as good cops should, for his superiors to arrive before he'd so much as touched anything. This was a lie and both men knew it was a lie, but it was said and accepted as the truth because that was the way of things.

The photographers had finished and the men had arrived to convey Stein to the city morgue. Hanson nodded his assent and watched respectfully as they carted the body out. He didn't bother to extinguish the cigarette. He somehow felt the deceased wouldn't have minded and, even if he would, the deceased was in no position to argue.

When Stein's mortal remains were safely on their way, Flynn moved in close behind Hanson's shoulder. Now he was with the living instead of the dead, it seemed he didn't consider he need stand like a soldier on parade any more. Had he been less of a beefcake, Hanson might have questioned this presumption, but the proximity of the cop's unattainable body was thrilling – all the more so because he was not up for grabs. Flynn was a great pet dog of a man, fetchingly eager to be of help, deferential and entirely unashamed of his morbid interest.

'I guess they'll have to cut him open and look at what he's made of. Do you think so, sir? He must have croaked while he was having sex. I guess you come across a lot of these fairy types, do you? It makes you wonder who else is going around looking at other men.'

His enthusiastic interest was too stilted to be believed. Maybe he was feeling nauseous and felt he ought to cover it.

Hanson was, despite everything, just as susceptible to propaganda as the next man. To him, a homosexual who dies in mysterious circumstances could not have been a good American. He already had Stein marked out as Public Enemy Number One. He was looking for secret codes, wads of roubles, photographs of the late lamented Joe Stalin – anything.

He had been holding something in his hand – something he'd picked up just before Flynn had interrupted him. He was about to discard it.

'Well, what d'you know?' Flynn said in a voice that suggested he had already earlier made the discovery for himself and was covering his tracks. 'That's lucky, isn't it, sir? The poor bastard kept a diary.'

Two

_____

It was just a large manuscript notebook. The months of the year (cut-outs from another source) had been pasted on little marker slips sticking out of the top. A label had been gummed on to the front with the word 'DIARY' written across in large capitals.

Hanson opened the book at January. The pages were completely covered with a close, precise script which showed the fussy personality responsible for it. Unusually for a diary, there were many alterations. Some of them appeared pretty major. It seemed Stein had been keen to get his prose just so, even when he was likely to be the only person who was going to look at the thing.

As soon as Hanson started reading, he knew he was going to have fun with this piece of evidence. What he was glancing at was hot stuff. He knew Flynn was still looking at him, watching his reactions, checking out his efficiency. Those reactions were not exactly for public display right now. He turned his back and focused on the writing. This is what he read:

JANUARY

I met him on New Year's day. I should have been at synagogue that morning and I'd missed for the first time in I don't know when. It just had to be an omen.

I'll call him Billy, but that wasn't his name. Twenty-six and packed with iron — he was, as they say, my type of guy. Later, I found out he took good care of his physique. Apart from all the good his job of work must have done for his body, he went swimming twice a week. Also, he played sports with some other fellas — fellas he said who would sure interest me.

His job was menial. He tended the gardens of those who couldn't be bothered to do it for themselves. That's what he was — a gardener — but I chose to see him as an ex-soldier boy, which he also was. Army guys are such easy picking. Most of them pretend to be normal, and some of them might be, but it doesn't mean they're not willing to pitch for the other side occasionally.

I'd found him in Marco's Bar and it was one of the quickest come-ons since Delilah snared Samson. I was surprised none of the other queens had got to him before me — he looked as though he'd been waiting for ever and a day. Maybe they were all still boozed-up from last night's celebrations.

Or maybe he only went for lookers — which, let it be said, is not the usual way of things. Most of America's finest will stick their dicks into any hole that's available, whether it belongs to man, woman or beast. They're not at all bothered about what they might have to look at while they do it.

I was in the front of the line when God issued faces and I don't give a shit for those who think I should pretend not to know it. I'm twenty-two (twenty-three this March — Jesus! How time flies!), dark hair and doe eyes of the most seductive brown. I have a slim body which I like to flatter by wearing a white shirt tucked into narrow-waisted pants. Sure, on this particular occasion I was wrapped up against the cold but I have a kind of crooked smile which seemed to be enough to interest Billy.

I live just a few blocks from Marco's Bar. I knew I had some bourbon left over from Christmas, so Billy and I went back to my place.

When I'd lit the gas and pulled the curtains, Billy changed his tune. In the bar room, he'd been giving out as though he was the good time to be had by all. You know: joking and laughing, you'd think he'd balled every whore in Harlem. Now we were alone he went all serious on me. He just sort of – well – melted onto the bed like he was Miss Leigh and he wanted me to be Brando. (I've been to that movie five times and I still haven't tired of it.)

I wasn't having that. He was a real hunk and I'd brought him back with the intention of getting my ass fucked. I wasn't so happy about having to do all the work. I looked at him and tried to figure out a way of getting round the problem.

He was pretending to be fast asleep, but I knew he wasn't for real because he'd only just fallen onto the bed. Still, he looked extremely appealing lying there. He had a slight auburn touch to his hair. If he'd been a real fairy, I would have accused him of dyeing it, but I believed his earlier pose (that he usually fucked with women) and, like all straight men, he must surely be a stranger to artifice. His eyes were green and his mouth was small. It was set in a permanent pout like a kid's.

I liked his skin: it was creamy, porcelain-doll skin. 'It clothed the bulges of his arms, making gentle mounds of solid power'. There! That's poetry for you, and it's not even nearly the cocktail hour!

I supposed the same could be said of his chest and shoulders but I hadn't been given the pleasure of knowing that yet: he'd taken his jacket and sweater off but he was waiting for me to deal with his shirt and undershirt.

I put my hand on his leg. He was wearing pants made of truly ghastly, coarse fabric which I loved to bits. They were a manly choice. To hell with elegance – 'manly' gets my vote every time.

He gave out a sigh and stretched his hands above his head. Oh well, I thought, I might as well see what he has hidden beneath the *wrapping. I undid the buttons on his shirt. He let me without even bothering to move.*

It's good to see a man in just his undershirt. It is, I think, a dandy piece of clothing: not too revealing, but skimpy enough to show the potential of the chest it's covering. I don't even mind string ones, though some queers think they're a bit common. Billy had on a tight-fitting cotton undershirt and, yes, his shoulders were like sculpted marble. He had tufts of reddish-brown hair under his arms. The sight of them made me want to push my tongue into his pits and lick the sweat. If I'd had known then what turned Billy on, I would have done it. I ran my hand over that cushioned flesh and I swear to God he purred.

His nipples were prominent under the cotton. I held back from going right ahead and sucking on them. This Mary was worth taking time over.

As I'd hoped, he had a bit of hair on his chest, but it wasn't too much, just a nice covering – something to stroke, something to kiss. I got astride him and unbuttoned my own shirt hoping he'd show a bit of enthusiasm for my body. After all, I'm much sought-after – just because Billy wasn't a fag didn't mean he wasn't about to appreciate the charms of a handsome guy.

Not a flicker!

I supposed he was just for being jerked off. I doubted he'd want me to screw him – straight guys aren't keen on having their butts invaded. It didn't matter anyway. I had made up my mind: he was going to fuck me.

I made him sit up while I got him fully out of his shirt. His body was absolutely limp – not a porcelain doll now: a rag one. Just my goddamn luck, I thought. As the hateful Conrad at Jack's Place always says, 'Bread and bread don't ever work. You have to have the sockets and you have to have the plugs, otherwise you might as well read fairy stories to him – at least they end happy.' (Connie doesn't care if she mixes her metaphors!)

I lay down next to Billy and tried to have him hug me close. He showed me his back and pulled my arms around him so we made

14

spoons. Was this the action of Mr Right? I should think not indeed! I started to get just a little bit annoyed.

'I guess you're just not into guys after all,' I said.

He opened his eyes and turned his head a bit toward me. Apart from that he didn't move so I ended up talking mostly to his back.

'If you're one of those straight boys,' I went on, 'don't you think you ought to get on with what you're supposed to do? I know the routine: you spill your spunk over me, knock me about a bit to show you didn't enjoy it and then vanish into the night.'

He smiled and, I must admit, it made my heart throb to see him do it. He had one of those faces you dream about. He was pretty, but not so pretty he looked like a girl. He'd been roughed up a bit: he had an even covering of stubble all over his chin and upper lip; his nose had a few freckles on it, and those eyes! It was like having a puppy looking up at you – except I've never seen a puppy with green eyes. What the heck – you know what I mean: big haunting eyes with a lot of sadness there. It made you want to hold him close and tell him everything was OK.

But everything wasn't OK so I kept my face stern and cross.

'I didn't say I was straight,' he said.

Of course – that was it! He was a bisexual! Connie would call him a bicycle (C. has a wit which is truly awesome). I'd come across his sort before (the pun is not intended). They like to stick their cocks into women but, when they go with another man, they expect him to treat them like they're made of gossamer.

In short, he wasn't going to be a whole lot of good to me.

'If you want cock up your backside, you'd best go back to the bar and pay some hustler like the rest of us have to,' I said.

'Is that what you want me to do?' came the reply.

The truth of it was, I didn't know. I was smitten – for sure I was – but it was no use being smitten if he couldn't give me what I wanted, and what I wanted was his dick. I decided to have a look at it before I made any major decisions. I unbuttoned his pants – he just watched me. He was – kind of – concentrating: as though he was just as curious about what was in there as I was.

I had to lift his hips up to get the pants down to his knees. He let me without resisting. His shorts were clean, thank God! They aren't always, believe me! I noticed his cock was only just waking up. I could see it uncurling under the cloth. Even semihard, it was massive.

I pulled up his undershirt so I could see his stomach. It didn't disappoint me. It was fabulous and flat with a tempting spray of hair starting at his belly-button, spreading as it reached the waistband of his shorts. I guessed there would be a real forest underneath: enough to plunge my face into.

I eased his shorts down but kept his dick covered, I wanted to tease him a bit. Sure enough, his pubes were wonderful: all thick and dense. I pushed my nose into them and got that musky smell of maleness that sends me half crazy with lust. I inhaled as deeply as I could and kissed the place were his dick was. It twitched inside the lovely white cotton. The time had come to say hello to it.

It was uncut and just as I like it: oozing with fluid. Even if the rest of the encounter didn't match up to my expectations, it was going to be worth it just for this. I pushed the thick, moist monster into my mouth and sucked as though my life depended on it. Billy lay back on the pillows. His hands reached to the sides of my head and he kneaded my skin with his fingers. He was loving it.

I didn't want him to come so I was mindful of any telltale signs. I know them all: an alteration to the rhythm of his breathing; the way he might tighten his belly; a throbbing in his cock, so slight you might miss it unless you know how boys work. Billy just relaxed and enjoyed. At least I'd hit on something to do where both of us could enjoy being passive in our own way.

He was ever so slightly sweaty down below. I like the smell of sweat. It's a big turn-on. It's the smell of manliness you never get from queens. I don't like fairies who look and smell like women; I like real men. Billy was the sort I could really go for. I'm not stupid enough to think he would have felt the same way about me. Straights and bisexuals aren't for keeps. The best you can hope for is a constant supply of different ones, not one alone who'll be your Red Shadow and let you walk off into the desert sands with him.

'*That's nice,*' *he said after a while.* '*Can I do it to you?*'

I said he could for sure. I lay back all ready for a whole lot of nothing – there was just no way he was going to be any good at it.

I just had my pants on, nothing else. I'd chucked my shirt and undershirt earlier. It's worth mentioning as well that, though I know it's not exactly good manners, I wasn't wearing underwear. I like the feeling of my cock swinging loose against my pants. It's particularly nice when it starts to get hard – you feel the air around it and you have all sorts of secret tinglings without the guy you're talking to in the bar having any idea what effect he's having on your nether regions.

Billy rolled over on top of me and surprised me by kissing. I don't mean I didn't like it: it was just not what you expect from a regular hard-working guy, not even one who's into other men. Punks do not kiss. I know – it's a bad attitude, but it's all mine and I can't help it. First it was just a light brushing of his lips against my cheek. Next came harder, more meaningful kisses. Then he pushed those cute pouting lips over mine and forced my mouth open so he could put his tongue into me.

I found my arms going round him, my cock going rock-solid and my poor heart not knowing where it was. I was in danger of falling for this one and I'd have to watch it. We were like two hungry men given their first meal in days – sucking, tonguing – lips, teeth, gums, faces. I wanted to eat him all up and it seemed he felt the same way about me. Any fears about having wasted my time vanished completely. This motherfucker was about as virile as they come.

You can't keep that kind of thing going for ever, more's the pity. After a long, long time, Billy broke off in order to come up for air. He smiled at me and lay there, panting slightly and running his hands through my floppy black hair.

I liked him doing this: it meant he appreciated me. Nearly all the butch he-men find my little-boy-lost look attractive. I may wear my hair too long – I get called names in the street often enough and my mother keeps going on about how much nicer I looked after I'd been drafted – but those same hoodlums who shout at me go all gooey once

I get them into the sack. (I don't give a flying fuck what my mother thinks, poor bitch.)

'I thought you were going to blow me,' I said. I was ready for it, I was going crazy for it.

'I am,' he said. 'Be patient.'

He let his hand slide down from the top of my head and, with his finger, traced the line of my eyebrows and down my nose, along my lips and back again. It was affectionate and that is not something I'm at all used to. Who'd taught him to do this? I wondered. He carried on, down my neck and to the front of my chest.

I don't have any hair there and if I did I'd shave it off. I like the feel of my skin as it is. It's like satin and there isn't so much as a blemish on it. I have big, brown nipples: smooth, no teats to speak of. (Not that I mind teats, but I don't feel deprived not having them.) Billy seemed to like my nipples. He kept circling them with his finger. Then he leaned up and put his lips against them.

It was a funny feeling. It felt warm in my stomach, which is not at all where I expected to have the sensation. This warmth spread as he got going with the suction. By the time he brought his teeth into play, I was stiff as a poker and about as pliable as a charmed snake. I had my eyes tight shut and my hands on each of his shoulders. I knew I was digging my fingernails into his skin, but he didn't seem to mind. The gentle nipping on my tit was one of the most wonderful feelings I had ever had. This was better than a quick fuck up against the wall in some back alley. This was making love – for the first time, I understood why the straights called it that.

When he'd sent me half mad with what he'd done to one nipple, he went over to the other. He licked his way across, not leaving off contact with my chest at all. I relaxed for a second or two while he was in transit and then tensed all over as his lips found their target. He wasn't teething it yet, just licking. He brought his hands up to the back of my neck and massaged the muscle there, breaking off momentarily in order to say, 'Relax, I haven't even started.'

I tried to do as I was told but I felt like I was wired and, relaxed or not, I was in seventh heaven.

'Do they do this sort of thing in your neighborhood?' I asked. It was meant to be a light question – a little joke to alleviate the intensity. After all, we were only two guys out for a bit of fun. It was supposed to be musical comedy, not grand opera. I wanted to stay in control.

He put the flat of his hand over my mouth to shut me up. I would have objected but I liked it too much. At the same time, his teeth started to do their work. I floated off into another place as the warm feeling rose up in my belly and grew bigger and bigger inside me. I was enjoying the strong smell of my saliva on his hand. He was in control of me; I could relax and enjoy my he-man.

He was nibbling away, sending short, exquisite bursts of pleasure through my body. All of a sudden he bit into me properly. It hurt like hell and I hollered. Of course it was only a muffled yell because he still had his hand clapped over my mouth. He pressed it harder against my face and bit me again.

It was strange but I didn't mind. Yes, it hurt, but the hurt had almost become an extension of the pleasure. It was like a love bite. Once you've had so much ecstasy, pain is the only place to go. I cried out again, but with much less conviction. Billy pulled his head away and smiled at me. His hand did not leave my mouth.

'You want it rough?' he said.

I could not bring myself to simply agree. After all, I wasn't sure just how rough he had in mind. I stayed where I was, staring at him and beginning to feel a bit ridiculous – what with his hand covering half my face.

His other hand traced a line down the front of my chest, down to my belly-button. He poked his finger into the crevice and pressed hard. It didn't hurt but it kind of worried me.

'You've got a choice,' Billy said eventually. 'Either you can fuck me and we can say our fond farewells, or you can learn some new games that I think you'll like. I wonder, are you brave enough?'

He drew his hand away to allow me to answer. I was excited: he knew it because he could see my cock responding – like his voice was an electrical impulse and my dick had been all connected up to it. I had *about as much control over my own penis as a dog over its tail when it hears 'walk'.*

'Are you saying you do weird stuff?' was all I could think of to say. It sounded such a silly question. Even if he got his rocks off by swinging from the chandelier, what did I care? (As long as he didn't have a thing for the recently deceased: I didn't fancy being found in bits under the floorboards.)

'Yes,' he said. He was smiling pleasantly. I couldn't picture him as dangerous. But then, I don't suppose dangerous people ever actually look scary. What the heck! At least he was being honest with me.

'What do you want to do?' I asked.

'I want you to imagine that I own you. I want you to do exactly as you're told, like you were a freshman being initiated into my fraternity; even down to giving me your ass if I decide I want it. I want you to serve me.'

His voice was deeper than it had been. I could tell that just thinking about what he was going to do was turning him on. I confess it did a whole lot of something for me too. I had not been to college and I'd had an easy ride in the army, which remains a disappointment to me to this day. The thought of having some strapping guy from the house – or squad – elite giving my ass what for with his cock is truly delicious. I was even interested when I heard about canings and other such punishments. Billy had touched on something in me that I had never previously thought to consider.

'I don't want to get hurt,' I lied, just in case he was planning on doing me permanent damage.

He smiled again. He stroked my face with the dry part of his hand and then turned it around and wiped my own spit onto my skin. A transaction had taken place between us: from that moment there was no way at all I was going to miss this experience.

'I might hurt you a bit,' Billy said. *'But I swear to God you'll enjoy every moment.'*

He got off the bed and went to piss. I listened to the loud stream splashing into the john and waited for the flush. I still had my pants on and I was wondering whether to take them off. Billy came back into

20

the room and stood in the doorway, naked and magnificent. I noticed a subtle change in his attitude. He was playing a part now – I knew it and I thrilled at it.

'What are you waiting for, punk?' he said. I felt a lump coming up to my throat. I wasn't sure what he wanted me to do so I just stayed there, waiting for instructions.

'I've just pissed. If you don't flush it away I'll ram your fucking head into it.'

Of course this was part of the game and seeing as I was still fresh at it, I messed up by protesting.

'Now hold it right there! I'm not sure I want –'

He strode over to me and gave my face a smack. It wasn't meant to sting and it didn't. It was just to put me in my place and let me know that from now on I was to do as I was told. I caught on pretty quickly, but he underlined the point just in case I hadn't.

'You're my pledge, boy. You do as you're fucking told and you don't give me any cheek about it! You flush that john or you get to drink everything that's in there. Do you understand?'

I nodded and was about to go and do as I had been instructed. The nod had not been good enough.

'When I address you, creep, you answer me and you call me "sir"! You get it?'

'Yes, sir,' I answered.

Though I felt a bit like crying, I knew I was loving every minute of this. I went into the bathroom and noticed I did it with my head bowed like I was in disgrace. I flushed his piss away and came back, still with my head down. I stood near to him with my hands clasped in front of me, respectful: waiting for him to tell me what he wanted from me.

'Kneel!' he ordered at last. I did as I was told willingly but at the same time feeling a bit of a fool. Strangely, even feeling stupid gave me a buzz. Billy must have known this because he made it even worse for me.

'I'm going to make you lick my feet. While you're doing it, you're going to put your hands on top of your head to show what a good little slave you are. I want you to clean all the shitty, sweaty, black bits from

between my toes. That's all you're worth because you're nothing but a creep. Isn't that right?'

His voice had changed again. It was slicker than it had been. He was playing the college boy. I hadn't a clue why it made my heart race to hear him talking like that. I did exactly as he said and set to work on his feet with my tongue.

I really tried to make a good job of it: going underneath and all round, swallowing down any bits of shit that had lodged there and licking everything as though I was his dog. All this time I kept my hands on my head.

It made me remember something which happened a long time ago when I was a kid. I'd done something wrong at school and the teacher said I was to be strapped for it. As was the routine, I went to the principal's study and, shamefaced, asked him for the strap and punishment book (the black ledger where all beatings and the reasons for them were recorded). I then had to carry this – and the thick leather strap – all the way down the corridor. I passed other kids who started whispering as soon as I'd overtaken them. It was absolute humiliation and far worse than the three or four licks I got for spilling ink or whatever it was I'd done.

This was the same. I was being humiliated in the same way. Even though there was only Billy there to watch, his presence was quite enough to make me humble.

There was nothing of the shrinking violet about him now. He was just about as powerful and masculine as I could have possibly hoped for. He lifted his feet so I could get my lips and tongue to the back, but otherwise he didn't make things any easier for me. He stood there without showing if he was enjoying it or not. He told me I was a pig, a slave, a filthy whore and all manner of other things. I revelled in it.

Either I'd finished my job or Billy had become bored with what I was doing to him. He told me to stop. I was to sit up but keep my hands on my head. He knelt in front of me and examined my face again just like he had done earlier: tracing the line of my features with the tip of his finger. Before it had been gentle and loving; now it had a hint of threat about it. He was deciding what to do with me next. After

22

a few moments of this, he unbuttoned my flies and laid the flaps of material aside to expose my pubes.

'Little fucker,' he murmured (though he made it sound like a compliment). 'You're not wearing any shorts. Well, that's a pity. I wouldn't let you keep them on of course, but it would have been fun to rip them off you. I think you deserve punishing for that, don't you?'

I didn't answer quickly enough. I think I nodded, but of course that wasn't the response he wanted. He slapped me across the face and gripped my chin hard with his fingers. It hurt, but it had the effect he obviously intended: I was forced to look him in the face.

When our eyes met, he spat at me – I mean really spat – loads of it, right into my face. It went in my eyes and ran down my cheek. Some of it ended up on my lips and I wondered if I was supposed to lick it off. Nobody had ever done such a thing to me before and, yes, I was still loving all this and wanting more.

'I said, you deserve punishing, don't you?' he repeated. I got it right this time.

'Yes, sir,' I answered.

I even flatter myself I'd put my voice in the right register: kind of respectful and humble. Like I was thankful for being given permission to speak, even though it was only to confirm I deserved a belting.

'Right,' Billy says. 'Get your ass over the bed. Spread your arms out and keep your face down. I don't want you wriggling or trying to protect yourself. You're to stay still and take your beating like a man. Do you understand, shitface?'

'Yes, sir,' I said again.

I expected him to take my pants down, but he didn't. Once I was in the position, (and feeling I'd walk through fire if this man told me to), he came and sat by the side of me. He started by gently stroking the seat of my pants. I wasn't sure if I wanted him to do that. I was impatient to have him beat me.

'You're going to have your butt licked with my belt,' he said. 'It's going to get really sore and you're going to take it. I'm going to train you like I've trained other boys before you. By the time I'm finished with you, you'll be obedient enough, and worthy enough, to lick my *ass. That's the most you can hope for, scumbag. You set your sights on being anything more than that, like a human being for example, and I'll lash your back with a horsewhip until you cry for mercy. You think about that when I'm beating you. Remember how you deserve every mark I lay on your ass because you're nothing more than a piece of shit. What are you?'*

'A piece of shit, sir,' I repeated.

'Good.'

He said this quietly like a doctor might who was checking the patient was good and ready for the scalpel. Then he stood up. I couldn't see him, but I could hear him taking off the belt from his trousers. Even today I get a boner when I hear that sound. I can get myself hard just by looking at some young guy wearing a belt around baggy corduroys.

I wanted to watch but I had been told to keep my head down and I wasn't about to try being awkward. (Though if I had, I guess I'd have gotten extra punishment and that didn't seem like it was too bad a thing to have happen to me.)

Billy trailed the leather across my buttocks. It didn't hurt and it wasn't supposed to. This was just a warning – something to make me concentrate on what was to come later and also to unnerve me. It succeeded in its first intent but failed in its second. I wanted him to give it to me as hard and as ruthlessly as he could. I even raised my pelvis off the bed a bit so as to make the target more easily available. He scoffed when I did this, but it got the desired result. The belt came swishing through the air and landed on my ass with a dull crack.

As I said before, my pants weren't all that thick. The belt cut through them easily, giving me a real sting which tingled after the initial impact and then faded into a glow across my backside. I don't think I moved or made any sort of sound. Not then at any rate.

The next one followed hard after the first. This was a bit more painful because it landed in part where I was already sore. I bucked a little but I was able to take it easily enough. Billy saw my movement and checked it by standing astride my legs and leaning over with his hand on the small of my back. In this way, he kept me firmly in place while he laid three or four more stripes across my butt. The fact that he was physically keeping me down made me fight against him. This effort, though it was pretty futile, helped me to deal with the stinging cuts. He didn't seem to mind my half-hearted protest and his hand was strong enough to cope with it.

'I don't believe you can feel anything through these pants,' he said. And with that, in one swift movement, he yanked my pants down to my ankles. He tore them a bit in the process but he didn't seem to be bothered and I wasn't about to complain.

There I was, practically buck naked (I still had my socks on and, though my pants had been taken down, they were still bunched around my feet). I felt his hand wander around the sensitive area he had been abusing. Then he carried on whipping my ass.

The strokes varied. Some were really hard and some even made me wish he'd stop. Others were quite gentle and wouldn't have hurt at all if it weren't that my skin was quickly becoming inflamed. He sometimes attacked the inside of my thighs; he made me spread my legs so he could get to them.

I felt I wanted to weep, but tears just wouldn't come. It wasn't that I felt at all sad or sorry for myself. It just seemed to be the thing I wanted to do. I think Billy would have allowed it.

After five minutes or so of this treatment, the belt started not to hurt so much. I wondered if he'd beaten me numb or whether I had just gotten used to it and my pain threshold had gone up. I could hear the sound of the leather hitting my skin and I could feel a tingle each time it made contact, but I was finding it more and more pleasurable.

I could feel my dick, squashed in between my body and the mattress of my bed – I tell you, it was hard as rock and ready to spill its juice just as soon as it was allowed. If I'd had any doubts about letting Billy thrash me, my erection would have answered them.

As if to have me learn this lesson for keeps, Billy gave me a real cracker. It made me moan out loud. In response to this, Billy lay right on top of me and put his hand against my mouth again. I licked it for what seemed like forever and then I licked it some more.

He kissed the back of my neck and stayed there for a moment or *two, after which he kissed me again and, using his old voice, he said, really softly, 'Thanks.'*

My beating was over.

Hanson put the pages down. Flynn had been trying to see what he was reading but a glance had warned him off. Hanson wasn't ready to be put in a position where this sort of stuff might end by being discussed between them.

'I'm going to piss,' Hanson said. He wasn't sure of it, but he thought he saw Flynn give a knowing smile.

The owner of the diner had invited them to make use of his toilet facilities. Hanson stood in the cubicle for some minutes. Maybe Flynn had known that he didn't want to piss at all: he wanted to do something about his hard cock. It felt very responsive. The skin seemed smoother than usual, the head more sensitive. It was the way his cock usually felt when he wanted to come and he was prevented from doing it. He rubbed himself briefly and then stopped. It would be a shame to shoot his load in these shabby surroundings. It would be better to go back to his apartment and enjoy a leisurely half-hour of self-abuse.

He flushed the bowl to make it look like he'd been in there for the intended purpose. Thanking the obsequious owner, who was waiting the other side of the door, he went back to the scene of the crime.

He padded up the stairs quietly. He had some thought in the back of his mind that he was going to catch Flynn out. This was not reasonable and not fair. Hanson knew this but wasn't going to let it trouble him.

He opened the door swiftly and silently. Flynn's wide shoulders were bent over the desk. His ass was projected temptingly, his trousers looked as though they'd been painted on, and his waist was narrow enough to suspect him of a corset. He straightened up quickly and pretended to be coughing.

He had not been quick enough: Hanson had seen him. Flynn

had been reading the diary and his hand was obviously and significantly rammed down the front of his trousers. It may have been wishful thinking, but Hanson had a fancy he had deliberately intended to be caught like that. He didn't seem nearly embarrassed enough. In fact, his look appeared to be challenging Hanson to do something about what he'd just discovered.

Hanson smiled. He was in with a chance.

Three

'Not exactly in the Samuel Pepys league, is it?'

Hanson wasn't kidding himself: he was doing a poor imitation of Roach and he knew it. He found the cop sexy and, when a sexy cop provokes you, what can you do but get hostile? He would push it just far enough to make the lovely lad squirm.

Remorse was absent from Flynn's expression and Hanson had an urge to put it there. If Flynn had been plug-ugly, Hanson would have overlooked his misdemeanour – a reprimand and call it forgotten. As the guy had the nerve to look like L'il Abner and behaved as though he could read every dirty thought in Hanson's head, damn it, he'd have to pay the price.

Sure, Flynn was still being nicely deferential and he hadn't gone so far over the line he couldn't be brought back, but if that was his idea of eating humble pie, Hanson wanted him to try a bigger slice.

There was ever that knowing look in Flynn's eye – a look that meant something to Hanson – and it unnerved him. This guy knew how to act the innocent but at the same time he was challenging Hanson to come clean and cut the crap.

Flynn removed his hand from the incriminating place where it had been. He blushed, a disarming habit on one so powerful. It had to be genuine and it would have melted the heart of stronger men than Hanson.

'Sorry, sir,' he said. 'I was just looking at what he wrote here.'

'Fancy yourself as a detective, do you?'

Hanson used the same heavy sarcasm that he loathed in his own superior. He didn't want to be a bastard but had little choice: sarcasm was the only weapon he could call upon. Flynn was certainly too desirable to sit down and level with. Hanson's 'pair' was a thin and balding detective who had a skin condition. Just as well, he thought. If he looked like the guys in uniform, I would never be able to concentrate on my work.

'Sorry, sir,' repeated Flynn. Then his pretence at respect flew out of the window and he stepped so far out of line he almost lost his place in the queue.

'The dirty fucker was having it all ways, wouldn't you say? I wonder how he set about getting people to do those things to him.'

Hanson could easily have demonstrated how this might be done but he thought better of it. He wanted to get out of this place. He told Flynn to have the room secured; after that, he was to stand guard in the corridor as penance for his sins. Flynn took this instruction without complaint.

Hanson asked him what time he was to be relieved of duty.

'Half after five,' he replied brightly. 'Only another hour.' Then, knowingly, 'Why do you ask, sir?'

'No reason.'

Hanson would have gone home, jerked off and eventually forgotten all about the beefy cop. He knew his interest was dangerously near to obsession because he'd read serious, psychological studies on the state of being a queer. There were two main sorts of homosexual male: the sex invert (he has make-up, dyed hair, whining voice and a powder puff in the shoulder bag), and the bisexual, sometimes called pervert (he often looks normal but can be very slightly effeminate; he wears hand-knitted cardigans and leaves the bar early in order to fix hot chocolate for his invalid mother). Inverts were. hopeless cases whereas bisexuals, as the description suggests, had the ability to cure themselves. Often they would not succeed.

Hanson was an aberration because he didn't fit into either category. He went for men who looked like men: real men, not queens or mommy's boys. This was tough. It meant no male person who caught Hanson's eye was ever going to reciprocate his feelings. Sure, there were more than a few heterosexual men who were willing to play at being queer, but they were not for keeps and it was strictly sex only. This was a shame because there was a mushy river of romance running through Hanson's cynical heart. He'd done his darnedest to get himself used to being single and lonely but he was always on the lookout for true love.

However, just because this guy had been groping himself did not mean there was any reason for Hanson to buy new pyjamas. Flynn was far too masculine and he was, after all, an officer of the law.

'You too − you're a cop as well,' said a voice in Hanson's head. 'So what if he's straight? He might at least be interested in a roll in the hay with you.' He dismissed the notion. Hoping for the impossible was a dumb thing to do.

Flynn stopped him just as he was about to leave.

'Sir, I guess it might not be worth mentioning . . .' (He said it in a voice that suggested it *was* worth mentioning, and then some.) 'You see, I was given this duty 'cos I'm one of the patrol who police the public toilets. I don't usually tell people this. It's not something I boast about, know what I mean?'

Hanson did know. He said nothing but raised his eyebrows and inclined his head forward, giving Flynn permission to continue.

'Well, sir . . . And I hope you won't think I'm out of line here . . .'

'Get to it,' Hanson snapped.

Showing his impatience gave Hanson a bonus: another of Flynn's hick blushes. Flynn swallowed and, for a moment or two, appeared to have genuinely lost his nerve.

'I apologise,' Hanson said. 'It's been a long day.'

He expected a sunny smile but instead Flynn was fast going sullen on him. So be it, Hanson decided. He was damned if he was going to crawl on his knees. Flynn stayed sulky and Hanson felt like a louse. Maybe crawling wasn't such a bad idea after all. He tried humour instead.

'I'll let you have a photograph of me for use as a dartboard.'

It worked. Flynn grinned and relaxed.

There didn't seem any good place to meet this guy. He had too much balls for a cop and not enough rank to be a pal.

Their eyes locked. Flynn was able to hold the look for an uncomfortably long time and it was Hanson who eventually hauled his eyeballs on to something else. Underneath the lumbering awkwardness, Flynn was showing flashes of confidence that were gradually transforming him. He had it all: arrogance covered with the thinnest veneer of conformity. His movements had taken on a masculine, loutish swagger. Even his uniform couldn't disguise a cocky, confident contempt for convention.

Rebellion was fast becoming the fashion for the troubled youth of the day. It was an aphrodisiac with the kick of a mule behind it. Hanson could well imagine why Flynn had been picked for the 'tearoom trawl'. He was the cheese in the trap all right – Mr Mouse would have no chance.

Unfortunately, the more confident Flynn grew, the more unlikely it seemed that Hanson would be able to exert any sort of 'protective' influence over him. He suddenly felt physically unworthy and had to affirm to himself that he was just as good-looking as Flynn – in a different way, that was all.

'I was going to say,' Flynn said. 'Stein: I might have seen him before. In fact, yeah, I'm certain of it.'

'Sure,' Hanson replied in a noncommittal way.

The news didn't after all surprise him. Manhattan's toilets would be crammed with Steins every night.

'That is to say,' Flynn went on, not sounding at all sure of any of this, 'I think I arrested him. But his name wasn't Stein. I remember because my aunt's neighbour has the same name as he used: it was Palmer – yeah, that's it – David Palmer.'

'You sure of that?' Hanson asked.

'I guess.' He said it like he was trying to please.

Hanson would normally have written the information some-place he would never look at again and gone home. It was no big deal. So what if the dead man had given the police an alias? Did it matter what he called himself when he was out hunting for men? Today, however, he was not behaving as normal. Today he didn't bother to write anything down but he did pretend to be interested.

'What d'you say we have a beer later on?' he asked. 'We can talk it over. If you're very good, I'll buy the first.'

'Sure,' Flynn replied. From the way he said it, it seemed he considered events to be headed where he wanted them and he was not the only one.

Hanson's own little triumph lasted for about thirty seconds before it gave way to another, not so pleasant, feeling. He got a picture of himself as that little mouse, sniffing away at a delicious morsel while, somewhere above him, a steel bar was all set to crack down and break his spine in two.

Hanson chose a bar he'd never been in before. He had no particularly good reason for doing this or for pretending (as he had) that it was where he spent most of his free time. It was a sultry, summer evening and the place smelt of male sweat and stale beer.

'I'm keeping my information to myself,' he told Flynn. 'My

pair is a lazy bastard and he looks on murdered queers as a good opportunity to spend time with his family. Also I do not want my boss getting to know my sources. He's sour and thinks he's due promotion. He'd take all the credit himself. And, just in case you were thinking of scoring points by letting him know what I think of him, he *knows* what I think of him. Understood?'

Flynn had only just arrived. He had been late. Hanson had waited half an hour beyond the appointed time. This was not his habit. A few minutes later and he would have given up. His relief when Flynn arrived was more than he felt comfortable with. The last thing he needed was to find he had a crush on some presumptuous prick-teaser. The description was unfair but Hanson told himself Flynn deserved it. What else do you call a guy who makes a living by tempting toilet traders?

As Hanson had predicted, Flynn out of uniform was not exactly Mr Elegance. He'd made some sort of effort with the knot in his tie but, this apart, his mother would have sighed in despair. Hanson, already smitten, was now on the way to devotion.

Hanson considered himself to fit very nicely into the boy-next-door type. He had the physical potential right enough, even if he was not quite gauche enough to make the image stick. He liked this image of himself: a comfortable example of small-town virtue who you mostly met on the silver screen. Though he would have preferred to be cast opposite Johnny Weissmuller rather than Judy Garland, Hanson saw himself gradually maturing into the domestic slippers–and–pipe sort: impossibly romantic (maybe); grouchy (only sometimes); always lovable. If he could squeeze the beefy Flynn into this perfect scenario beside him, everything would be perfect.

Flynn would need keeping in check of course. He was surely far too impulsive for his own good. Hanson felt again that strong urge to look after him. His fine, moral intentions were given the lie by the pleasant brush of his erection against his trousers. Hanson had taken a tip from Stein's diary: for the first time in his life he was in public without his underwear.

'I have no reason to speak to your boss,' Flynn was telling him. 'There's not so much I can give you on Stein anyhow. Let me lay it on the line: I don't feel ashamed of what I have to do. No sir! And, if you think it's a bit of a crazy thing for a cop to admit to, that's also fine by me.'

'I know – *somebody* has to police the tearooms . . .' Hanson began.

Flynn pounced on his words. 'You know "tearooms"! I didn't realise you guys in the detective branch concerned yourselves with homosexual offences. Not unless the Reds get themselves involved.'

Hanson lit a cigarette to give himself time to cover the slip. He caught Flynn's change of expression but soon found it was the smoke that was interesting him. Hanson's knowledge of homosexual slang had gone unnoticed.

'Sorry,' he said. 'Do you want one?'

'Thanks,' Flynn replied, accepting the cigarette and a light. He puffed gratefully and then ruined the man-of-the-world effect he'd tried to create by coughing. Hanson was reminded by this that he was a lot younger than he looked. His blushes contradicted the effect his hefty body created; he was eager and clumsy. Mr Maternal tapped Hanson on the shoulder once again and he felt like hugging Flynn for ever and ever.

'I'm supposed to be giving it up,' Flynn confessed. 'I've got a bad chest and Mom reckons these things don't help it, but I think they do.'

Two youths, bikers, pushed through the door and strode up to the bar. They acted like they owned the place (which would have been nothing to boast of if they had). They were too openly aggressive for Hanson's tastes. He noticed Flynn cast a glance in their direction and the glance *may* have meant something more than 'Jesus, what jerks!'

'Tell me about how you keep an eye on these faggot pick-up joints,' he said. 'Don't you worry too much about what people think about you doing it. Don't even care about what *I* think. After what I've seen today, I think I can safely claim I'm familiar with the territory.'

Flynn may have been concerned about Hanson's moral position, but, if he was, he didn't show it. It wasn't too surprising, given what Hanson was supposed to be investigating. Sex was going to be on the menu whether he was talking with a hustler or an elder of the Mormon church.

It seemed Flynn had prepared what he was going to say. He took another drag on his cigarette and coughed again. Lowering his voice to a conspiratorial whisper, he began his story.

'There are the well-known places. The queers sometimes visit three or four of them in one night. Some do it in the toilets, some fuck each other in the open. You know the Ramble in Central Park? That's a fag place. The ones who do it in the john are easiest to catch. You see the same faces come back two or three times in an evening. That's how you know what they're about – nobody needs to piss that much. When you go in, they look you up and down to see if you're interested. Then they start pulling on their dicks, trying to get you to have a feel.'

Hanson nodded and tried to look calm. Flynn, who was perhaps surprised his audience hadn't vomited all over the table, continued.

'There are uniform men who try to keep an eye on the cans, but if they go too near the queers all vanish like magic. Personally, I think fruits recognise a cop for what he is whether he's in uniform or not. I've noticed the looks I get sometimes: real suspicious. They have coded warnings: "Lillian", names like that. Heck! I've been called worse things.'

Hanson had never dared go cruising public urinals, but he knew something of what went on. Not that he minded hearing it all over from Flynn. He should have been keeping the conversation relevant to the Stein case but, because of his throbbing dick, he was getting careless.

'Do you wait for them to make the first move?' he asked.

'You mean do we use entrapment? Some cops do, for sure. I'm not so dumb I'm gonna say if that means me or not. At least not without my lawyer present.'

'Of course,' Hanson assured him. He really wanted to hear about Flynn's adventures with his dick but he would have to get the story in bits. Still, they had all evening. He stirred his beer with his finger.

He was in luck. Flynn carried on.

'Yeah, for sure: some cops stand there like they wanna piss and flash their meat at anyone standing next to them. I guess that's about as bad as what the queers are doing, don't you? I mean, if you were a normal guy who's come in there to piss and some guy gives you an eyeful of dick, what difference if it turns out he's a cop? You're still going to be mad at him, don't you see?'

Flynn was showing yet another side to his character: he was an earnest, fair-minded sort and these were qualities a cop needed like a hole in the head. It could have been the beer talking, but maybe not.

'What's *your* take on all this?' Hanson asked. 'What do you think of men who like men in the way they should like women? And what do you do when they seek out their jollies in the public john?'

'Not a problem where I'm concerned,' Flynn replied. He realised his opinion might be thought too liberal, so he qualified it: 'That is, I don't think it's exactly *right* or nothing. We have to do something about it.'

For him, this contradiction seemed to answer the question. Hanson could not leave it alone. He asked again, 'So? What d'you do about it?'

'If you tell 'em not to do it, they're going to do it all the more. It's like with the booze, don't you think? Pretty soon the mob gets in on the act and all hell's broken loose. Now alcohol's legal again, the gangsters are all washed up and everyone's happy.'

No, Hanson thought, I'm not even going to try to follow this logic. Aloud he said, 'So you'd legalise it?'

'In public – no way! But what harm if they keep it behind locked doors? It's not like there aren't enough guys around who want to make it with girls to get babies. I'd say there's probably too many who want to do that. Sometimes I think the queers are just Mother Nature's way of keeping things even.'

Hanson had not before considered the subject in this way. Now he did, it made good sense. He was all for coming clean about his own sexuality and seeing if Flynn could cope with the good news. Confession was good for the soul and may have its fringe benefits.

Even the way Flynn was sitting seemed provocative: leaning forward, his large hands on the table right next to Hanson's, his head slightly on one side. Jesus! He was irresistible: a rough diamond; an impudent, bearlike coquette. Whoa, boy! Hanson thought. Leave it right there!

It wasn't as though he hadn't met them before: young men with too much testosterone swimming through their bodies. Just because they had a brain didn't mean they used it. They were always likely to turn nasty. It was because of these guys that women ended up with unwanted offspring and queers with empty wallets and broken jaws. It counted for zilch that this particular charmer was a cop. Hanson had no illusions when it came to the morals of men in uniform.

'Sir, is this off the record?' Flynn said sharply. 'I wouldn't want it noised around this is what I think.'

Maybe he'd guessed Hanson was a liberal and was saying all this to suck up to him. Hanson decided to be less than liberal and so put freethinking to the test. He imagined what Roach's reaction would be and gave a modified version of it.

' "Live and let live" is not exactly a catchphrase around here,' he said. 'Sometimes I think that's a real shame; other times I get cynical. You argue for tolerance – another Oscar fucking Wilde crawls out of the cheese. Only last week we've had that randy priest with his fingers in the choirboys. Now every good-looking guy in the district is scared of going to Mass. Maybe I shouldn't say nothing. Father Quirk hasn't been found guilty yet.'

'He will be,' Flynn said. He might have thought this was hard luck; he might have thought the law sucked – Hanson couldn't tell. He tried getting the conversation back on more interesting lines.

'So, tell me more about these places – "tearooms" or whatever you like to call them.'

'What else do you want to know?'

The question was loaded. Flynn drained his glass and placed it on the table between them, meaning he wanted it filled.

Hanson obliged. He was trembling slightly and it was not unpleasant. He was excited: his mind was trained on things sexual.

Fate was not kind. Arriving back with the drinks, he found Flynn had been joined by another guy – his buddy, Tony, from way back, so he said. Flynn was acting up a lot: trying to impress and failing dismally. He leered at every female derrière that sashayed past them and laughed too loud at his friend's not very funny wisecracks.

Hanson sat quietly wearing a pained smile and trying not to be a stuffed shirt. He was disappointed. He was sure Flynn was much more sensitive and thoughtful than he pretended; he didn't need to lower himself like this. Hanson wished in his head Tony would take a hike, but Tony was not too hot on telepathy. By the time they were rid of him, it was late.

'One more for the road, my friend?' Flynn suggested.

He was drunk but he was done with playing the hoodlum by now. The harshness had left his voice round about the time

Tony had left the bar. Even so, Hanson could recognise liquor talking when he heard it.

He agreed to a Scotch on the rocks and, while Flynn was at the bar, he chewed his fingernail and considered.

What the hell was he doing here? There didn't seem any way he and Flynn could stay friends. Hanson had worked too damned hard to get where he was just to throw it away by making a pass at some rookie cop. Having a pretty boy tell him dirty stories about what men got up to in the public toilets was all well and good but that was where it had to stop.

Flynn was back with him now. Hanson managed a hearty, masculine cough. He didn't know why he did it and he didn't need it, but it was quite a good one all the same.

'Sorry about Tony,' Flynn said. 'He's quite a guy.' He lowered his voice conspiratorially: 'I guess he's not always on the right side of the law, but I reckon I just don't know nothing about that.'

This was not a clever thing to say in front of a superior. Hanson raised his eyebrow. Flynn covered his mouth jokingly.

'It's this damned drink. I guess I'm not used to it. What the fuck? My career is in your hands. First, I must warn you: my mom is big with the Almighty. Treat me nice or you won't get to heaven.'

Hanson shook his head and took a sip of Scotch. Flynn had bought himself the same with a beer to follow. Though he knew it was plain stupid, Hanson was already planning to offer him yet more booze back at his place. He reckoned the invitation would be safe enough. Because of Tony they weren't done with their work. What harm in a nightcap? Anything else depended on how much Hanson worried about Flynn's mom and her friends in high places.

With this in mind, he banished the Stein case from his conversation for fear there wouldn't be enough of it to last out. They talked about everything and nothing: Tony, the bar and even the good and evil of watching television. By the time the bartender closed his doors, their work had been forgotten. Flynn was happy in a haze of booze and Hanson was beginning to feel like the big bad wolf.

The night was airless and thunder was not far off. Flynn wiped his sleeve across his forehead and eased a finger around the inside of his damp shirt collar; rain spattered on to Hanson's face. They would normally have parted quickly as there was no reason to hang around and every reason not to. Flynn must have sussed that there was unfinished business because he made no effort to say goodbye.

'Thanks for the drinks, then,' he said at last. 'I dare say I wasn't much help, huh?'

'We need to talk more about the Stein thing,' Hanson agreed. 'We didn't finish what we had to say.'

'It was Tony's fault,' agreed Flynn. 'He likes to talk and – Jesus – can he talk! I thought he'd never go.'

Hanson smiled faintly. They must either make a move or get drenched. Maybe Flynn thought he needed permission to be excused. If so, he wasn't going to get it.

'I've got some more Scotch back at my place,' Hanson said, far more quickly than he had intended to. 'How about you and me go back and you give me the rest of the story?'

'Sure.'

The dark clouds parted and the angels came out to play. Hanson was floating off the ground and his heart was thumping. He had expected at least some resistance. At one point, he had even considered pulling rank.

His guilty conscience chased after his delight, caught it and threw it in the trash. If it was so easy, it must follow Flynn was innocent as a newborn babe and even the thought of getting him into bed was going to rate as a venal sin. As if this weren't enough, Hanson's bitch of a conscience also decided to have fun by causing him to be fretful: had he put his muscle magazines away? He thought he had but he couldn't be sure. If they were still lying about on the table, it could be make or break and with Hanson's luck it would be break. Flynn would not need to be the world's best detective to work out the significance of *Physique*.

This whole evening had turned into one hell of a gamble. Hanson took in a deep breath: 'faint heart never won fair lady' – did faint heart have any sort of a chance with fair cop?

Four

———

Hanson's apartment was in a creaking mansion block which leant sleepily against its neighbours. It had a cold, spacious landing on each floor and a cage-lift going up the centre of the stairwell. The other residents fitted into three categories: actors (and one elderly actress), old-timers (one of whom owned the kitty-cat who was responsible for the distinctive aroma in the lobby) and middle-aged whores (who passed off their profession as nothing more risqué than a hectic social life). Hanson had something in common with them: like they did, he kept his profession to himself. When he first moved in, the only young and single male in the block, he'd had to suffer frequent lascivious glances from these scarlet matrons. Not any longer. They soon got to ignoring him, assuming for some reason that he was a chorus boy.

The living room had high ceilings and windows that rattled in tune to the passing traffic. Lucky for Hanson, he'd left in a hurry that morning so the place was untidy enough not to betray him as being house-proud. The bed doubled as a sofa but he hadn't folded it away. Hanson hurriedly straightened the sheets, remembering not to make them too neat. Flynn grinned and threw himself down. He lay back and closed his eyes.

'Jesus! Jesus! Jesus!' (He was fond of that name.)

If this had been the movies and if Flynn had been a woman, Hanson would have lain beside him and got seducing. It wasn't and he wasn't, so he perched on the edge of the mattress near Flynn's feet. Flynn had good, solid feet. He'd kicked off his shoes, one by one, and the smell of those feet made Hanson's cock stand hard. For reasons best known to God, the sweat-dampened socks were driving him nuts. Sitting together like this, with Flynn so relaxed and comfortable (and almost bare-foot), it was kind of intimate: special. Hanson wanted to kiss Flynn's toes, smell his socks, lick his ankles.

The muscle magazines had not, after all, been left on the coffee table: they had been stuffed under the bed. Hanson noticed one poking out. He tried to push it back with his heel but unfortunately chose the very moment when Flynn decided to sit up and, in a slurred voice, ask for a drink. The sitting up must have taken all his available energy. He bounced back down again.

Hanson went to get him a glass. The measure was just slightly too large, not so much it would make Hanson's intentions obvious or get Flynn so woozy he would pass out. Luckily, the honoured guest hadn't asked for any sort of mixer because, apart from tap water, there wasn't any.

'What were you were trying to push under the bed?' Flynn asked. His eyes were fixed on the ceiling, the glass rested precariously on his chest.

'Nothing very much. I just like to keep the place tidy, that's all.'

Flynn didn't look like he believed him. Hanson knew he would have to stand guard or, you could bet dollars to dough-nuts, Flynn would go snooping. He almost thought that might be no bad thing. This whole game was becoming stupid. The excuse of work had been long forgotten – surely they both knew what all this was for and were just taking time getting round to admitting it.

Flynn edged up next to him: too close. Hanson was incapable of acting natural. He felt like an actor who had forgotten his lines: his brain was reeling. Flynn was becoming more and more obvious but still Hanson didn't dare come clean.

'No need to keep the fuckers under the bed,' Flynn said at last. 'You gonna let me see?'

'They're not what you think they are,' Hanson replied hastily. It had only just come to him: Flynn must have thought they were girlie mags.

He was wrong, Flynn thought no such thing. 'I know what they are,' he said. 'I can recognise another fucking homo from five blocks away. Jesus! I've had enough fucking practice.'

He was so goddamn sexy! He looked like a soldier, talked like a thug and his words were music to the ears.

For Hanson, the world slowed down its spinning and every movement seemed to take an hour. Flynn sat up. His hand wandered over the front of his trousers. Then he pushed it down inside: feeling himself, his tongue flicking briefly over his lips. He never left off looking directly at Hanson. He was smiling now, his tongue had gone into freeze-frame. There was no possible chance of resistance.

'How long have you known about me?' Hanson asked.

'Does it matter? You must think I'm dumb. I've had your measure more or less from the start.'

Hanson was about to challenge this.

'I'm right, aren't I?' Flynn sounded reasonable as he went on. 'I don't mind – I know you have to be careful. We all do. You tell me you're not hot for me if you can.'

Flynn had the upper hand here. Hanson suddenly felt stupid. He had to remind himself that he had been nothing if not sensible. Anyway, this man was his subordinate: he still had the upper hand.

It didn't matter for long. One glance at Flynn's wrestler's

body (his shirt flap had escaped from his trousers, his tie and top buttons were undone) and Hanson didn't give a damn about the upper hand. He was excited – not just sexually aroused, more than that. Well, as his father before him had said, 'You always appreciate the things you have to work hard to achieve.' Hanson was stiff with lust and dizzy with infatuation.

He was now lusting openly for Flynn's body and Flynn was taking it all in. He was quite the knowing tempter. He feasted on Hanson's gaze, pushing his hand harder and harder down the front of his trousers. His cock wasn't perceptible beneath the corduroy, but the thought of its being there was enough. He moved his hips in a slow-motion pastiche of a fuck. His other hand went inside his half-loosened shirt. With the precision of a stripper, he undid the few bottom buttons and lifted his vest, keeping what was under it a secret. He rubbed and scratched his stomach slowly, luxuriously. Hanson got a glimpse of his hairy belly for just a second and the sight sent his heart into his mouth.

Flynn had a square, thick neck. Hanson had never before appreciated the erotic qualities of the neck. The physical power on view brought out the romantic side of his nature. Here was a man who had strong arms to melt into; here was a man he could trust; here was a man he could really love.

Hanson shook himself off his pink cloud and let less high-minded thoughts take over. Here was a man who could fuck him for ever and then come back for more.

He checked himself only to remind his conscience that Flynn also had his goofy, innocent side. That wicked grin he had adopted just had to be a pose. His true character had been seen in the innocent blushes he'd been unable to conceal. Sex, the black sheep of the emotions, vied for supremacy with her younger sister. It was a poetic thought but Sex won hands down.

Hanson copied Flynn's action, bringing his own hand down the front of his flannels. He knew his prick was real obvious now. What did Flynn think of guys who didn't bother with underwear? Did it matter what he thought? They were on a nonstop train to Paradise.

Hanson reached down slowly with his other hand and produced one of the muscle magazines. He handed it to Flynn, who took it without even glancing at the cover. He laid it by his side.

The room was a bit cooler than the street but not cool enough. Hanson had a pedantic need for everything to be just so; he hated himself for it, but what could he do? He excused himself − a bit awkwardly − and dashed into the bathroom to get an electric fan.

While in there he checked himself in the mirror. He considered his own attractiveness and decided he could honestly award himself nine out of ten. He was not beefy like Flynn, but, in those few years when he could have been building up his bulk, he'd managed to naturally acquire a strong, slimmed-down masculinity. He was good-looking, not pretty as he had been in his teens, but handsome.

If Flynn was able to flaunt his looks to get his way, Hanson decided to be just as immodest. By the time he was back in the room, he was feeling like he was gorgeous.

He'd managed to get rid of any guilt he might have felt about seducing an innocent. Flynn knew what he was doing and everything was as safe as could be expected. The both of them might just as well make the most of it. Hanson was going to enjoy this and to hell with the consequences.

Then, somewhere in the back of his mind he caught a glimpse of the mousetrap again. The spring was straining for release.

Flynn was flicking through the magazine. His flies were now undone and his shirt fully open, hanging off his shoulders like a woman's stole. His cock was discernible through his underpants and he didn't seem to care. It was almost as though he was used

46

to having it on show. You could bet your life he didn't patrol the tearooms with quite the same reluctance as other cops.

This thought brought Stein back into Hanson's mind. He put him right back out of it immediately. This wasn't police time and he was damned if they were going to waste it by discussing who might have murdered that poor loser. His conscience pricked him but he wasn't going to let the wound bleed.

He plugged the fan into the socket and knelt on the floor in front of Flynn. He dared to feel over that lovely instep. As he did so, he kept his eyes fixed on Flynn's face, hoping for an invitation to go further.

Flynn didn't even look at him. He went on turning the pages of the magazine, occasionally stopping to examine in more detail some model or other who took his fancy. He didn't pull his foot away and he didn't say he minded but, as far as encouragement goes, that was all he was giving.

Hanson didn't carp. He gently pulled Flynn's sock from his foot. It was like removing skin and finding underneath another layer: pale, secret skin. Flynn's toes were satisfyingly large, and his instep would have done justice to a dancer: it was a big foot but it could have belonged to a Greek statue. The sock in Hanson's hand was giving off its powerful smell of manliness. He buried his nose into it and inhaled. Flynn glanced up from the pages and smiled – it may have been a mocking smile but Hanson didn't care. Flynn stuck his other foot forward and, taking this as a cue, Hanson pulled the remaining sock off. It stuck slightly and wrinkled around the heel. Hanson took his time.

Once he was barefoot, Flynn returned his attention to the magazine. His feet were right in front of Hanson's face. Giving in to some unconscious desire, Hanson buried his face in the socks and then rubbed them hard against his cheek like you might with a sponge when you want the water out of it. He gave out a low, ecstatic moan. Flynn ignored him.

Feeling really brave now, Hanson leant forward and kissed Flynn's ankle. Flynn responded by pushing a toe into Hanson's mouth and wiggling it around. He still didn't show any great interest in Hanson's attentions – not even when his toe, so gently held in Hanson's mouth, was sucked harder and harder. Hanson sucked it like it was his only source of food after days of starvation. It felt so hard and goddamn live in his mouth. His tongue felt every detail: the razor edge of the toenail, the hard skin where the joint rubbed against the shoe, the two or three hairs which came out of the knuckle. He could even feel the minute ridges on the pad: the toe's equivalent of a fingerprint. Flynn kept on moving his foot this way and that, showing he appreciated the attention but, for all the movement it showed, his upper body might not have been connected to his lower. He just went on reading.

Hanson licked and sucked at the large, hot feet for a full ten minutes. He was enjoying it though he started to want for something more. He could feel his dick and knew it was pointing upward, showing obscenely through his trousers. Flynn still hadn't looked in that direction; was he the narcissistic type who would just lie back and stare at the ceiling? Hanson decided he wasn't going to let him. He came up for air.

'Did you like all that stuff in the diary?' he asked.

Flynn looked up as though he had been miles away and was surprised to see someone else in the room.

'Stuff?'

'The way Stein enjoyed being knocked about – all that.'

'Oh – yeah, I don't mind.'

Flynn was very embarrassed all of a sudden. His colour rose in his face like a glowing lamp and he went back to the pictures. Hanson snatched the magazine from him and was gratified to find this got his attention.

'Why spend all the time looking at pictures? There's the real thing here.'

He climbed on to the bed and knelt up on the mattress. His crotch was inches away from Flynn's face.

Flynn was utterly seductive – lips parted and moist, breath steaming hot, eyes still with the knowing, flirtatious glint about them – but he made no move. Hanson crept forward, keeping a distance between himself and the tempting warmth of that mouth. His shaft was standing almost flat to his belly and it was so engorged its shape could easily be made out under his trousers. It was there for the taking, but Flynn had to demonstrate his desire for it.

He did, in as much as he brushed his hand against it. Even this slight contact was beautiful. Hanson hissed with pleasure. He needed more. Grabbing Flynn's wrist, he pulled it back to his cock. This time Flynn took more care to please. He gently pinched the outline, all along its length. Then he pressed his finger against the head, pushing and prodding at this most sensitive place.

'Get 'em down,' he said.

Hanson thrilled at these words. He yanked his trousers down to his knees and pulled his shirt and vest high up his chest. This deliberate exposure of his abdomen, his chest and genitals, made him feel more naked than if he'd stripped completely. It's meaning was unequivocal – his body was prepared for the pleasure of the other man.

Flynn studied the flesh made so available to him. He looked it up and down; he felt it gently with his hand. Starting with Hanson's chest, he lightly glanced over each nipple and then traced a line to the navel. Hanson took much pleasure in this appreciation – he knew his torso was hard and well formed. Flynn drew him close and kissed him hotly. Afterwards he moved back.

'Do you like hairy guys?' Flynn said.

His hand reached out to Hanson's pubes. He was fingering through them with the attention of the connoisseur. He leant over and kissed the tip of Hanson's cock. It responded by weeping some pre-come, which Flynn licked up, causing more to follow.

'I love hairy guys,' Hanson replied. 'When I was a kid, I fell in love with King Kong and I've been crazy for him ever since. Is it possible you have a beautiful face and all that too?'

Flynn didn't reply. He turned his back and unbuttoned his shirt. Once this was removed and his vest with it, he turned to show Hanson a wonderful covering of black hair, dense in the centre of his upper chest, around his biceps and under his arms, smoothing out and fading away as it spread over his solid torso. A thick black line of it ran from his belly-button down to his belt. Hanson had expected a mat, but this was better: it was defined, enhancing the contours created by his muscle. Hanson gave an appreciative whistle. He reached out.

Flynn caught his wrist. 'This is against the law,' he said facetiously.

'Perhaps I should arrest you,' Hanson said, touching the downy covering lightly. It was beautifully soft, like stroking the fur of an adorable pet animal.

Swirls of hair surrounded Flynn's lovely round, dark nipples. Hanson squeezed and then kissed each of them. Then he leant back, trying to implant the image in his mind. He wanted to recall this man's beauty for ever.

The details of that chest were not sharp and focused as in a photograph, he decided. They were created by many brush strokes of hair as they might have been had they been the work of an impressionist painter.

Hanson gave another low whistle. 'King Kong is gonna be devastated, but I guess I'll have to tell him we're through.'

'It gets even better.'

Flynn unbuttoned his flies and, lying flat on the mattress, stretched his legs and raised them. It was an invitation for Hanson to remove the corduroys.

If it was an artist who had created the covering of Flynn's chest, the same genius had also been responsible for his legs.

Athletic, sturdy legs they were, tanned and shapely just like the rest of his body, and completely covered in the soft, dark, brush strokes of hair. They grew enticingly dense at the top of his inner thighs where his penis, the centre of interest of this masterpiece, lay hidden, swathed in dazzling white cotton.

Hanson indulged himself once again by standing back to get the full effect. He was lost in admiration and he didn't give a damn if this encouraged Flynn's conceit.

'Forbidden goods,' Flynn said, grinning. 'You wouldn't get any of this if you was normal.'

Hanson pulled his own shirt off. He was thankful his chest at least half matched the one on offer. He felt he was in an unspoken competition with this beauty and losing. Any part of his body that wasn't as healthy, handsome or sexy as Flynn's was setting him further back. They were playing games again – 'I show you mine, you show me yours.' He consoled himself yet again with the thought that he was not less attractive than Flynn: just different.

The two of them spent the next few, blissful minutes feeling each other's naked front. Hanson laid his cheek against that soft down and kissed it gently. Somewhere in his head a violin was playing and roses were growing up the walls. He would have liked to have taken Flynn's hand and walked naked with him into a glorious sunset while, behind them, the credits rolled.

Flynn held Hanson's head close into his own body – carefully, as if it might break. They stayed like that for some time until he became impatient to continue his own exploration of Hanson.

Flynn's underpants had been so tightly stretched over their upright prisoner. Now the thing inside them was wrestling to be free. The white material had become rucked and slack; his cock was twitching inside like it had been caught and couldn't find the way out. There was a damp patch showing where the head of it was: pre-come was already leaking out.

Hanson could glimpse Flynn's balls through the gap at the

51

top of his legs. He remembered opening presents when he was a kid: that moment, before the wrapping was entirely removed – a glimpse of the gift inside – almost a shame to open the thing completely.

He didn't – not yet at any rate. Instead, he lay on top of Flynn and kissed him with passionate fervour. Flynn's groin was radiating heat and Hanson's back was licked by the cool airstream from the fan: hot body and cool air.

Hanson's own prick was stimulated by the unfamiliar brush of burning, cotton-cased cock pressed so hard against it. He eased upward, supporting his weight with his hands. Slowly, he gyrated his body over the younger man's. The body hair beneath him was drawn by static to meet his skin. It tickled and kissed. Again and again, Hanson's belly met the one under it – fleetingly – before pulling away. His penis sought the other one as if by its own accord.

The preliminaries were over and done: Flynn scrabbled to get himself naked. The two organs kissed and, unable to sustain this enigmatic pleasure, Hanson collapsed on top of Flynn with a frantic, desperate run of grinding and rubbing.

Now his hands could no longer caress: they pressed and held. Now he pushed hard against Flynn's skin until his fingers met the resistance of the bone beneath. If he hadn't felt that solid, physical proof, he might have imagined this was all a drunken fantasy and Flynn was a figment of his imagination. No, it was real: Flynn was real.

They held still for a moment. Hanson snatched a kiss. Flynn, still on his back, held him at bay with strong hands. There was an unspoken challenge between them. Then Flynn wrestled Hanson over and took the top position for himself. He went straight for Hanson's penis and held it in his fist, tight and secure. His face had an expression that said 'dare me'. It could have been read as threatening but Hanson didn't care. If Flynn wanted to play it rough, he was beautiful enough for it to be worth it.

The fist relaxed and the fingers crept down — down under Hanson's cock before slowly and carefully encasing his balls. Hanson exhaled and let his body go limp. Flynn had arrived at the most erogenous part of his body. When his balls felt human touch, Hanson was in heaven.

The fingers played with the tightening sac. As the skin contracted, Hanson's pubic hair bristled. He wanted this subtle sensation to continue but it could not. It was a preliminary. Once they were on that road, 'all the way' was the only place to go.

Flynn's thin fingers encased his scrotum. Then he squeezed gently — very gently as if he was testing how ripe this fruit was. Hanson sighed dreamily and sought the back of Flynn's neck with his hand. He stroked and pressed. Flynn rolled his head and stretched his neck. He didn't let go of Hanson's balls.

Flynn's other hand took hold of Hanson's cock and gave it a few preliminary strokes up and down. As he often did when an orgasm was approaching, Hanson tensed his legs and held his breath. Flynn must have noticed this. He disengaged his head from the attentions of Hanson's hand and brought it down to the waiting cock.

He kept one hand there at the base, with just two fingers encircling Hanson's penis and holding it tight. Flynn's other hand slowly made firm its grip on Hanson's balls while he stimulated the cockhead expertly with those sometimes sulky and arrogant, but always beautiful, lips.

Hanson had kept his eyes tightly closed. Subconsciously aware he was being studied, he opened them and lifted his head to find Flynn watching him closely as he sucked cock. The guy was impossibly cute, with his large Mediterranean eyes gazing up, eager (so it seemed) to see he was doing the right thing, and his mouth stretched like it was full of lollipop or something.

This lovely bastard is sucking my cock, Hanson thought. *My* cock.

The sensations swept over him in waves. Several times over

Hanson felt himself coming; nothing could stop it. Then he would feel the urge ebb away and his body would go limp again. As this relaxation took over, another tension grew, surging up as the warm, slick tongue and the wet, hot mouth pulled and sucked at his shaft. His balls remained encased in the gradual, tightening grip. Over and over he approached a threshold where it would hurt to go further, and over and over Flynn let go and began again with the gentle tantalising touch that was sure to intensify. He seemed to have the knack of doing this in perfect unison with the rush of pleasure that kept flowing through Hanson's body.

Bliss cannot last for ever. Despite the increasing intensity of sensation round his genitals, the surge eventually came from nowhere. Hanson's spunk raced up and out of him before he could warn it was coming. Flynn moaned, a low contented sound which came from deep inside his throat. He swallowed Hanson's come, rubbing the excess around his face, taking it directly from the seeping cock that had given it.

Hanson raised himself and kissed Flynn purposefully. Flynn gripped his hand and pushed it down to his own needy cock. Hanson held the burning flesh, appreciating its stubby shape and impressive girth.

Following Flynn's example, he bent down and licked the top of it. The cock responded by twitching in his hand as though it had a life of its own. Hanson licked it again.

Flynn proved to be more impatient than you might have thought from all the expertise he'd just shown. He pressed Hanson's head to where he wanted it and moved it fast and forcefully up and down.

Flynn's prick was just the right shape and size for sucking. It was neither so long it would make a man gag, nor insignificant in size. It felt comfortable inside Hanson's mouth, blunt and wide; it was good to have it inside him. He relished the taste of its fluids and the heady smell of the groin around it. He noticed every pulse as the inevitable climax built. He wanted to drink this guy's spunk; he wanted semen to fill his mouth; he wanted to taste the essence of his Adonis.

Hanson always thought the male body was at its most lovely when in the throes of an orgasm. Looking at Flynn's, he made no exception: he surrendered to pleasure so absolutely. Hanson sucked him as he screwed his face into a passionate grimace and shouted. Then his voice disintegrated into breathy pants.

'Oh yes! Yeah, man! Suck my cock! Yeah, let me come! I'm going to come into your fucking mouth! *Yes!*'

This last was a howl of pleasure. It brought the semen into Hanson's mouth in a gush. Hanson was aware of a slight sting at the back of his throat and then the faint, indefinable aftertaste. He swallowed the come and was grateful to get another burst, then another. Each spurt made Flynn buck. His hands were on Hanson's shoulders and his nails dug in like a cat's claws.

It was over at last and the two men lay close to each other. Eventually they climbed into the bed and embraced lovingly. Hanson felt sleep beckoning. He gave in to it gratefully.

He woke in the early hours to find Flynn's side of the bed empty. He felt the indentation in the mattress – it was cold. Panic got hold of him, chasing the sleep out of his brain.

He told himself not to be so juvenile. If the guy had gone home without kissing him goodbye, it was hardly the end of a true romance. Flynn had, at best, been a one-night stand. So what if it turned out he was only a half-night stand? Hanson would survive. The dream he'd just woken from had involved the pair of them and a whole lot of romantic slush that Hanson now felt ashamed to remember.

He sat up and switched on the bedside lamp. The door that led to Hanson's tiny study (the landlord had called it the bedroom but *you* try getting a bed in there), was showing light underneath.

The apartment was stuffy and smelt of garbage from the cans below his window. Hanson got out of bed. He was getting apprehensive and he didn't know why. It was obvious what had happened: Flynn couldn't sleep — (then why get out of bed and go prying around some other guy's room?).

There was a possible explanation: Flynn didn't want to disturb him. Yes, Hanson thought. He was restless and he didn't want to wake me — so he's gone and sat at my desk where the lamp won't bother me.

He kidded himself he really believed this. At the same time he was careful to tread quietly so he could catch Flynn in the act of . . . doing nothing? There was something farcical in this, prowling around his own apartment in the dead of night. He opened the door swiftly, as he had before when he had caught Flynn reading Stein's journal.

Flynn was fully dressed and sitting by Hanson's desk. Letters, notebooks and Hanson's private documents were scattered in front of him.

It was like a rerun of the last time Hanson had caught him snooping but this was far more serious. He'd heard Hanson approaching, but too late to cover what he'd been about. He managed to look challenging rather than guilty.

At least — as always — he had the grace to colour deep red.

Five

Roach's mood was hovering somewhere between bad and foul. It was the usual reading for the early morning and those who might otherwise have to suffer it knew better than to approach until after he'd shaken off his hangover.

Hanson was on his own for the rest of the week – his partner had called in sick. It suited Hanson fine – he preferred to work alone. He was rocking on his chair (just like his mother had always told him not to) and amusing himself with a game of 'get the ball of paper in the basket'. He was losing. This seemed appropriate. Life was a whole crock of shit and the sun would never shine again.

Flynn had spent the rest of the previous, fateful night in the armchair. He had not said goodbye and they had not arranged to meet again. Hanson had not slept a wink. Thinking he might catch Flynn engaged in further treachery, he had let him creep about the place and leave before first light. The bastard hadn't even written a note to say 'thanks for the fuck'! It was too bad.

He galvanised himself into some sort of constructive mental action. He went through his own feelings as if they were on card index. The one that seemed to demand priority was the one marked 'Why the hell was Flynn prying into those private papers?' There didn't seem to be any sort of answer to this but, if Flynn could snoop, so could Hanson. Without a whole lot of hope that it would reveal anything, he placed a call to records.

'This is Mark Hanson, the new man in DI Roach's squad. I want some info on one Henry Flynn. Henry Flynn is a cop so it shouldn't be too difficult to turn up.'

He didn't like his own tone and he was well aware it wasn't the best way to charm people into efficiency. It didn't even make him feel better. The woman at the other end of the line was probably used to assholes. She was brisk enough and appeared not to have taken offence. She rang back within ten minutes.

'How are you spelling "Flynn"?' He told her. 'Yes, that's what I thought,' she said. 'I'm sorry, sir, we have no records of a Henry Flynn. Your source must be inaccurate.'

'You sure?'

The voice became testy. 'Quite sure, sir. Of course he may belong to another department. Do you wish me to investigate further on your behalf?'

'But . . .' He was trying to figure this out and she was not going to hang around to wait for him to do it. 'I'll call you back,' he said, but she had already hung up.

From inside his 'corner', Roach tapped on the glass partition that separated him from lesser mortals and beckoned Hanson, who had started rocking again. Hanson nearly fell off the chair. He reached for his jacket and straightened his tie. There was no call to do this – it just made him feel less of a worm.

Roach started talking straight on in there with no preliminaries. It was as if Hanson's entering his office had placed an invisible needle into a record groove.

'The way I see it is this: a faggot fairy is dead and my heart is bleeding. We have three alternatives: we can say it was homicide, in which case some shitface is gonna want a culprit; we can say it was suicide, in which case we have to convince the coroner; or we can say it's what happens when fruits start getting their rocks off in dangerous ways, in which case we needn't do nothing. Here's a little test for you — which do you suppose is the best use of our resources? I give you ten seconds.'

Hanson was thinking emptying a bucket of sick over Roach's head might be a good use of resources; he was thinking how satisfying it would be to smash a fist into Roach's fat, pudding of a face; he was thinking would this be the perfect time to let him know the girls in the typing pool always prefixed his name with 'Cock'?

Instead he said, 'I guess we could find out the truth.'

He knew this was not going to be the cleverest answer he could give. Roach looked as though he'd swallowed a glass of piss. He recovered enough to say, 'I am not hearing you right. I thought you just said something not very smart.'

Hanson ignored the threatening tone. He was pushing his luck but he didn't care. He did not wish to live any more. Flynn, the only man he was ever going to love, was a treacherous bastard who'd tried to steal things from him. Now, if the woman in Records was to be believed, he had been lying from the very start. He was probably some jumped-up newspaper reporter who'd scented blood. It didn't matter what he was — it sucked and Roach could do his worst.

'Give me charge of the case,' Hanson went on blithely. 'If I crack it, I'll swear I owe it all to you. If I don't, you can kick my ass round the block, which is something you would enjoy.'

Roach looked at him as though seeing him for the first time. He was amazed, but maybe just a little impressed.

'You got terminal stupidity? Or have you just visited Planet Krypton and come back with the Superman rock?'

'The first.'

Roach nodded a 'thought so' nod. He went back to the racing page as though Hanson had dematerialised. Hanson waited for an answer but it wasn't going to come of its own accord.

'Do I get the case or don't I?'

Roach didn't look at him. He put a circle round *America's Finest* in the 3.30.

'You get it.'

Hanson left the office in a brighter mood than he'd entered it. He still thought Dame Fate was a bitch, but maybe she had her nicer moments. He was going to begin his enquiries.

He drove to an address in Amsterdam Avenue. It was a far more up-market apartment than he'd supposed it would be. It seemed Gregory Stein had rejected his roots, big time.

'My son was not a pervert!'

She was a neat woman, small and sharp-featured. She must have practised that tone of voice on her children. The years she'd spent alone since they'd grown up had not destroyed its effect. It said, What I say goes and don't you dare try to disagree.

Hanson did disagree but he wasn't going to argue with her. If she thought her son was a saint, then so be it. He could remain blessed in her memory if not in the police records.

She said she had not seen her Gregory since the previous Fall and Hanson had no reason not to believe her. She went on to give her views on what Hanson should be doing about the killing. She equated all homosexuals with the worst possible kind of demon. Consequently, she believed her son had been murdered by Stalinist satanists who would very likely have gone the whole way and eaten his remains if they'd had time before their dinner date with Vlad the Impaler. There being no actual evidence to support this theory did not sway her one bit. She repeated many times that she was a good, Jewish woman and God would look after His own when the trumpets sounded.

'I can see you are a well-brought-up young man,' she said to Hanson. 'In time you will know that there are wicked people in this word — wicked, wicked people. I've seen what it's like in Harlem, I know what goes on. My son was a God-fearing American. He went to synagogue every sabbath, rain or shine. I know he will be at peace and his killers will be in torment for ever. I have to be content with that. It's all I have left.'

She began to sob again. Despite thinking her opinions would not look a hell of a lot out of place in Dixie, Hanson felt very sorry for her.

He closed his notebook in a way that he hoped indicated the respect with which he was supposed to hold her words written inside it. He thanked her and was about to go.

'You are very young,' she said. 'I expect your girl is proud of you.'

Hanson smiled thinly and said nothing. She came up to him and put her hand on his arm. 'I know you'll get to the bottom of all this. People are so cruel. They're saying all sorts of things about Gregory. I'm relying on you to prove them wrong.'

He nodded and left the room feeling like the biggest god-damn fraud since the Wizard of Oz. If he was to do anything, he would prove these people right: he would send nice, prim Mrs Stein into a lifelong nightmare. Nobody would thank him for doing it. His boss — his country even — would rather he gave them the usual line and left the case unsolved. The arrest of some nutcase who murdered faggots was of no importance to anyone; maintaining this woman's delusions about her off-spring was.

J Edgar Hoover and some big knobs from the FBI were in town. Roach was wetting himself because of it. Though there was no reason for the FBI to show interest in a squalid killing, Hanson had been told nothing was to move on the Stein case until they were safely back in Washington. The Bureau direc-tor's draconian attitude to morality was well known; it wouldn't do to be seen to be championing the faggot cause. If justice was to be served for Gregory Stein, Hanson was on his own.

Sex was the key to all this but it was a key that kept locking doors instead of opening them. Homosexual men were often the victims of blackmail. If this explained anything, it may mean Stein had killed himself for fear of being exposed. Not possible, Hanson concluded. How does a man manage to commit suicide by tying himself up and then strangling himself? It didn't make any sort of sense.

Then there was that goddamn nursery rhyme that kept coming back to haunt him: 'Peter, Peter, pumpkin eater . . .' What the hell had that got to do with anything? 'Had a wife and couldn't keep her . . .'

Other phrases and images floated through Hanson's brain: things people had said, the torn page with the pornographic drawing on it. With these thoughts came memories of Flynn's face, Flynn's voice, Flynn's body . . . Hanson was beginning to get a headache. He climbed in behind the steering wheel of his car and massaged his temples.

Then one of the floating thoughts came right up and waved a flag at him. Mrs Stein had said her son had attended synagogue every sabbath. Hanson recalled that his Paul, his Jewish ex-boyfriend, had done the same. It had always caused arguments between them but Paul was more scared of his mom's recriminations than he ever was of Hanson's.

Hanson remembered one particular row. He could hear himself saying, 'Why does it have to be every bloody week? God is not going to punish you if you miss just one Saturday!'

The Jewish sabbath was on Saturday – and, as Hanson clearly recalled, New Year's Day had been on a Friday that year.

Later that day, leaning against the edge of his desk like he'd seen Bogart do in some movie, he picked up the telephone and dialled a number. He was connected immediately.

'This is Detective Mark Hanson. I've just taken over the Stein investigation. Get me the journal we took from his apartment.'

On Hanson's desk was a framed picture of his sister. He let

people think she was his girl. He took it and placed it face
down in a drawer. Without having thought through the consequences, he knew he'd made a decision. From then on he
wasn't going to pretend any more. Not unless he absolutely
had to.

Stein's journal looked out of place in the fluorescent light of
the office. Hanson speculated on how many of his colleagues
would like to spend an hour or so going through its contents.
Would they find it stomach-churning or cock-erecting? Himself, he would rather have taken it somewhere private; but, if
he was going to get any answers to all this mess, he was going
to have to look for clues, not for turn-ons.

He opened it some way in and leafed through a few pages.
Each entry seemed to describe a complete sexual encounter.
Two or three names were changed – crossed through and an
alias written over the top of them. This seemed rather odd as
the originals were still clearly legible under the lines he'd drawn
through them. In other places (as in the instance of 'Billy') Stein
had admitted to concealing the identity of whoever he'd had in
his bed.

Hanson stopped where Stein had apparently met a new
boyfriend.

*Stuart called and absolutely insisted I go with him to one of those
parties he'd mentioned. It was in a beautiful building in West End
Avenue – v. exclusive. He took me down a long dark corridor with just
one door at the end of it. I followed like I was Alice and him the
White Rabbit. Come to think of it, that's not a bad way of putting it.
There was sure as hell a Wonderland waiting for me behind that door!*

*It was so dark. I could hardly see the hand in front of my face. Sex
was all around us, I could sense it as soon as we went in. I could
almost smell it. There was no noise to speak of; I couldn't hear any
chattering or clinking of glasses. Everybody talked in whispers. Sure,
there was the occasional groan or throaty sigh, but all you heard apart*

from that was a reverential hum created by a hundred men hypnotized by lust.

Stuart was acting like a tour guide in a church. You know what I mean? Seen it all before and sure as hell isn't going to let a few people on their knees stop him talking out loud. He walked straight on in there, not bothering that the place was pitch-black. He obviously knew his way around.

'You don't have to get rid of your clothes yet, but if you want to there's a place for them through there. If you go naked, don't be surprised if they all treat you like you're communal property. That's the code — those who keep their pants on are the ones who are calling the shots. Those that don't get treated like shit. Being treated like shit is good but, either way, you're certain to have a good time.'

In that kind of ambience I didn't at all mind using my hands to find my way around. There were dim, red bulbs and I could see enough to know there were men every which way I turned. There must have been twenty or thirty people I guess. Some of them were in couples, some in larger groupings. There were all types and sorts.

The singles just stood around looking at each other, waiting to get in on the action. Stuart and I were getting lots of attention, and it seemed to me I was getting the most. I think Stuart was too brazen and they considered me the better option. I suppose they were waiting to see what kind of meat I liked on my plate.

There was everything on offer: some dressed like anyone you'd meet in the street. You know — white shirt, collar and tie. A small number of them were actually wearing drag — the full thing with make-up and wigs. And yes, some guys were actually walking around bare-assed — completely naked! They didn't seem to have any self-consciousness about it — it was as though their birthday suit was just another costume they'd put on.

Like Stuart said, the naked ones were there for the taking. Let me just tell you about one couple.

First guy: well, he was about thirty or so and handsome as you please — he was clothed; he even had a hat perched on the back of his head. He had a cigarette dangling from his mouth and he had to squint to keep the smoke from his eyes. His pants were bunched around his ankles and his dick was rammed right up the rear of this exquisite apple-faced beauty — the sort who looks like he spends all day in some field doing healthy things. He was on his hands and knees taking everything that was given him. He was panting with pleasure.

The one who was doing this to him took off his belt and put it between Beauty's teeth. He used it like a rein, to pull his head this way and that — you just wouldn't believe it! I certainly wanted some of the action. Before this, I would always have said I preferred being the top man — the rider — but if I said it now I would be lying. I really, really wanted to be that horse.

I knew I could have stripped there and then, but I was too nervous to do it just yet. I accepted a glass of gin and stood by the wall trying to look as though I was used to all this. Stuart wandered off. Just before he did, he put his hand over my groin to check I wasn't so nervous my cock couldn't get hard. As soon as he'd done it, he grinned all over his face. My cock is nowhere near as shy as the rest of me.

'You'll soon get into the swing,' he said. 'Have fun, you hear me? And don't do anybody I'd do.'

That was the last time I ever saw him, which was a pity because he had really kissable lips — if I ever meet him again I'll spit in his eye and pretend he did the dirty on me. I know, it's not fair, but it's how I cope with rejection . . .

I hate to ruin a good story, but I didn't find my prince on this particular occasion. He will arrive in his own good time, I'm certain of it. Instead I got bothered by a queen. Let me say I have nothing against fairies who like frocks, but I wouldn't say my dick responds to satin and lace. Besides which, he was old enough to be my father. He came mincing up to me, all-over perfumed fat, squeezed into a backless bead number, complete with a boa. He stood right up close with his arm threatening to wrap itself around my shoulder.

'I've had enough of this orgy. I think you and me had better go somewhere quiet and get to know one another. My car's waiting.'

Fucking cheek! But I'm so nice, I didn't want to offend him; so I *said I was with somebody and somebody was the jealous type. It didn't put him off one little bit.*

'Let me set your mind at rest, pretty boy. I saw who you came in with and he's not going to stand in the way of our pleasure. Do you know, I actually think he would be pleased to give us his blessing? These New York fags are so accommodating. Now suppose you quit making excuses and get yourself ready. Like I said, my car's waiting.'

I thought he was just odious and I hated Stuart for not rescuing me right away. It wasn't even as though this punk had any taste or anything! He looked like he'd thrown his costume together out of castoffs. I could just tell, under all that badly applied make-up, that was one boring little shit trying to get his dick into me. He acted like he owned the place; he seemed to suppose all he need do was snap his fingers and I would come running! It didn't occur to him I might actually have some thoughts in the matter.

Stein went on to do what he claimed he hated to do: he ruined his good story. Much space was wasted on this righteous indignation. Hanson turned the pages, looking for the next occasion where the action hotted up. Ten pages later found Stein at an orgy in a suite at the Plaza. This time he had a better idea of how to get what he wanted.

Let me confess it: I'm a masochist. I like to be bossed around but I like to know the person who's doing the bossing is going to look out for me. I have no special yearning to be mauled by elderly nasties who think they're somewhere in between Clark Gable and God.

Hanson scanned the page. Stein was complaining about another unwanted admirer. It seemed he was now an old hand at sex partying but hardly ever wrote about himself as an active part of the proceedings. He always fancied the guys who were busy and he seemed to have a knack of attracting rich older men who weren't to his tastes. Then a familiar name caught Hanson's eye.

It had taken me some time to figure it, but then it came to me in an instant. I wouldn't leave things to chance: I would bring along my own little sadist to look out for me. I knew exactly who would play the part best.

Billy was a little dubious at first. He said he didn't much go for group sex — you never know who's going to recognize you on the street at some later date. I thought he was going to let me down but it turned out he was really interested — just didn't want to show it too much in case I thought he was gone on me.

To digress: just after I first met Billy, I had this dream. I was being gang-fucked by four statuesque Olympians and Billy was standing there overseeing it all: he was my master and I was his slave. When I woke I found I'd come in my sleep. I haven't done that since I was a little kid.

Considering it was his first orgy, Billy behaved like he was doing it nightly. He soon sized up what was what. He'd gotten himself a drink and made it quite clear I wasn't going to be allowed one until I deserved it. Then he told me I was to strip naked before he even considered letting me do anything else. I tried to undress slowly so he could enjoy the tease but he wasn't about to mess around. He hit me across the face.

We were in the bedroom. On the bed was a couple of guys sucking each other and there was another three of them having fun on the floor. Just through the door there were people chatting and eating sandwiches.

Some young men were looking in to see what was on offer. They immediately got interested. They stood around the doorway, waiting to see what was about to happen.

I was on show.

'I told you to strip, not do the fucking dance of the seven fucking veils,' Billy said. He was all too aware of the others around us and I knew he was getting off on all this just as much as I was. I'd made a special effort and was wearing undershorts. I stripped down to them: no point in having underwear if you just cast it aside at the first opportunity.

There were five other naked guys in the room but in my shorts I was getting more attention than any of them. My prick was rock-hard and I was trembling like I do when I know I'm in for a fucking. Billy walked all the way round me like I was an exhibit and he was thinking of buying me. He pinched me in various places, maybe to see if I reacted or maybe to test how tight my skin was. He lit a cigarette and held it right next to my nipple. I could feel the heat from it getting more and more intense. I knew it wouldn't do to back away so I just grimaced and tried to bear it. Billy's mouth curled into a really sexy sneer.

'You finding that just a little too hot, boy? You think standing that bit of pain makes you into some sort of fucking hero? You don't know nothing. I'm gonna have your butt red-raw and your pretty-boy back covered in welts. That's before I get all these gentlemen here to fuck your shithole until you scream. You understand, boy?'

I was shivering uncontrollably and, stupid though it seemed, I put my hands in front of my genitals to protect them. Billy grabbed my wrist and twisted it painfully behind my back. He repeated his question.

'I asked if you understand me, boy!'

I said I did and remembered to call him 'sir'. It turned me to Jell-O standing there almost naked with so many males looking on while I was talked down to by this young buck. I noticed how my cock was showing through my shorts and I wondered what would happen if I pissed myself right there in front of everybody. Billy almost brushed the cigarette across my nipple but pulled it back just in time. It felt like he'd burned me and I didn't care.

One of the guys who were watching came up close to Billy and felt his butt like he was really turned on by all this and he wanted to ball with him. I lowered my head hoping that if I acted real respectful Billy would give me over to this guy and have him screw me. He was in his late twenties; he had slim, pointed features and soft brown hair which made him look younger than he probably was. I couldn't make out what color his eyes were, but they were like two lumps of coal with long, curling lashes to decorate them. He had padded, wet lips and an attractively damaged nose. He was dressed in a T-shirt and jeans and wouldn't have looked out of place on the dockside. Billy glanced at him and then returned his attention to me. He allowed the groping and I noticed it became more serious.

Billy pulled on the waistband of my underwear and released it back with a snap.

'You gone all bashful, shitface? You think you can hide your dicky in your shorts? If you don't get them off in two seconds you won't have a dick left to show us. One – two . . .'

I still didn't take them off. I just pulled them down to my ankles. Doing that made me feel the more abject, more like I was being forced into all this. It seemed Billy considered I obeyed his order. He hit my cock with the flat of his hand and it sprang back at him. The other guys were coming in closer. Their hands were reaching out for one another's body but the focus stayed absolutely on me. I could have read menace into their expressions; it felt like I was being bullied by a gang of uncouth street kids.

'How is he at sucking dick?' said the Docker. (I'll call him that, though he might have taught math at Harvard for all I know.) 'Can that pretty mouth do for me what I think it can?'

'Sure,' said Billy. 'If he's not up to standard you go ahead and let me know and I'll knock shit out of him.'

He said this nicely as though it were something he did every day of his life. The Docker nodded and, leaving off Billy's ass, he unbuttoned himself and felt inside. His cock came flopping out, semihard and getting stiffer by the second. It was big enough to call deformed. It was oozing fluids and it had a loose foreskin which peeled back as the snake grew. I waited. Even though I was dying to get it into my mouth, I wanted to have to be forced to do it.

The two guys on the bed had left off what they were doing and were coming to have a look at my poor body. I was surrounded by men who were handsome as hell so I didn't argue when lesser specimens came to watch from the edges. I wondered if it would have made much difference if I had objected, but I wasn't to be given time to worry about such trivia.

The best of them were crowding in on me. I was an animal and they were the hunting party. I knew I was cornered and they knew I might *make some futile attempt to escape. Neither they nor I thought for one moment I might succeed, but I wasn't going to be allowed to try in case I damaged myself. My body was soon to belong to them and it was no longer up to me to play fast and loose with it.*

Billy looked to the right and left of him and gave an 'Oh, I get it' smile. Still behaving like hunters, they had me pinioned in a flash. I didn't see who gave the order for it, but I suppose it must have been Billy because, just like I'd hoped he would, he'd stayed in charge of all this and the rest of them seemed to accept it.

They had my arms behind me and one of them secured my wrists with handcuffs. He must have come prepared — maybe he was an off-duty cop. I've never been cuffed before. It was a weird feeling: different from being tied with rope where there's always the chance you can work it loose. Here I knew there was absolutely nothing I could do until this son of a bitch decided to unlock me.

They were right up against me now, all grinning like handsome apes. They started poking my genitals: just light prods to let me know they could really hurt me if they wanted to. Billy got my head in a cradle hold and squeezed his finger into my mouth. As he prized it open, another of them pushed me down to my knees. The Docker stepped right up in front of me and forced his pecker into what we were all pretending was my unwilling face.

Billy had squatted down with me, keeping hold of my head so he could steer my movements and stop me from pulling away. He kept whispering things into my ear like 'Taste that, fucker. It's gonna be going right up your backside. It's gonna split you in two, and you won't be able to do nothing to help yourself.' Or 'That's it, shitface! You suck that meat. Suck it good. How does it feel to have your wrists in metal?'

I spluttered a bit and once or twice nearly choked. The man's cock felt like it was bigger than my mouth and it was poking right down into my throat. I was trying not to graze him with my teeth. I wanted them to know I was going to give them no trouble at all.

His eyes glazed over. He looked as though he could have been on drugs. Maybe he was, or maybe the loving care I was giving his cock was enough to send him to heaven. I loved his tight, flat stomach and the real profusion of hair spreading like a mane around his dick. His belly-button (which I could see every now and again when his shirt rode up far enough) was beautiful: just like the name says — a button. I wanted to lick it — maybe later I would be allowed to.

Billy was fumbling with his own flies. Two of the others had their cocks out ready and waiting. I hoped this wasn't just going to be a case of having to do everything five times over. Somehow I thought not. They looked like they knew what they were doing. In any case, I had full confidence in Billy's powers of imagination.

Eventually, the Docker pulled out without coming. Another of his friends took his place. This guy was broad and just the tiniest bit on the plump side. He wasn't as sure of himself as the others. He kept looking to them for encouragement. He had sandy hair, like Billy's (I think so, it was very dark), and an honest kind of face. He was the sort you could take home to meet Mom and she would always say, 'He's such a nice boy. Why can't you be more like him?'

His dick curved upward. It was solid enough and it looked hungry. It was the color of a plum at top and nesting in fine hair at the base. His pubes smelled vaguely of good, male sweat. He held me at the sides of my head and steadied himself by standing with his legs astride (at least, as far astride as he could with his trousers hobbling him).

'You go for it, Franky,' one of the others said. 'It's your big day next week. Get your old man seen to. It's gonna be the last time you ever do.'

There was general laughter and Franky responded nervously. I felt sorry for him. Can you beat that? There I was all naked and with my hands fastened behind my back. I was about to be used as a spunk receptacle by all these guys and I was feeling sorry for one of them. Billy seemed annoyed that Franky was delaying things.

'Go on, kid,' he said. 'Make him eat cock.'

Franky almost gulped and nodded like he was being ordered to do this by his sergeant. He put his dick into my mouth and I sucked on it powerfully. It tasted a bit of salt.

I could tell what I was doing was pleasing Franky because of his increasing body movements. The other guys seemed to think this whole thing was funny. Did Franky's 'big day' involve throwing rice and a woman in white perhaps? He was obviously new at the man-to-man game and was successfully embarked on his first test. I eased up. I didn't want him to spoil his image by coming too quickly.

The Docker was whispering a suggestion to Billy. Billy gave his consent and Franky was stopped in his tracks. He looked puzzled, poor thing.

'Was I doing it wrong . . .?'

I almost ruined everything by joining in the general laughter. No, they assured him. What he was doing was just perfect, but there was something else he ought to try.

They turned him round and presented my face with his butt. Franky was slowly persuaded to bend over. They told him this would be the ultimate in sexual experience. One of the ones who hadn't been sucked by me made Franky suck him instead.

I was given Franky's hole to lick. One of the men was holding his cheeks apart for me and Billy was standing by to see I did exactly as I was told. He shoved my head against the knob of flesh. I went for it like metal to a magnet.

It was clean, for which I was thankful. The only taste I got from it was sweat, which I thought was just beautiful. I could hear Franky's satisfied grunts as he did justice to the other man's cock. I tried to get my tongue right inside him. I don't know why, but I was keen to show him as good a time as I could: call it my wedding gift to him.

The muscle around his shithole was rough to my tongue. Inside, he was smooth and slippery. It was hot in there too. I pushed inside as far as I was able and nearly suffocated myself in the process. Billy could see I was trying my best and made sure I was given every opportunity to satisfy. He made Franky bend further, causing the guy he was sucking to have to squat.

A third man took his position behind me and I felt a finger probing into my own hole. He didn't use any spit to ease it in and it hurt me quite a bit. Still I went on licking Franky's most private place. I knew the finger was just for starters and, sure enough, the guy soon pulled it out and prepared to fuck me properly.

I really like having a guy's cock up against my asshole. It's that anticipation of being speared — feeling the hot, wet thing next to me, all set to go inside. I pushed back against it and got a cuff across the face from Billy.

'You don't get impatient now, do y'hear? This nice gent's going to fuck your ass when he's ready to do it, not when you are.'

I grunted a 'yes, sir' and tried to cover my mistake by licking Franky's butt even more furiously. Apparently he'd had all he was going to get because the Docker made him move away from me.

Franky did what he was told without complaining. He just stood at the side, watching with a look of absolute seriousness across his open face. He was pulling away at his shaft, slowly and intensely. One time, he put his hand behind him and felt his own backside. He was remembering my tongue up there and wanting more. I knew this, and he knew this, but it was evidently not going to be up to either of us to try to cause it to happen.

The lanky gazelle behind me was not going to hang around for ever just to prove a point. He got me by the upper arms and steadied my body ready to be impaled. I was having difficulty keeping balance, shackled as I was. I nearly fell over when he went inside me. The other guys grouped up around me. This time it was Billy's cock that found its way into my mouth.

The thin rod of heat in my shithole was fucking me hard. I had taken the pain of it willingly. It soon fired off into an aching fullness which branched out all around the insides of me. I rocked up and down, feeling the hardness which fueled this charge. At the same time, Billy's blunt penis was filling my mouth. Franky dared to come closer and, accommodating him, Billy allowed his cock in there along with his own. I don't know how I managed it, but I was able to blow both guys while I was being fucked by a third. As well as that, a fourth was wanking himself over my bound wrists.

Man meat in my anal passage makes me feel real good and I was hoping it would keep going all evening. It was not possible: volcanoes *were designed to erupt. Pretty soon the lava was flushing through my insides in a rushing, hot stream. I pictured it filling me up and prayed to God that the bastard would stay inside me when he was through. He pulled out, leaving me feeling bereft.*

Another guy, the one who had had to content himself with jerking off, came and took his place. I groaned as his penis crawled up my back passage.

This guy's cock was easier to take because my gut had been loosened already. It didn't feel so much fun until he started fucking me. He was rapid and brutal, slamming at my ass like a man possessed. I could hear his 'oooh yeahs' and his little snorts of pleasure. I tried to grip his fat cock with my gut and, if the increase in speed was anything to go by, I succeeded.

He came quickly and, as Franky and Billy pulled out of my mouth, he put his cock in there, making me lick it clean for him. I took good care to do it properly. When I was done he patted my head as though I was his pet pooch. I wanted to lick his whole body all over and push my head into every private place he had — he was glorious and completely golden, like a picture I have of Icarus, who flew too near the sun. I knew he had a Bronx accent but I didn't care.

Billy was taking his place behind me and I prepared for another impaling. Each time it happened, I had found it easier to adjust to and Billy's penis slid into me without my body resisting it at all.

When there is nothing in you that's fighting it, the slippery, piston-like motion of a man's cock inside your body cannot be bettered. The physical warmth spreading up that neglected part of you connects to your heart and your brain. It's like you love the whole world and you would do anything for the man who's giving you this joy. Of course (as I'd known from the moment I'd chosen him to accompany me here) I had been a little in love with Billy ever since New Year.

Franky, Docker and company were grouping round me in a tight circle. Hands were patting my backside and stroking me. I was wrestling against the handcuffs, not because I thought this might get me out of them, but because I liked to feel their restraint to the very full.

Somebody, and I think it was Franky, got hold of my cock. Soon enough my approaching orgasm had caught up with Billy's. The Docker kissed me; I felt Billy tensing, ready to shoot his semen into me; hands were everywhere. I sucked on Docker's mouth, giving strangulated cries as my come raced up and out.

It was over. Franky made me lick clean his semen-soaked hand. Billy soon replaced it with his cock and I cleaned that as well. The guys all patted me like I was a racehorse who had just won them lots.

Pretty soon, me and Billy were on our own again. He left me manacled but he cradled me in his arms and stroked my hair. He kept kissing my forehead and squeezing me. I could have stayed like that for ever.

★The drag queen was there again and he'd brought a friend. The friend was much too good-looking to be anything other than a hustler. Mr Drag is getting on my tits. If he reads this he'll know he'd better watch his back. Fuck him! I've got Billy.

Hanson was about to leave the office when his phone rang. He recognised the voice as belonging to the frosty woman in Records. She was not sounding half so sure of herself this time.

'Detective Hanson? I – erm – I'm sorry to have to tell you, I did indeed make a mistake when I informed you earlier about our not having a Henry Flynn. I really am terribly sorry, I hope you appreciate it's not a usual thing for us to get it wrong . . .'

Hanson wasn't in a forgiving mood.

'You've caused me a whole lot of trouble and now you just come back and say "sorry"? That's crap!'

The voice stiffened: 'There is really no need for language.'

Hanson would have played semantics with her but he couldn't be bothered. He demanded to know what information she had on Henry Flynn. Here she became cagey again.

'I'm afraid I can't give you anything to speak of. He's been with us for some time and –'

'Some time? How long?'

'I can't tell you that right now.'

Hanson grinned to himself. 'You've lost the file, haven't you? Go on – confess it and do your soul some good.'

There was a long pause during which Hanson thought he heard some whispering. Then she came back on the line: 'That is correct, sir. I regret to say we have mislaid Officer Flynn's file.'

Hanson uttered one last expletive to keep her happy and slammed the phone down. A lost file! It happened, sure it happened – all the time.

Hanson considered his position: did this mean he could get back to being smoochy with his delectable mountain of muscle? No, he decided. If Flynn ever came back to him there would have to be conditions. Delectable mountain of muscle he may well be, but Officer Flynn still had some explaining to do.

Hanson forced himself back to the matter in hand. Thinking he may as well make good use of the frosty service, he asked the woman to look him out the file on sexual deviants. He had a mind to start meeting with others of his own kind. If it didn't solve the case, it might at least be fun.

Six

Next day, in a bar where the customers liked their membership filed under 'D' for 'discretion', Hanson took his place on a wobbling stool of quite ridiculous proportions. Next to him was one of the contacts Old Frosty in the Records department had turned up for him. She was a Jean Harlow lookalike and would have been extremely convincing had he not known her secret: she had the wrong equipment under her dress.

He pushed a drink over to 'her' and she smiled at him in what was meant to be a coy way. It looked like she was already imagining what it would be like to suck his dick. He tried to behave as though being given the eye by a man in heels meant no more to him than a peck on the cheek from his old auntie. In fact he looked like he'd prefer to snuggle down with a skunk. She didn't seem to mind; in fact she laughed. Her voice was throaty and attractive. It would sound like contralto if you didn't know the secret.

'Honey, you're cute! What d'you say you come with me and you find out what your dick's for? I won't even charge you.'

Hanson was annoyed at being embarrassed, annoyed that she

found it amusing and annoyed that a male person should be wearing a dress.

She was the most likely weirdo on the list of perverts he'd been given. She'd been arrested in dozens of police raids on dozens of queer bars: she had a record the length of her fingernails. When he'd phoned, Hanson had kidded her he was a reporter on the *Times* and he was looking for background to pad out his article on the Stein murder. (She'd never heard of it of course but what did that matter?) He would have kept up the pretence but her carrying on as if they were equals had got his goat.

'I might just charge *you*,' he said, flashing his ID.

From her scream, anyone might think he'd flashed something else at her.

'You're a cop? I didn't know! How was I to know? Oh Jesus! I wouldn't have tried pullin' you if I'd known. I thought you were some poor dumb hack! Fuck!'

Hanson didn't want the whole place to know who he was. He tried to hush her but she was building up to hysteria and enjoying it. He grabbed her by the arm and yanked her off her stool.

'Come on, sugar,' he said grimly. 'Looks like you've just pulled.'

He marched her out, cursing under his breath as he did it. Everybody in the place was scowling in Hanson's direction. Though they made no move to help the captive queen, being on the receiving end of their disapproval was not exactly comfortable. The bartender sighed and went on with his work. He'd seen it all before. Hanson had effectively blown it with that particular bar: in there, a plain-clothes cover would be as much use as a toupee with the tag out.

Naturally, he placed all the blame at the door of his new friend. 'You dumb jerk!' he shouted, pinning her up against a wall and shaking her till her fake rocks rattled. 'I did not want every pervert in that bar to know I am a cop! Why couldn't you just have kept your fucking mouth shut?'

If she was going to take anything lying down, it wasn't this. 'You assholes are all the same!' she screamed right back into his face. 'You pretend you are who you ain't; you come and threaten us; you arrest us and then you expect us to *help you*? Go screw yourself and let go my arm. I want my lawyer.'

Hanson let her go and tried to calm himself. He was annoyed with himself, not this freak. This was no way for a detective to advance his career. He tried to sound reasonable.

'I apologise. You're not in any kind of trouble. I just wanted to ask you a few *fucking questions, that's all*!'

It wasn't the best attempt at keeping temper hidden. He'd managed pretty well – until the end of the sentence, when the swear word had lighted the blue touchpaper and a small explosion had taken place. The freak should have known she was going to have to tread careful if she wanted a quiet life. It appeared she wanted no such thing.

'Are you trying to tell me you looked me up to ask me the way to Times Square? You must think I was born yesterday, mister!' She held out her wrists and heaved a resigned sigh. 'OK, get it over with, Mr Asshole. As if I don't have enough bracelets to sink a battleship. Get them on and read me my rights. That is, if I have any.'

Hanson felt truly ashamed. He didn't like to admit to having things in common with this person, but he wasn't a million miles away from her perversions and she was, after all, one of the city's oppressed. He tried to glue a smile across his face but it looked like he was sucking citrus.

'I'm not gonna arrest you. I need some information. Do you know of somewhere else we can drink?'

She scoffed. 'Yeah, Big Chief Sitting Duck, that's me. Sure – we'll just go to a nice, quiet bar where nobody's gonna notice that I'm me and you're you and we're sitting together. Then when the nice, polite maître d' has brought us our champagne and oysters, I'll give you the names and addresses of every queen I know in the city. Next day you'll be going round giving all my friends a great big kiss and tellin' 'em how it was me who sent you 'cos I know what a charming, upright and decent kind of *fucking asshole you are!*'

She gave these last words all she could and Hanson was kind of put out by her anger. What was the reason for it when he was just doing his job? He would have to try a different approach.

'I'm not vice, I'm from homicide. That case I said I was writing a story on? It's a real case and that's the God's honest truth. There *has* been a killing and I'm investigating it. I've no interest in what you and your friends do together behind locked doors. Now, are you going to take me to some queer bar where they're not going to be prejudiced about my wearing pants?'

This last was meant to be a funny but she wasn't amused, not even a little bit. She looked Hanson up and down as though he were trying to sell her life insurance. He really wished she didn't have the upper hand here – he thought it should be him.

'They're gonna be more prejudiced about your profession than your pants, big boy.'

'Do you suppose I'm gonna tell them what I do for a living?'

She shook her head. 'I guess not. What do you want to ask me?'

'Different things. For instance, there's a nursery rhyme: "Peter, Peter, pumpkin eater . . ." That mean anything to you?'

She looked at him like he'd gone crazy. 'If you want me to rock you to sleep in your cradle,' she said, 'I can think of better songs to sing.' Then she appeared to have made a decision. 'Let's go,' she said.

She turned on her diamanté-studded heel and tripped sassily off down the street, her hips undulating like a fairground ride. Hanson followed three paces behind her (as is right and proper when walking with a queen). He knew what this must look like: that she'd just picked him up and they were off to some squalid dive to do the business.

They arrived at a backstreet joint which was full of smoke and the smell of old cabbage. It called itself a restaurant but, if your dinner had been through that kitchen, it was probably not the best idea to try eating it. Hanson's companion seemed to know the bartender. There were yelps of delight from both of them and so much kissing you'd think they were Italian.

Hanson was introduced: 'He's just a trick – but he's a really famous writer. He's even had movies done of all his books.' Hanson thought this way over the top, but false modesty about false achievements would be just wasting time.

The bartender commented on how very nice-looking he was. Pearl (for that was what the freak was calling herself) would have pushed this further but she caught sight of the thin line of Hanson's lips and realised this was not a good idea. She made out he was the shy sort and they were going to sit at the back where it was darker.

'Don't do that,' Pearl said when they were alone.

'Do what?'

'Keep looking all disapproving like that. People will either know you for a cop or think youse an evangelist fallen into sin. We get quite a few of them in here.' She dipped her finger in the sugar and sucked on it. 'OK. What is it you want to ask me? Shoot.'

'Lots of things. What do you know about orgies?'

Pearl squealed and made everybody in the place look at her. Hanson was beginning to get used to this.

'OK, you don't have to piss your knickers. There's one you may have heard of that maybe happens regularly. It's at a private address in West End Avenue . . .'

'You want a piece of action, mister? I thought you was just after some killer.'

Hanson hushed her sharply. He was beginning to think this

whole thing was a very bad idea indeed. Perhaps he should ditch this particular Pearl and try opening another oyster.

The bartender had arrived with the drinks. He set them down and smiled at his two customers as if he were their matchmaker.

'Enjoy,' he said in a voice that would not have disturbed a cobweb.

'You give me something to know I can trust you,' Pearl said when he'd gone. 'How am I to know you ain't planning on busting some place where perfectly innocent people are doing illegal things to each other?'

'You can trust me. I'm not interested in what men do with their dicks. I just need somebody who knows people, somebody with their ear to the ground. I'll pay you.'

'Honey, I took that much for granted. But before I accept one dime off you I need to know that you ain't gonna muddy my name with my friends.'

Hanson imagined she would sell her own mother if the price was right; he had a really low opinion of this queen. He was being prejudiced as hell and he'd saved himself just enough moral fibre to know he'd no right to be.

He wondered how it would sound if he tried the more open approach: if he said he was currently in love with a dream boy with a dark, hairy chest. He decided it would weaken his image.

Flynn was back in his head again now. Damn it, Hanson thought. He was like a tune that wouldn't go away. They called the feeling lovesick and 'sick' seemed about right – Hanson had a terminal case.

Mr Detective struggled to take over his personality. He sat back, just like Bogey, and lit a cigarette. He let a thin wisp of smoke emerge from his lips. If he hadn't been so handsome he would have looked the part fine.

Pearl was annoyingly unimpressed. She drummed out a clickety tattoo on the table with her turquoise nails and half closed her eyes.

'Ain't no use looking across at me like you're gonna crap. I need something I can trust in.'

If she'd meant to make him feel ridiculous she'd got what she wanted. Roach would surely have run her in for lewd behaviour. Other cops would have got her into the privacy of a cell and then beaten her senseless. Hanson was proud of his own, reasoned methods but they were sometimes damned difficult to maintain. He had to try to think of a way to get the trust of these folk.

Your folk, his conscience shouted from behind the locked door where he'd shoved it. Just because you look normal doesn't mean you're not one of them.

He scribbled his number on a note and pushed it across the table. Pearl looked at it; kissed it, leaving the shape of perfect pink lips on it, and slipped it into her fake cleavage. Her mouth curled up at one side and down at the other: the kiss had not been exactly sincere. Hanson got up to go.

He was on his way out of the door when a queen sitting at a table nearby waved his arms like windmill sails and shouted to him, 'Andrew Roscoe, can it really be you? Well fucking Mary! Fucking, fucking Mary! I thought you had walked out of my life for ever! How are you?'

Had this been said in any other place and by a person with less of a lisp and more of a body than this guy had, Hanson might have stolen the unknown Mr Roscoe's identity. As it was, he said his name was not Roscoe: he'd never even met anyone called Roscoe – if he ever did he would send him the queen's regards. The queen in question did not seem to believe him.

'Pretending not to know me! I thought you might. How is that bitch you live with? I suppose he gave you hell after I left! You should have called me. I really was very keen on you but, hey! Life's like that!'

They were getting attention on all sides. The bartender was

simpering away; Pearl was rising from the darkness, intrigued by what was happening; other customers were looking to see whether the attractive young man would go for the drag queen or the old flame who wouldn't burn out.

Pearl was soon at Hanson's shoulder. She was accusing.

'Ain't you gonna introduce me to your friend?'

Hanson muttered that the guy was mistaking him for somebody else. The queen was getting peeved. He protested he would know those deceitful eyes anywhere and did Hanson still have the smallest dick in Manhattan? Pearl shook her head from side to side very definitely.

She turned to the queen. 'How long is it since you two were together?'

The queen assumed Pearl was a jealous new partner and played up accordingly.

'I don't know why he's gone for you, bitch. Does he imagine that screwing a broad with a dick makes him a normal man about town? He liked it better with a real man, I can tell you.'

Two or three presentable specimens of American manhood sidled up. They were wondering why Hanson was going for either of these people when there were better prizes to be had. Hanson gave them a weak smile but resisted the temptation to go further.

Pearl had seen this smile and knew exactly what it meant.

She laughed, she shrieked. Soon she was doubled over and holding her sides. The queen had no idea what was so funny and Hanson thought she was putting it on.

'So have hysterics – be my guest.' Hanson said. 'This man has made a mistake. He thinks I'm called Roscoe: I'm not called Roscoe. Somehow I don't see that as hilarious but maybe I'm missing something.'

Pearl gave him a playful push against his shoulder. She swallowed her laughter and wiped a tear from her eye, smudging her mascara. The effect was not flattering.

'Hon, why did you not tell me you're a friend of Dorothy?

You imagine youse the only one in your profession who's been doing it with the sons of Adam? God, *nooooo!*'

She turned to the queen. The mock gentility with which she began slid beautifully off the tracks at the end of her speech: 'This gentleman was just asking me if I knew of any good parties. I thought he was after going to them in a working capacity. Now I understand him correctly, I have decided to accept his kind offer and go with him to one. I'm terribly sorry, it looks like you and him are all fucked up!'

She beckoned for Hanson to follow her. The queen called out after them.

'Andrew, can't we see each other again, when you've done slumming it? I'm in here most nights.'

Hanson leant back through the door.

'Go fuck yourself,' he said.

Hanson caught up with Pearl. She was still smirking. What use in protesting innocence? She wasn't going to believe him anyway. Better try to still her wagging tongue.

'I never invited you to nothing! And I do not want it spread around what I do with my personal life,' he said.

She shrugged. 'Any fag who can pass for normal wants to pass for normal. It's the way of the world, sweetheart. I ain't gonna tell no one. Say, I like your little friend. If he wasn't so ancient and maybe just a little less poisonous, he'd be cute.'

'So, you gonna help me?'

She stopped and put her exquisite hands on both of his shoulders.

'What do I get from this deal?'

He wasn't going to ask her to name her price. Things weren't supposed to be this way at all. She had been calling the shots from the start and he wasn't at all happy about it. He had a mind to tell her she was damn lucky to get away without being charged but he knew it wouldn't make her roll on her back and play dead. He reached for his wallet.

'Half now and half later,' he began.

She stopped him. 'Put your cash away, handsome.'

If he looked surprised that was because he was. She licked her lips. 'Sure, I want paying for what I do,' she said, 'but I'll take payment in kind.'

Hanson glanced up at her sharply. 'Now hold on right there . . .!'

'You want to know about orgies? I tell you, darling. If youse gonna escort me to the ballroom then you can promise me the first dance. Is it a deal or is it a deal?'

Hanson wanted to slap her but he was too well brought up to hit a lady.

'Yes,' he said. It was a deal.

Later, he showed her one of the book covers with the photograph of Stein. It wasn't the best likeness — his publishers had done their best to make him look like Dick Van Dyke — but it was enough like him to be of use. She studied it and shook her head.

'I have a memory for faces. You have to have if you dress like I do and plan to carry on breathing for a living. This one I have not seen.'

Hanson had to admit it: up to now Pearl Silverstone (formally known as Eddie) was being about as much use to him as Little Orphan Annie. He tried giving her an edited description of a chapter from the diary to see if it rang bells. In response, she suggested they take three or four hustlers back to her place and recreate the scene.

Hanson had several copies of the photograph with him. (Stein would be able to look down from heaven and know his unsold stock was coming in useful.) She agreed to take one and ask around.

'People will think I'm trying to track down a lover. It will give me a kind of melancholy character. Maybe, when I ask folk, I should dress in black and cry a lot.'

Hanson was idly wondering what kind of male body lurked beneath the glitz. He had just about decided he didn't care and that Flynn, with all his faults, at least stuck to one gender. She was psychic, if just a little wide of the mark.

'Later, big boy!' she said vampishly. 'First you have to find out who killed this poor sucker.' She put her hand up to her mouth as if shocked by a sudden thought. 'My God! The streets aren't safe to walk no more! You will protect me, won't you?'

It was not a convincing performance. A thought came to Hanson: 'Has anybody ever tried to blackmail you?' he asked.

Pearl laughed quite genuinely.

'Oh yeah? You think some guy is gonna come across and say, unless I split my welfare with him, he's gonna go somewhere and tell that I'm a man wearing a dress? Hon, it would be like threatening to expose the Hudson as a river.'

Hanson tried to be patient. 'I didn't say has anybody done it? I said has anybody tried? Even a vague threat. Come on, think.'

Pearl adopted a 'thinking' pose. She clenched her fist and brought her chin down to it as in Rodin's statue. She stayed like that for so long a dog nearly left a message on her leg. Just before Hanson was about to disturb her she came up with an answer.

'There was a guy some time back. He asked me where my family was. I said I didn't know and I didn't care. Then he said, kinda conversational like, "Do they know you come in places like this?" I said I didn't know and I didn't care. He wasn't a queer: he picked a fight with someone who tried it on with him. I don't know who he was and it makes no difference. If youse gonna start checking out everyone who hates queens, you'd better open up a very big file.'

Hanson was aware of some punks grouping closer and closer around his car. Soon they would be near enough to scratch the paint. He said a quick goodbye to Pearl and sprinted back to rescue it. The kids followed him into the driver's seat with catcalls and insults.

'Hey! Shitface! You a cocksucker?'

'Kiss my ass, motherfucker!'

As asses go, the one on offer wasn't the worst to kiss but perhaps the punk wasn't really sincere. A small stone hit Hanson's windshield. He flinched but kept looking straight ahead. In the mirror he could see Pearl walking defiantly towards them. The kids turned their attention to her and ran on in front to block her path. She walked right through the middle of them as though she was a Broadway star and they were adoring fans.

Hanson headed next for the Plaza Hotel. He didn't hold out any hopes of his visit being of use but Stein had been there without his trousers and so it would be stupid not to try.

The receptionist was smart and brisk, with razor-edged politeness. Hanson showed her the photograph. She glanced at it briefly and returned it.

'It would be impossible for me or any of our other staff to remember this gentleman from a photograph. What name was the suite booked under?'

Hanson admitted he had no idea at all. Her face told him what she thought of his efficiency.

A man, who had been watching from across the foyer, came up to the desk and accidentally placed a newspaper on top of the photograph. Hanson wasn't going to make any big deal out of it because he had plenty more of the book covers. Anyway, the man was young and attractive and probably had a terrible life.

He thanked the receptionist and headed for the door.

At the reception desk, the man moved his newspaper and picked up Stein's photograph.

The receptionist looked tight-lipped but she made no move either to call Hanson back or to take the photograph herself.

'How fortunate I happened to be passing,' the man said. 'The gentleman will no doubt call back for this when he misses it. There's no need to tell him I've taken it.'

She didn't question him. He was one of the guests from suite 104. Nobody asked questions about suite 104.

FBI Agent Herbert Goddard left the Plaza Hotel and crossed the street. He went directly to a phone booth and placed a call to a colleague.

'Goddard here. Listen, I thought you said the Bureau had cleared up that case where the fag writer got himself killed? Yeah, well maybe the Bureau didn't clear it up enough. There's a gent been asking questions at the Plaza. I'd like to know who he is and I think maybe you would too.'

Seven

It wasn't such an unusual occurrence in the Village: a man (who would normally have been the 'no-nonsense' type) looking furtively about him as he walked through the streets. Though he looked like he had no physical reason to fear, he showed his nervousness in the way he curled in on himself, the way he jumped every time a stranger came too close. His whole demeanour had the imprint of fear written large across it. Those who were more used to the ways of this area of New York would at once know him for what he was: a 'happily married' man on homo leave of absence.

He would sometimes stop and light a cigarette. This was a dangerous luxury for him. Standing in one place for more than a second or two meant someone, somewhere, might recognise him. This was a place for bohemians and perverts – and artists.

The last description came to James Brisbane as if it were his salvation. If, at some boring cocktail party, anyone was to remark, 'Say, didn't I see you in the *queer* part of town last week?' he would say, 'Sure. I was going to meet my friend, the artist.'

James (Jim to his friends) was taller than he ought to be. His was a kind, honest face but not out of the ordinary. He supposed any physical attractiveness he'd had to be a thing of the past. He had resigned himself to being with Geraldine and the kids. Normality was his lot and he would have to make do. Every time he had 'those thoughts' he had tried to deal with them in a descending list of preferred ways. He would

1 take a cold shower
2 go for a run
3 fuck his wife
4 masturbate without thinking or,
5 give up kidding himself and fantasise about men while he jerked himself off.

If he had to resort to 5, he would afterwards go through 1 to 3 as a kind of penance.

Such was the life of James Brisbane. He was the first to agree: it was a dreadful waste. 'Dreadful waste' didn't mean he had any big ideas about his looks. If asked, he would have said quite the opposite, but he'd had one or two compliments from women. He'd always wondered about getting something similar from men.

He'd dared to actually do 'it' with other guys only a handful of times a century or two back when he was still in his twenties. Then he'd been told he was cute (in a tall, slim brush–salesman kind of way). Now he had reached the great age of thirty, he considered he was cute no longer.

He didn't know what the hell he was doing in the Village anyway. There was no way he was going to be able to pick somebody up; he wasn't even sure he wanted to. He wouldn't have come here at all if Geraldine hadn't gone to visit her family. He'd felt bad about it but there was nothing he could do to stop himself. Every time she was away from home the old urges resurfaced in him.

The ghost of his younger self told him it was a shame to

waste the opportunity. Practical, older and wiser Jim did not agree. The shame was, for him at least, that there was no longer an opportunity to waste.

'There, look,' the ghost argued. 'That guy is looking back at you.'

It was true, but that was no reason to let his cock rule his cranium. The guy may be a rough, or a cop in plain clothes or Lord knew what.

Jim was all mixed up. He wanted the thrill of danger but he didn't want to take any risks. He knew with this attitude he was going to wind up with a whole lot of nothing. How was anyone to know he was available if he didn't do something to show it? It wasn't as though he *looked* like a fairy.

He had been in one or two bars. He had been reliably informed they were bars where 'things go on'. He'd been terrified every time somebody had tried to get talking to him.

They were sad sorts of places he'd chosen. On the dance floor, male couples swirled about, haunted expressions on their pale faces. Every so often the cosy red glow would be broken by a warning flash of real light, sending the couples scuttling away to be wallflowers. A stranger would enter and, once his eyes had strayed in the kind of direction that proved he wasn't a cop, the lonely boys would gradually resume their licentious foxtrot.

Jim saw it for what it was but it still seemed impossible to be part of it. A dance and a hug would have done him just fine. He remembered an old joke about a pious man who prayed to God for a lottery win. He never got a dime and eventually began to lose his faith. One day God appeared to him and said, 'Look, you gotta meet me halfway – at least buy a ticket.'

He tried. Several times he'd tried to buy that ticket. Now he was out on the street again. He dredged up the remains of his courage from deep inside. This time he would do it, he would ask someone for a dance. He headed back to one of the places he'd already visited. He was fully determined on smiling nicely and talking to everybody who was interested. Hell, they couldn't arrest you for making polite conversation.

A sandy-haired guy who he'd seen earlier was in there. He was smoking and looking around as though he were window-shopping for someone to talk to. He recognised Jim and smiled openly. Jim breathed deep. It was now or never. There was no need to fear this guy: he was surely a nice person and he must be interested or why else smile like that?

They went through the usual routine of 'was the seat taken?' and 'no, it wasn't'. At first Jim pretended he was happy with his own company and he'd just happened to sit there because there was a vacant chair. Inside, his head was buzzing. He was going through every opening line he'd ever heard and discarding them all as being either corny or obvious.

He was still hoping the other guy would make the first move. Then Jim knew he would be able to throw off his shyness and be so accommodating you wouldn't believe. He kind of guessed the other man was having very similar thoughts to his own.

At last, in a cracked voice quite unlike his usual one, Jim asked, 'Do you know this place? Are you regular here?'

It was not a good line at all and he wished he'd gone for, 'Looks like rain, do you know where I can get a cab?'

The guy nodded and sipped some funny kind of cocktail he had. It was full of ice and maraschino cherries; no self-respecting male would dare drink such a sissy-looking concoction.

'I wouldn't ask but it's my first time. I notice you have a very interesting-looking drink . . .' Jim was mentally kicking himself at every goofy word that came out. 'I never know what to ask for.'

He smiled – or tried to. The effect was like he'd just done something in his pants. The guy was twenty or so and Jim was wrong about his being on the timid side: he looked plenty self-assured now. Maybe Jim's making such a mess of things was encouraging him. Maybe he was thinking, At least I'm nowhere near as stupid as this dork . . .

Jim tried to shut up, but his tongue had got the better of him and refused to stop prattling. By the time he'd regained control of it, he'd exhausted all his small talk and wouldn't have been surprised if the youth had got up and left. Instead he looked Jim straight in the eye and said:

'I'm Arnie. Do you have a place we could go?'

Arnie said he had to stop by somewhere on 33rd Street. It was out of their way but Jim was not about to complain. To his surprise, the 'somewhere' turned out to be a public lavatory. Arnie was glancing at his watch as they approached as though he pissed by appointment. As the hour drew close he began to sprint, leaving Jim some way behind.

He was in and out of the john within half a minute and he looked a hell of a lot more relaxed coming out than he had when he went in. Jim did not ask questions: he never asked questions.

For some reason he didn't know, he had a sense they were being watched as they walked off down the street. Like Lot's wife, he disobeyed a warning about looking back. A figure was standing square in the middle of the pavement, staring at them. For Jim, it was like seeing a ghost, though the kid was made of flesh and blood right enough. He was handsome – beautiful even. He was probably Puerto Rican: dark-skinned with curly black hair, flashing eyes and gleaming white teeth. He was wearing a loose vest and jeans. He looked the streetwise sort. He seemed to be scowling, but that could have been Jim's imagination. Arnie paid him no heed.

They carried on to Jim's place in silence.

Jim had never done it in his own apartment before. He hated himself for betraying his wife like this, but she wasn't going to know and he couldn't turn back now.

As he struggled with his latchkey in the door, Arnie pressed up behind him and squeezed his buttocks. Jim pulled away and scolded him in an indignant whisper: they weren't in the Village now. But once inside it was a different matter.

Jim turned into the Incredible Hulk. He enveloped Arnie in a bear hug which near squeezed the breath out of him. Pretty soon they were writhing together: hands, arms, lips, tongues all wrapped in one great tangle. Arnie's cute-boy chequered shirt rode up his back. Jim grappled with it, desperate to get at what lay underneath it. At the same time Arnie scrabbled to undo Jim's shirt. Jim was all too keen to rid himself of it; buttons flew about the place but who minded? Next he kicked aside his shoes as Arnie helped him get his vest over his head. This done, Jim stood there, stripped to the waist and feeling like Goliath.

There was a pause in all this as Arnie lay back to see what he'd come home with.

'Not bad,' he said. 'I love all that.'

He reached out, a slower movement than before, and stroked the flat, dark hair that ran down Jim's chest like feathery seaweed on underwater rocks.

The calm did not last. Jim, keen to check out what lay beneath that lumberjack cotton, fumbled desperately with Arnie's shirt. Arnie, who wasn't all that good at the patience thing, ripped it off. More buttons flew, Arnie's vest was torn away. The two men sat up and studied each other.

The action slowed again. Their sharing of each other became tender.

Arnie went first to Jim's ear. After nibbling the lobe (something that caused Jim to whine with delight), his tongue went to work licking and probing inside. Jim demurred at first but a steady hand against his head persuaded him to stay still. He could hear a sound like some giant cat lapping milk next to a microphone. Arnie was tickling like crazy but Jim didn't care: he was going weak at the knees. After a minute or two, when it was over, Arnie kissed him lightly on the cheek.

'You liked that.'

It was a statement, not a question.

Jim drew Arnie to him and held him quietly. He felt pleasantly emotional. It was getting dark now, the room was grey. Jim preferred it like this. He did not want to see the familiar things that spoke to him of his family.

Holding eye contact, an unspoken dare governing their actions, they raised off the sofa and both dropped their trousers. There was a brief cuddling before their shorts followed. Jim considered this the ultimate human contact. Had he crawled across the Sahara and at last found water, he couldn't have been more relieved.

His hand was taken and placed deliberately and firmly between Arnie's buttocks. There was sweat down there, which helped it slide along. Jim had his eyes closed; he let his fingers see for him. His fingernail clicked against the hair.

Elsewhere, his cock was getting to know its new friend as their two bodies rocked against each other. Arnie stooped a little and began licking around Jim's neck. The movement allowed Jim's finger to find its target. It slipped inside the grasping ring of flesh and he felt the warmth close around it. He tried to simulate what he intended to do later with his cock but Arnie wasn't lubricated down there and it was difficult just yet.

'I'm gonna suck you,' Arnie said.

Again it was a statement.

Jim steered him back on to the sofa. Pedantically, he draped his own shirt over some cushions, arranging them first to support Arnie's back. While he was plumping them Arnie, who was now sitting directly in front of him, leant forward so his head knuckled into Jim's chest.

Even this accidental contact set them off again. Arnie's tongue took a tour around Jim's midriff while Jim massaged Arnie's neck. The massaging got harder and harder until Arnie was forced downward towards Jim's groin. Jim closed his eyes and raised his face up to the ceiling. This was bliss.

The wet lapping of Arnie's tongue was now well below Jim's

belly. It wasn't long before his cock was enveloped by slippery wetness.

Arnie's tongue did not stop moving. It found parts of his cock Jim didn't even know existed. Inevitably, it left off for a while, but only so it could take a visit to his balls and then go even further underneath. Once Jim had relaxed, this delicate sensation was wonderful to him. If only sex was always so good.

Arnie went back to his cock. Jim, who had been crazy about having his testicles licked, was now undecided what part of his genitals he liked being attended to best. He shifted. Arnie stopped what he was doing and looked up questioningly. Jim smiled and without either having to say anything, the two men readjusted themselves. Arnie lay back on to the cushions and Jim got on top of him, letting his balls dangle over Arnie's open mouth.

Arnie continued to surprise by moving Jim so he was sitting with his ass squarely across that mouth. If Jim had thought for even a second he wouldn't have done it but he soon realised what bliss it was to have his ass licked. He swore to God he'd do penance for his sins as long as God let him go sin some more.

Arnie's tongue went right inside him: inside his hole. His nose was pushing between Jim's buttocks, his hands were pulling them wide so it could get in further. This was a part of Jim's body that no one had ever seen, not even Geraldine, not even Jim himself. James Brisbane was allowing someone he had met barely an hour ago to lick his shithole – and he was loving it. If he had died then and there, he would have said he'd had a complete life.

He tried to get rid of the analytical steam train that was chugging through his brain. Just enjoy, he told himself. Just relax and feel. He would have done, but in some ways the thoughts of shame were giving him an added kick. This activity would be off-limits to the most wanton hustler and Jim liked that fact very much indeed.

All good things have to end but Jim tried not to let his disappointment take hold. Arnie had finished with licking his shithole but who was to say what other pastime he had in mind? The two men held each other for a brief rest.

'I'm not really a homosexual you know,' Arnie said. 'I'm not a fairy.'

'Neither am I,' Jim returned. He wondered why this needed to be discussed at all.

'Just don't think it,' Arnie said.

Jim gave him a real good, meaningful kiss to say thanks for everything so far. All the time he was doing it, he reminded himself that the lips he was kissing had only seconds before been loving his own backside. This was the next best thing to kissing his own ass.

'I think I'm crazy about you,' he said and he thought he meant it.

Arnie gave him a 'yeah, yeah' kind of look and lay back. Jim was instantly worried.

'Something the matter? I didn't mean . . .'

'Sure. Forget it.' Arnie was evidently not the romantic type.

Jim tried to compensate for being such a jerk by giving Arnie something back for all his hard work. He got him to turn over, meaning to return the favour and lick Arnie's asshole for him, but somehow he just couldn't.

Instead, he spat on his hand and rubbed the saliva into the hole where his finger had already been once that night. When it was sliding in and out without any problem, Jim made Arnie lie on his back with his legs up and wide. Arnie did as he was asked, holding his legs in position and showing his asshole as if to say, 'Here it is. Fuck me.'

Jim put his dick against the tight ring of muscle and tried to get it inside. It was difficult. Arnie tried to slither down the cushions to allow him better access but Jim still couldn't get himself where he had to be. He asked Arnie to go on all fours on the floor. By the time he'd done that, Jim's nervousness had taken over and his dick had gone just a little soft. He couldn't get it up and he couldn't get it in. Arnie rolled over on to his back and grinned.

'You're not used to doing it with men, are you?'

Jim started to apologise but Arnie stopped him.

'That's OK. There sure as hell isn't a rule about it. If my wife could see me now!' He noticed Jim's reaction to this. 'Yeah, I'm married too. Who isn't, for Christ's sake? And I have a kid. That's why we men look after each other, don't you say so?'

Jim nodded. He had detected something not quite right about Arnie's tone of voice but he couldn't tell what it was.

'Do you think I look like Montgomery Clift?' Arnie asked suddenly. He did a little but he wouldn't fool the fan club. Jim was wise enough not to say so.

Arnie was lost for a moment; a wide-eyed look came over his face.

'Did you know he's a queer as well?' he said. 'Truly: I have a friend who knows somebody who's fucked with him!'

Jim didn't know and he didn't much care. There was little chance of having Montgomery Clift over to dinner and still less that either he or Arnie would have the pleasure of him or any other movie star.

'You don't believe me, do you?' Arnie was saying. 'It's true, so help me God. I met a guy called Gregory who's really hot on movies – all queers are hot on movies. He told me Montgomery Clift is queer.'

Jim lay down on the floor beside Arnie and curled up to him in a foetal position. He contented himself with kissing whichever part of Arnie's body presented itself to his lips while Arnie chattered, his conversation getting more and more zany as he went on. Jim would have noticed how odd it was if he'd been listening but he'd stopped doing that as soon as the movies were mentioned. Jim was not hot on movies – he was not a typical queer.

★

They must have lain like that for quarter of an hour or so. Arnie could talk for America. Jim had woken up his brain enough to admit this guy was maybe a little too young for him. Jim was long past the stage where everything in the world impresses and you think Hollywood is capable of breeding real people. No, he thought, he wasn't crazy about Arnie after all: he was just in lust with him.

His dick was now completely flaccid. The pleasures of postcoital petting had started to wane. He felt an urgent need to get back to being his normal, everyday self. With this in mind he got up and pulled his shorts on.

'I'm sorry. It's time I asked you to go.'

Arnie looked hurt. That was too bad — nothing could be done to help it. Jim was suddenly *so* in control: so matter of fact; so heterosexual.

'Come on, please,' he said. 'Get dressed. I can't . . .'

The reason his voice faltered was the change that had come over that nice, babbling kid he'd just been curled up with. Arnie had not taken kindly to being ordered. He wasn't a cute queer any more: belligerency had transformed his face.

'You shouldn't do that to me,' he said. 'It's not a good idea, man.'

Jim made a desperate stab at polite persuasion. His wife would be back soon he said.

'Bullshit!' came the reply. 'You already told me she'd be away for days, remember?'

Jim went to the telephone and reached for the receiver. Arnie's hand slammed down hard on top. He was standing far too close; he was still naked. He leant even closer, his hand firmly planted over Jim's, which continued to grasp the receiver.

'I don't think the cops would be much interested in the problems of a fairy who gets into hot water by trying to lay a normal guy, do you?'

Jim was really scared now. Arnie came right up so you couldn't have placed rice paper between them. His breath smelt. Funny – Jim hadn't noticed that before. Arnie drew back, keeping his hand where it was. His tone reverted to being friendly but the abruptness of the change meant 'friendly' was not to be taken at face value.

'Don't you worry,' he said. 'Think I'm gonna tell everyone about you being queer? No, course not! I'll keep it between the two of us, shall I?'

He slowly released his grip on Jim's hand. Jim did not try to dial. He knew when he was beat.

'How much do you want?' he said.

Arnie sounded genuinely apologetic. 'I swear I didn't come here to get money. I'm not a criminal, man! I've even had this sort of trouble myself.' Then he must have thought better of defending his own good character because he got down to business. 'I wouldn't ask for a cent but I've just got hitched and you must know how difficult things can be. I won't ask you for much this time – say twenty dollars?'

Jim nodded, choking back his fear and anger and managing to look like he was still cognisant. His voice was a little shaky but it almost passed for normal. 'What do you mean, "this time"?'

'You and me have an understanding now. I don't say nothing about what you tried to do to me and you just make sure I don't get hard up. So, let's say my girl could do with a new coat – I come to you. My kids want a holiday – I come to you. Hell, I'm not greedy. We'll get along fine, won't we, Jimmy boy?'

He smiled like he really meant that last bit. Then he added, 'You know, you're lucky. I'm new at this game. Others would charge you more. I won't. I'll fix up a postbox address. Hell, it's easy enough to send money, don't you think?'

Jim sat down on the sofa where he'd just made love to this man and buried his face in his hands. The enormity of his mistake was sinking in.

Arnie was still shirtless but he was already on his way out of the door. He paused, getting Jim's attention back with a 'Hey!'

Jim looked up. Arnie stood loosely, his weight all on one leg, his clothes held casually over one shoulder. He was all muscle and smooth shape: shirtless torso; symmetrical face. Seeing him standing there caused Jim's dick to stir again. Even though he knew Arnie for a bastard blackmailer, he was still a handsome bastard blackmailer.

'See you around,' Arnie said.

The door closed and Jim was left alone.

Eight

Hanson had got it bad. He had taken to sitting by the phone as if doing that might make Flynn call him. Whenever it did ring, Hanson pounced on it, pathetically hopeful and always disappointed. At the very least, he needed to be rescued from the Billie Holiday record he found it necessary to play over and over. Four days of this behaviour was seeming like four months. Still he did it: every time the phone rang, Hanson pounced.

This time it was Pearl. In a reversal of the usual precautions, Hanson had given her his home, rather than his office, number, figuring she was more likely to embarrass him at work than camp out outside his apartment. She was reasonably brief, if a little overenthusiastic.

'Can we meet, hon? There's this guy who's got trouble with a telltale. God, what is the world coming to! Blackmail is such an ugly habit, don't you think? I told him you was a queer cop and you'd be sure to understand. I think you ought to see him.'

Hanson grimaced and, giving her a place to meet, told her he was on his way.

★

She was standing at the corner of the block, where he'd told her. Alongside her was a conventional-looking fellow who was not without a certain appeal and who could have taught Eeyore the donkey something about looking miserable. Hanson drove up and opened the door for them. Pearl climbed in, all excited, but her companion could be described as reluctant.

'Come on, honey!' Pearl told him. The guy's problem could have been with her perfume, which was extremely sweet and extremely vile. 'This one's tame. I told you, he's just as bent as you and me.'

Hanson scowled but got nothing back but a simpering wince. Pearl explained that she'd had to move heaven and earth to get her friend even to trust *her*! It was maybe the knowing look Hanson gave the man at this point that eventually persuaded him into the car. Even so, he looked like he expected Sam Giancana to be sitting right in there alongside him.

Pearl introduced him to Hanson as Jim Smith. His choice of surname showed he lacked imagination but he was cute if you liked the lanky, Harvard type.

'I found him during the course of my enquiries,' Pearl said. She sounded like she'd been having the time of her life. 'He's got himself involved with a very dangerous individual. I guess you'll be making an arrest right away . . .'

Hanson told her to hush up. He would rather hear it from Mr 'Smith'.

Jim was drunk. He was in shit and he didn't appear to think he could dig his way out of it. He trusted Hanson not at all – that much was obvious. He told his sorry tale without expecting his listener to be able to supply it with a happy ending.

He had been blackmailed, he said. It was someone he'd taken home with him. He feared it was not going to stop at just one payment. He was a married man with kids, who'd never intended screwing with another man . . . et cetera.

Hanson was sorry for the guy, but he really couldn't see what could be done to help. Pearl was busting to speak. She was behaving as if Hanson were her own personal genie who she was loaning to her new friend. Hanson thought she was rubbing the wrong lamp.

'I'm sorry,' he told the victim. 'The news is not good. The only thing you can do is make an official complaint against this bastard. When he gets caught, regardless what happens to him, you're going to be exposed in the process. What can I say? Your best hope is that he blackmails someone who turns out to be in with the mob.'

Pearl had managed to stay quiet for almost thirty seconds. (She'd been making strange little gurgles every time she forced back the words.) Now she exploded with righteous fury.

'That's no answer! Fuck! You call yourself a law enforcer? What is this poor guy to do? He's coming to you so you can arrest this shit – put the asshole away where he belongs . . .'

Hanson said it slowly so it would have a chance of registering with her. 'It just isn't possible without putting Mr Smith here at risk.' She turned to Jim and shrugged.

'The law stinks,' she said. 'I knew it all along but hope does indeed rise eternal. I guess your best bet is to pay some other hoodlums to rough him up. I know a number you can call. How about it?'

Hanson warned her to stop right there but she was not listening to him. Eventually, just to get some peace, he agreed to take details.

Did the blackmailer have a name? Yes, he was called Arnie something, Jim couldn't say what. Was he tall? Short? Thin? Fat? He was average. What did he look like? He'd said he looked like Montgomery Clift but Jim wasn't so sure he wasn't kidding himself. Had he said where he lived? Maybe, Jim couldn't remember. Anything else he said that might be useful? He'd said he wasn't a homosexual . . .

That was all Jim could come up with right now. He didn't want to think about it any more.

Hanson pretended this was all most helpful and said he'd do

his best to get 'Arnie something' on whatever other charge he could. There was always a chance he was not paying his taxes.

This promise brought weak cheer to Jim's face. Hanson felt sorry for him. In these cases, it was a pity it was always the criminals who got the sex, the money *and* virtual immunity. Hanson patted his arm and was surprised when Jim responded forcefully, holding on to his hand.

Hanson gave him the X-ray-eye treatment. It might not have been what he should be concentrating on at that point but what was he supposed to do? If he was to be denied his romance with Flynn, he would just have to start looking for it elsewhere.

If Jim thought this was an unusual method of policing, he didn't say so and Hanson's obvious interest even stimulated his memory some more.

'I just remembered something else,' he said. 'This Arnie, he said he had a weekly appointment – with a homosexual who was paying him to keep quiet. When we first met he insisted on stopping off at the john on 33rd. He was only in there two seconds. I mean really – just two seconds. Maybe he was collecting something. Maybe that's what he was doing in there.'

Hanson said maybe this was so. He smiled and squeezed Jim's hand. For a moment he thought he was going to get a kiss in return.

Pearl, who should have been selling apples to Eve, piped up again.

'Say! Maybe you two guys need a little time to talk. How's about we go back to my apartment and do what we have to?'

Hanson refused the invitation even before she had finished speaking. Jim, too, was quick off the mark but, to Hanson's surprise (and maybe to Pearl's), he accepted. His eyes fixed on Hanson, whose cock twitched into life. He was falling into bad ways without caring who was there to catch him.

'OK,' he said. 'Your place it is.'

He said this to Pearl and with as much insouciance as he was able to muster right then. She was giving him the 'Momma knows best' look. He added, 'But I warn you . . .'

Pearl opened her eyes wide and asked innocently, 'What? What do you warn me?' But Hanson didn't rightly know.

Pearl's apartment was in a dilapidated block in West 10th Street. The sidewalk outside was infested with kids in various states of stickiness and grime. Like Hanson had seen her do with the other punks, she sailed through the middle of them as though their catcalls were shouts of adoration.

The steps that led up to the main door might as well have been booby-trapped: not a single slab of stone was in its original place. The door itself had once been painted blue but that must have been very long ago. Now all that remained of this covering was a few blistered streaks. Pearl pushed at it gingerly, wise to the fact that it wasn't healthy to make firm contact with it. It opened to reveal an interior that was every bit as quaint as the outside. Hanson grimaced.

'Nice,' Jim said.

Pearl went on ahead shouting for them to follow her on up to Apartment Five. The stairs were dark and dangerous and Hanson was beginning to regret this whole thing.

It was curiously cool in there. If anything, on the first floor the gloom became more dense. There was one tiny thing that relieved it. There, above the door of Apartment Five, was a little red electric bulb, covered in glitter. It didn't exactly give out any light, but it was trying to be cheerful. If its purpose was to advertise what sort of tenant had the place, then that little bulb could be proud of a job well done.

Pearl had gone into the apartment and shut the door behind her. Hanson tried to open it but it was locked. He knocked, there was no reply.

'I'm sure she – he – said Apartment Five,' Jim said. He sounded flustered, as well he might. 'He did – I mean *she* did.'

Hanson was not so timorous. '*It* did say Apartment Five and *it* is up to something.' He hammered on the door. Pearl's voice came out of the depths.

'I'm just a little busy right now. Would you mind waiting, caller?'

After five minutes or so, just as Hanson was about to give up and go home, the door was opened violently. Much to both their surprise, it wasn't the blonde drag queen who posed before them, but a lithe and handsome young man, stripped to the waist and wearing jeans that revealed more than they covered. His face, which still had vestiges of make-up on it, lit up.

'Hi, gorgeous! I don't *believe* this! You've come to see me! And you've brought your friend . . .' It was Jim he went for, acting as though it had been months since they'd met. He gave a simpering smile towards Hanson, who returned it in kind. Jim was pulled inside while Hanson was left to follow if he cared to.

It was truly an amazing transformation. What had made Pearl convincing as a woman made Eddie, her alter ego, into an extremely handsome man. It was like meeting your best friend's brother and seeing a cuteness in his features that you never realised was there all along in your friend's face. Eddie's high cheekbones, his twinkling green eyes, his full lips were all cute and then some. He had the sort of face that ensured he was going to keep young and beautiful far longer than he ever deserved.

His age was difficult to determine. As Pearl, he was twenty going on sixty, but that's drag for you. His curly, dark-brown hair was cut short, maybe because he was starting to lose it at the back. Hanson decided to be charitable and place him on the flattery side of thirty.

Jim, who looked nervous and excited at one and the same time, had stumbled his way across a pile of rugs and cushions and had seated himself in a convenient armchair. He was attempting to assert his masculinity by sitting with legs apart and a hand clamped squarely on each knee. Eddie vamped over to him and breathed into his face.

'You sure do look butch, honey! I love the way you real men behave — not a bit like us faggots, huh?'

He went for Hanson next. He pressed up against him and pulled him in by means of his tie. Hanson tried to push him off, noticing as he did so just how hot Eddie's sexy, rippling body was. It was also surprisingly muscular — quite broad about the shoulders and with hefty biceps. Hanson supposed he might once have been a dancer.

'I thought you said we were coming here in order for me and Mr Smith to be alone together,' he said, though he was not entirely sure he still wanted this to happen now he could see what extras were on offer.

It was a bad tactic. Eddie complained loud and long. It poured out in a torrent of invective. The physical improvement vanished and Pearl was with them once again.

Hanson attempted to quiet him but it was not going to be possible. Eddie turned his back on both of them and walked off, pushing theatrically through a beaded curtain into another room. The beads rattled back into place as though they were applauding him. When they were finally still, there was absolute silence.

Hanson was sure Eddie was standing the other side of that entrance waiting to see what they would do. He glanced at Jim, who grinned almost happily. Hanson reckoned the poor bastard deserved a treat after all he'd been through. The poor bastard in question got up and stood just behind him. Hanson reached out and brought him close. Jim's arms wrapped around him from behind and Hanson felt wet, beery kisses on the nape of his neck.

'We have to sort that little Mary out!' he said at last. He wanted it to sound apologetic but Jim seemed to think the whole game was going great. Drawing in a deep breath, Hanson went through the beaded curtain. Jim followed.

★

The bedroom wanted to be tasteful but didn't know how. It was a room that, just like its tenant, thumbed its nose at convention. It was ostentatiously draped in lace and chiffon. Greek-style statues stood here and there. They were probably bland and inoffensive but in this light they'd pass for vile. There were several heavily fringed Spanish shawls: one over the table, one serving as a counterpane on the bed, one over the back of the large armchair in which Eddie was curled.

He wasn't looking at his guests. He was making a point of it. His head was turned deliberately and awkwardly away from them. He'd formed his mouth into a perfect pout. His chin rested on his hand while his other arm went round his legs, which were hunched up to his chest. It was the kind of casual anyone could see takes serious effort. It was maybe coincidence that it showed off the lines of his body very nicely into the bargain.

'Come on,' Hanson said in a bored voice. 'Cut the crap.'

The only result this got him was a haughty sniff and a slight toss of the head.

It now seemed more or less inevitable that they were going to have a threesome. Would screwing Eddie be like screwing a woman? Did it matter? His face did not look feminine right now. His eyebrows were naturally artistic; so what if he did pluck them? He could only have been accused of improving on perfection. His wrists and forearms were thin, even though heavy exercise (ballet?) had had its effect on the rest of his limbs. He had a long, graceful neck and a fine, pointed jawbone. Without the shrill camp, he would have had all the boys buying him flowers.

Hanson saw that Jim was taking stock of the room at the same time as appreciating the physical charms of its occupier.

Eddie had turned his head towards them in the most regal way possible. He had been regarding them for a minute or so. Now he deigned to speak.

'So, boys,' he said. 'You gonna fuck my ass or just stand there?'

He rolled back in the chair, his tongue lolling crudely out of his mouth. He grasped his thighs and pulled them up towards his chest. His jeans gave up their struggle to stay whole and tore down the crack of his backside with a satisfying rending sound. Eddie put his exquisitely artistic fingers into the hole and pulled the fabric wider apart. Underneath lay his perfect, smooth skin encased in shining white silk with tiny rosebuds to decorate it.

Luxuriously, he pushed the satin into his anus with his finger. The material stayed in there, puckered like a magician's hand-kerchief all ready to make something disappear. When Eddie opened his legs just a fraction wider, it popped back to its full tautness.

'Come on, boys. Mama's waiting.'

Hanson looked at Eddie and marvelled again at his perfect mixture of the masculine and feminine. Without his drag, he was dynamite: a power-packed miniature he-man with eyeliner and lady's underwear.

By this time Hanson had got the measure of Jim, who he figured was game for this but didn't want to take the initiative. Feeling it was maybe time to get rid of his coat and hat, he knelt beside the chair. Eddie stole his fedora and perched it on top of his own head – it looked a million times better on him than it did on Hanson.

Hanson put an exploratory hand inside the ever-widening hole in the jeans and crept it up Eddie's thigh. It was a tight squeeze in there and didn't give him much by way of satisfac-tion. However, doing it had broken the ice and encouraged Jim forward. He squatted at the other side of Eddie. Within seconds they were giving each other full, deep-throated kisses and Hanson was left to watch the show.

He made the most of what was available to him. Bringing his mouth to the front of the satin panties, he licked around until the material was one large damp patch. He could feel and smell the lovely organ beneath but he was going to take his time before he uncovered it. Eddie's hands were wandering in there with him. He gently and deliberately set them aside. This was going to be his province for the while.

Jim, helped by Eddie — who never left off kissing him — was hurriedly ridding himself of clothing. Hanson saw this and did the same for himself but more slowly.

Now it had nothing to do down below, Eddie's hand found its way to Hanson's shoulder and began to dig in. The finger-nails were sharp as claws and Eddie must have known it — he scratched slowly and painfully. Hanson bore it without protest. The stinging — which followed like an aftertaste — felt good to him.

He checked the two kissers and saw Jim also had marks along his shoulder. Still with the rest of his face fully engaged in kissing Jim, Eddie's eye gleamed out to check Hanson's reaction to all this. Finding him suitably aroused, the eye closed and the fingernails did some more damage.

The temperature was rising and nudity was not optional. Eddie raised his hips off the chair and fumbled, but his jeans were too tight to undo easily and Hanson had to pull them off for him. Eddie nearly came off the chair with them. There were shrieks of laughter from him and an unfortunate break in the passion. It at least gave Jim chance to drop his pants.

Eddie's (or maybe Pearl's) panties were ridiculously small and his dick was poking out over the top of the elastic. He made no attempt to do anything about this. He rose and went over to the bed, where he collapsed like a broken puppet. He was going for the artistic pose, come what may. He kept looking from one man to the other, no doubt wondering which of them was going to fuck him first.

Following Jim's lead, Hanson stripped down to his under-shorts. Jim lay alongside Eddie and got busy on his tight, perfect nipples and hard, well-shaped upper chest. Hanson went for the tip of Eddie's dick with his mouth. The satin, which after all had never been designed to cover a bulge, became a useless irritation and just had to go.

Eddie's tidy, curly pubic hair smelt of talcum powder with a powerful musk behind it. Hanson took the seeping shaft into his mouth. He pulled the foreskin down, exposing the glistening dark head with its pinprick opening.

Eddie's ever-wandering hands were now down the front of Jim's shorts. Hanson let Eddie's cock slip from his mouth and climbed up on the other side. He immediately found Eddie's finger and thumb tightly rubbing at the head of his cock.

The long fingernails nicked him and made him wince. There was a whispered 'Sorry, hon,' and Eddie kissed him. It was different from kissing other men – it was more sensual. Frantic fucks are fine but Eddie promised something different. His kissing was tender, gentle – an exchange of softness.

Jim rolled over the top of Eddie's body and, pulling Hanson's shorts down, started to lick his balls at the same time as Eddie rubbed his cockhead and kissed his lips.

Hanson tried to hold both men to him at one and the same time. He was now sandwiched between them and everywhere he moved there was a mouth or a hand at some tender part of his body. He felt Jim pushing into his hole; he felt Eddie scraping very carefully over his nipple. He felt his cock, his balls, his ass, all swirling in a whirl of touch and stimulation. All the while he took care to give back to the other two what he was getting. His lips and hands never left off kissing and squeezing whichever part of whoever's body presented itself to him.

Then Eddie eased himself away from them and, in a businesslike way, plumped up three pillows and set them in the centre of the mattress. The other two men were in no doubt what this meant. Hanson received Jim's unspoken permission to be the one who was to have Eddie's ass first.

Eddie lay with the small of his back supported by the pillows. He made no more of all this than if he'd been having his nails painted. As before, he gripped his thighs with both hands and raised his beautiful, hairless legs upward, arching his feet to form a perfect line.

Hanson lay full length on top of him and allowed Jim to guide his throbbing dick into the hotness that waited for it between Eddie's legs. Hanson groaned when it was fully planted in there and embraced Eddie, who placed delicate hands on Hanson's shoulders and slowly began to move in and out.

Hanson's strong hips moved with him. As he got into the swing, he felt Jim's tongue licking around his buttocks. His pace quickened with the excitement. Jim's tongue flicked around – he was trying to find his place in the rhythm. Meanwhile, Hanson's dick was simmering inside Eddie, who was gripping him so tightly. Behind them, Jim pushed his face into Hanson's backside and rode up and down with him, pressing his tongue hard and square into the centre.

Hanson didn't plan on coming just yet. He slowed down and gave Eddie a reassuring kiss. Eddie looked up at him questioningly.

'Do you like things a bit spicy?' Hanson said. He felt Jim remove himself from behind and crawl up his back. Hanson pulled his cock out of Eddie's ass and moved over to let him lie full length again. The three of them hugged together.

'What you mean, spicy? Ain't this spicy enough for you?' Eddie said, making it sound like he was open to suggestions.

Jim was rubbing away at his cock, priming himself for the next bit of action. Eddie disengaged himself and gripped his own, slender penis.

'What you mean?' he repeated.

Hanson tried to stroke Eddie's cheek but he turned coquettishly.

'Whassamatter?' Hanson asked. 'No harm in putting it to you is there?'

'I heard of spicy,' Eddie replied. 'Spicy means you get into the perverted stuff. You a pervert, Mr Detective?'

Hanson laughed and lay on his back. His cock was going soft; he waggled it around to get it hard again.

'I'm no pervert,' he said. Then, as if as an afterthought, he said to Jim, 'How about you?'

Jim was lying flat on his back. He was taller than the other two and, though not as muscular as Eddie or as boyish as Hanson, he was sexy enough. He was stroking himself, narcissistically enjoying the trail of hair that defined his chest. He was pleasantly loose-limbed and, now he'd lost the hangdog expression, he looked relaxed and handsome.

'I don't mind what you like to do,' he said. 'But I like it better when it's just . . . just fun. Know what I mean?'

Hanson nodded. 'I guess you wouldn't be into tying a person up and putting their head in a pillowcase then?'

Jim was wide-eyed and incredulous. Eddie seemed to think Hanson had gone crazy.

'Why would I want to do a thing like that?' Jim asked.

'Get yourself over here and start fucking!' Eddie demanded. 'We don't need none of your vile fantasies.'

Hanson got off the bed and stretched. It was a bluff – in a split second he'd jumped back on top of the other two men. He let out a good old yell.

There were squeals of delight from the other two and, in seconds, they were back at it. This time the lovemaking was more robust, less careful.

Hanson's dick was building up to spurting its juice. It may have been Eddie's hand that was on it but, whoever it belonged to, it was sure having the desired effect. Hanson began to pant: short, heavy gasps. He noticed Jim biting his lip and pumping furiously at his own cock, his face screwed into a grimace. Eddie pushed in between them and closed his mouth around Hanson's sex. Hanson kissed Jim – deep and long. The juice came gushing out of him into Eddie's pulsating mouth.

Jim pulled Hanson close. His dick was all ready and within seconds he too had come. The semen splattered over Hanson's

115

belly and across Eddie's face. Within seconds Eddie had returned the favour: their bodies were a delicious mess of semen and sweat. The three of them lay back, exhausted.

'Personally,' Eddie said after a while, 'I think this sex thing is overrated. I'd rather have a nice bath.'

Nine

Jim received a menacing little note exactly a week after his inadvisable encounter with Arnie. It told him tonight was an anniversary. To celebrate, he must send a specified number of dollars to a mailing address. The icing on the cake (as it were) was a little poem that Arnie had included. The words were familiar and innocent enough, but their meaning on this occasion was quite clear:

> *Humpty Dumpty sat on a wall;*
> *Humpty Dumpty had a great fall;*
> *All the King's horses and all the King's men*
> *Couldn't put Humpty together again.*

Jim was a timid man in many respects, but he had a great sense of justice. Some folks he knew would say his sense of justice was strong enough to override any other consideration. His sense of justice did not take kindly to threats of blackmail. I mean to stay on that goddamn wall, he thought, and no damn punk is going to push me off.

The only trouble was, Arnie had not been helpful enough to

include his own address and the best thug needs to know how to find the man whose face he has to rearrange. Arnie was out there somewhere, but how to find him?

The answer fell out of the sky and hit Jim fair and square: the Puerto Rican he'd seen staring at them from the john in 33rd Street. At first he'd thought the image was with him because the guy had been extremely attractive and, well, he *would* remember him, wouldn't he? Not so. He was attractive, sure – but he may prove useful in more ways than one. Arnie had visited him once at his 'place of work'; there was a good chance he'd visit again. The john on 33rd was as good a place as any to start looking for him.

Unfortunately, in the meantime, he would have to pay Arnie's demands. He mailed the money as he had been told and prepared to sit around all day letting his nerves eat him up.

The evening was long in coming but come it did. Jim set out for 33rd Street.

Seven days ago he had been a novice; now he was a harlot. In the time it took God to make the world, Jim had screwed a blackmailer, a cop and a drag queen. Though he was telling himself he had other motives, it had not escaped his attention that he may just be about to get lucky with a fellow 'Humpty Dumpty'.

Out on the street, Jim's mood changed. He was nervous, but it was an excited nervousness. Maybe the weather had something to do with it: it was one of those bright evenings in the late summer when everything, even the garbage that blew about his feet, looked worthy of sticking in front of a camera. Usually Jim got this way when he was drunk, but today he had no excuse. It was all to do with the light, he decided. There was something about the setting sun that would do it for anyone or anything.

In his head was an avenging angel with his sword of justice all ready to smite Arnie and make him cower. However, his

118

angel was a little in danger of being sidelined: it jostled for priority with the wolf that Jim had unleashed in the name of his libido and the wolf was winning the tussle. The angel tried playing dirty: 'What about Geraldine?' it said. 'What about your wife?' Jim took from his wallet a picture. He'd once said he'd keep this picture for ever. On the back of it was written, 'To my husband: our first anniversary – September 16, 1952.'

Jim didn't even flinch. He ripped the picture down its centre, so separating its two subjects. Symbolically, he had set the both of them free.

He examined every passable male he encountered for signs of interest. Sometimes the passable male would notice and Jim's heart would rush into overdrive but it was always a false alarm. It was some long time later he fetched up in 33rd Street. He suddenly stopped, a few yards short of the men's room.

At first glance, the place looked innocent enough, but, once a casual observer had casually observed, it proved to be doing better business than *Oklahoma!*.

It was half after six. Jim figured Arnie would be collecting the rent at seven. He had just about half an hour to wait around. He wanted to join the party but he didn't dare plunge into the pool. Instead, he settled himself in a shop doorway and waited.

The minutes crawled along as though they were drugged. Men continued to go in and out of the tearoom, most of them going in and not too many coming out again.

6.35 . . . 6.40 . . . Jim needed to piss. Pissing was legal, wasn't it? He decided to go for it. He approached the door of the john and was immediately cruised by a middle-aged man with a hairpiece. Jim went in.

There was a line of men at the urinals. They all turned to look as he entered. What were meant to seem like brief glances lingered over him like they'd been put into slow motion. When the men turned back to their cocks, it was with a studied interest which showed they were doing more than pointing Percy at the porcelain.

Jim noted, too, the row of cubicles, most of them with their doors ajar. It was clear that visitors were welcome in any and all of them. He went to join the line at the urinals. He sensed in the other men a sexual charge mixed with a vague melancholy. The sex made his heart thump; the sadness swept over him like a warm wave.

He couldn't piss. It was impossible with the man next to him so obviously stroking a very stiff dick and trying to get a peek at Jim's. It was like a routine: by turns, the man looked across at Jim, down to Jim's cock, then back to his own. His own was impressive and seemed to grow larger each time he returned to it.

There was no way Jim could get hard and, for this guy, he decided he didn't want to anyhow.

He noticed two or three good-lookers. They were looking at Jim and at each other along the row of backs. The spaces on both sides of each of them were engaged. When there came a vacant space next to one of them, Jim wondered what the protocol was. He found out when Guy A moved into it and, without any preliminaries, began to blow Guy B right there in front of everyone.

This action seemed to kick-start the activity. The man next to Jim gave up on him and got going with his other neighbour. A guy who may have been a student (and who looked so wholesome you wouldn't believe he'd know what his dick was for) went into one of the cubicles. Bumps and the sound of panting emerged from the cubicle seconds later. Another (older) guy moved close and made a play for Jim's cock but was turned down. He joined in the activity further up the line.

Jim was left to sing solo. He was wondering whether all this was for him and how the fuck he was going to follow Arnie home without being seen, when a vision came out of the end cubicle.

It was the Puerto Rican and, this close up, he was remarkable.

He had doll-like eyes and a greaser's hairstyle. He wore jeans and a dirty shirt, whose sleeves had been rolled up to his slim, curved shoulders. Tufts of jet-black hair peeked out from his armpits. His body had yet to form fully but he moved in a slick, coordinated way which showed he was the sort who took enough physical exercise for it to develop in its own good time. He was smoking a tiny home-made cigarette. The fingers that pinched it were large and stained with nicotine.

Jim felt sure the youth would recognise him. There was no sign he had, though it seemed he was only too willing to get acquainted. He leant back with one leg against the wall. It looked like a pose he had practised and, if he had, the practice had been worth the bother. Jim was the only one who was free to appreciate it and he felt sure it was all for him.

The youth clicked his tongue as Jim came near. His eyes took a tour of Jim's body. Jim was certainly interested but he couldn't bring himself to give a public performance just yet. He brushed up against the guy's crotch and, although he got a lustful grunt in response, he could do no more. He nodded towards the exit, expecting the guy would obediently saunter off and he could maybe follow him to Paradise. There was no move.

Jim took the lead himself and crossed the floor. He could feel coal-black eyes burning into his back. Even though he had a feeling like he was stepping into quicksand, he stole a quick glance behind to see if the guy was following.

He wasn't – but there were compensations: he was grinning at Jim quite openly. Jim stopped by the door, wondering whether this would all end in tears and whose tears they were going to be. He tried to hook the young guy in with another encouraging look before going out into the street. There, he lit a cigarette and waited.

The kid joined him within a few moments. He stood close, kicking his heels, his thumbs hooked into his front pockets.

Ten to one he would have the IQ of a gorilla, but so what when he had the body of a panther?

The youth's face was lowered, but his eyes were flashing over to Jim every two seconds. He had more sass than a stripper. Jim risked grinning back and, for the first time, they really connected. They both started laughing at the stupid routine.

Jim offered him a cigarette. He accepted and, without making a thing of it, took the whole pack. Jim was feeling too good to carp; he even gave up his lighter knowing he probably wouldn't get it back. He didn't.

The youth inhaled smoke, deeply, quickly, so as to appear tough. He had to narrow his eyes and disguise a tiny cough, but other than this he looked the part well enough. 'Chico,' he said, offering his hand. It was a cute attempt to copy the formality he'd seen in others.

'Jim.' He squeezed Chico's hand. The squeeze was returned and Chico's eyes, fixed on his own, said all the rest that was needed.

'Let's go,' Chico said at last. He jerked his head in the direction of a back alley. Jim didn't much fancy doing it up against a wall any more than he did inside a public toilet but he wasn't about to let Chico go find someone else.

Once they were in the relative safety of the deserted backstreets, Chico slowed up. Jim drew alongside him and allowed himself the luxury of feeling Chico's butt as they walked. Chico carried on smoking but responded absently by testing the hardness of Jim's cock. He didn't make any move to either help or hinder the groping hand on his backside. Jim was enjoying the thrill of danger. He was all ready to pull away if anybody saw them, but a powerful mix of temptation and frustration was building inside him. After they'd walked a few blocks he was ready to do it just about any place.

'I don't hang around the john if I trick,' Chico said. 'You

can meet with bad company in places like that. Tonight, I met with good company – am I right?' This was said with a sly, lopsided grin which melted Jim's heart. He asked Chico where they were headed. Chico shrugged.

'I live with my mom and sisters,' he said at last. 'We'll have to go in the yard. OK?' After a pause he added, 'I know what you're thinkin'. You think I maybe can't look after myself and it's a shame.'

Jim was amazed – Chico had got it about right. Chico laughed and his laughter was harsh.

'You folks are all the same. You think I *want* you to feel sorry for me? Let me tell you, I don't. I want your cock up my butt, that's all. When you've come, you can fuck off back where you came and tell your posh friends how you just tricked with a bit of rough.'

Without warning, he grabbed Jim's wrist and pulled him to one side. The two of them flattened against a wall as another couple walked by. Jim hadn't heard their approach at all.

He thought the subterfuge was a bit overdramatic, until he realised it had two purposes. Chico's hand went for his fly and, with a few deft tugs, Jim's dick was free and begging to be touched. He made Chico's task easier by loosening his own belt. Chico knelt in front of him and closed his lips on Jim's shaft.

Jim grabbed Chico's brilliantined head and guided it up and down, up and down. The suction almost hurt but he wanted it to be harder still. He spoke short, disjointed sentences of encouragement: 'Yeah, that's it. Get my . . . Suck my . . . Yeah!'

The orgasm evaded him. Once or twice he felt it surging up, but it subsided before it reached its peak, leaving him wanting. Then he had to pull out of Chico's lovely mouth and get his cock back to a full state of erection with his own hand. While he did this, Chico sat back on his heels waiting patiently – too patiently – as though this hold up meant little to him. Jim said he was sorry — it wasn't usually like this. Chico shrugged and said, 'Up to you, mister. You call the shots. Why should I care?'

It wasn't the reaction Jim expected. 'Let me get this straight,' he said. 'Are you doing this for kicks?'

Chico raised his eyebrows and shrugged again: if Jim wanted him to be doing it for kicks, then he was doing it for kicks.

'What I mean is, do you want me to pay you for blowing me?'

Chico sprang to his feet and was at Jim's throat in a second. He had hold of his collar. His face, previously so handsome, was now contorted into an ugly grimace.

'You're fucking right I want paying! Don't you try and say I haven't done what you wanted, mister! I'll have your fucking balls off!'

Jim told him to go easy. He didn't like to admit to being scared of the kid and he was getting plain fed up of being threatened by everybody he ran into. He was thankful his wallet contained only a few dollars. *Just about the going rate for having my cock sucked* he thought dryly.

'OK — it's OK. I just wanted to know, that's all. For sure I'll pay you.'

Chico had turned sulky now. He let go of Jim's collar and stood beside him, his dark brows knitted in a fierce, sexy frown.

'You queers are all the same. You can't get it up and you blame me for it. Then you try and get away without paying. 'Tain't right.'

Jim let him fume for a while. He needed the break to get his thoughts back on track. He put his cock away and reflected that he should have stuck to getting information about Arnie. This unpleasantness had served him right.

'Have *you* ever paid someone for having sex?' he asked.

Chico glared at him like this was the biggest insult in the world and he wasn't going to bother to grace the question with an answer. He squatted on the ground and doodled patterns in the dust with his finger.

Jim tried again: 'I saw you leave money for someone in the john.' Chico was on his feet in a second. His fists clenched and his face looked like thunder. Jim held up his hands in surrender. 'It's OK,' he said. 'I'm nothing to do with that man. I'm having something of the same trouble: we can help each other. Am I right? Is someone squeezing you for cash?'

Chico pushed the sleeves of his shirt up to his shoulders showing his biceps to their best advantage. He came over as guileless enough but Jim was sure he knew how good it looked: he understood how to make the best of himself. His hair flopped into his face and he flicked it back with a toss of his head.

'Maybe,' he said. 'Maybe not. What's it to you?'

'I told you,' Jim replied. 'He's something of a problem to me. I have two options – one's legal, one maybe not so much, but I have to know where this man can be found.'

Chico had scoffed at the word 'legal'. He didn't seem too impressed with the other idea either. 'The law can't do shit. You try the other thing and I'll come and visit you when they lock you up.'

'I know this cop,' Jim began. Dealing with Chico was like dealing with a firecracker. The word 'cop' had got him angry again.

'He's safe. He's a queer cop,' Jim assured him. 'I know. I've been with him. I think he wants to help us.'

Chico's eyes were darting about as though he expected Arnie to appear at any moment.

'I hang around the john most nights,' he said. 'It's where I make my money. Sometimes he comes in there and has me for nothing, sometimes he wants money off me, sometimes both. He said if I don't role over and play dead, he'll set the cops on to me. My mom and my little sisters: they need me home. I can't let them put me in jail.'

Jim nodded and he hoped he looked sympathetic. Chico snorted in disgust.

'So you're gonna set a queer cop on him? That's perfect. I wish you luck.'

'It doesn't matter,' Jim said. 'I have another means of sorting it. If I know he can be found around that place, then that's enough for me.'

'Give me the cop's number,' Chico said. 'Maybe I too should have the protection of a queer lawman.' He caught Jim's doubtful expression. 'Your man is safe from me. I have much to lose. Who knows? I might even be able to help.'

Hanson thought he was in danger of becoming addicted to weird sex. The session with Jim and Pearl had whetted his appetite and now he wanted more. If he had been completely honest he would have admitted to trying to block out his true feelings, which were deeper and much harder to deal with. He was still a romantic at heart and he wanted Flynn back. Sex was good and it made him feel much better, but there was more to life's rich banquet than sex and Hanson wanted his full portion.

If things worked out like they did in the fairy stories, Flynn would come charging back into his life on a white steed. He would cast all Hanson's doubts away in one heroic gesture and they would live happily ever after.

In fact, there was no such luck: Flynn had disappeared into thin air.

The woman in Records didn't have the file on him but stuck to her story, which sounded more suspicious each time she gave it; Roach didn't know who he was and claimed he didn't care; none of the other uniformed guys had heard of him. There was one isolated confirmation from a fellow officer: 'Flynn – yeah, I know a Flynn, sure I do. Great guy. I often see him.' Pressed further he said, not very convincingly, that Flynn could not be contacted – he was taking some leave right now.

Either something was going on or Hanson was falling victim to the general climate of fear. Since McCarthy had been on the warpath, America was no longer the land of the free.

At first, he had taken to waiting by the phone, believing the magic call would come any second. It was stupid behaviour and he couldn't keep it up for ever. Now when it rang he picked it up despondently as if it had been years since he ever heard anything good from it. Romance can be sweet and it can be hellish. Hanson was getting to be a connoisseur of the latter kind.

Life's banquet is not a set menu. This surprise course came to Hanson when he had all but given up.

It was not often he got a call on his home number from somebody he did not know. When the phone rang and a young, slick voice spoke – a streetwise, city voice that wasn't going to take any crap – Hanson was interested. The caller wasted no time with preliminaries.

'I met this guy. I picked him up in a john. I thought he was after doing business but he said he wanted to nail some punk who's squeezing him for cash.'

Hanson tried to interrupt him to ask where the hell all this was leading but the voice went on regardless.

'Listen, I'm telling ya. The guy I had was real nice. He paid me even though he got nothing for it. He said you were OK. He said you would listen and not mind that we'd been doing what we was doing.'

The voice wanted to meet with him in the Blue Parrot on 53rd Street.

'You know it?' the voice said. 'Cops don't usually go in those sorts of places unless they are out to make trouble but maybe you're different.'

'This cop goes into any place he wants,' Hanson replied, 'and you can forget the trouble.'

'Maybe when we meet I can give you something that might interest you,' the voice said. It sounded like it was flirting. Hanson was happy to flirt back.

'I just want to get acquainted,' he said suggestively. 'Then you can tell me your story. How will I recognise you?'

'Oh, you'll recognise me,' the caller said. 'I'll be there at ten. You got a date.'

In his present mood, Hanson could resist anyone as long as they weren't breathing and male.

He had about an hour before the 'date'. He decided he would go early and get settled. This was a dumb idea and dumb ideas always begin life sounding like good ideas. Hanson checked himself in the mirror, decided he looked a little rough, but was still good enough for some, and left his apartment.

In the corner of the bar, a man was having difficulty squeezing into a small chair. He was just too plump. His body was attempting to burst out of his tight clothing; his vest showed through his shirt. It was stained and damp with sweat. As if this weren't off-putting enough, he had greasy hair and small, peevish eyes. Small wonder that he looked surprised when Hanson came and sat down opposite him.

'Hi, fella,' he said eagerly. 'You here on your own? Don't you worry, I don't mind who I talk to. I'm Dermot Cannadine and I'm pleased to make your acquaintance.'

He talked fast and bright. He was not an obvious homo but Hanson was getting used to latching on to the telltale signs. Dermot had taken stock of every single man in the bar. He hadn't a chance with any of them so he'd settled for an empty table in the corner where he could watch the action. Now Hanson had joined him he must have been thinking it was Christmas.

'Careful if you sit there,' Dermot said. 'I'm something of a man-eater, don't you know?'

Hanson thought he could just about resist Dermot's body. The truth was he reckoned Dermot was just about the kind of guy who might be able to give him useful information. Hanson felt good about this thought: it meant his professional integrity was still intact – just about.

'Nice to meet you,' he lied. 'S'matter of fact I'm trying to trace somebody. He and I used to room together some time ago. I know he was in New York last time I heard from him. I think he wrote me that this was one of the places he used to hang out.'

Dermot's face fell. Hanson was not going to be the easy picking he'd hoped for.

'What makes you think I come in here regular?' he said morosely. 'I don't know the folks who drink here. Anyone would think I went around asking everyone where they lived or something.'

'Just take a look and see if you recognise him,' Hanson began. He took one of the Stein photographs out of his wallet.

'You a cop?' Dermot said sharply. Hanson kicked himself. He should have learnt by now that ordinary folk do things different. He tried to salvage the situation.

'No, course not. I meant what I said, I'm trying to find –'

But Dermot Cannadine was gone. Out of the shadows another man emerged and came to sit in the place where he had been.

He looked like a geek, but when he took off his glasses it improved him no end. Hanson thought his face vaguely familiar. He had none of those telltale signs of being queer but Hanson somehow knew for a fact that he was.

'Now I don't want you to bullshit me,' the newcomer said. 'I knew I was going to run into you sooner or later and it's maybe lucky for you it's sooner.'

'Who are you?' Hanson asked him. He was pleased to have this guy join him whoever he was, but they might as well do the formal thing.

'Yeah, sooner or later,' said the stranger, taking no notice of him at all. 'I sometimes think every homosexual in New York winds up in here before long. You was asking questions at the Plaza wasn't you?'

Hanson looked around to check that other people weren't

interested. There were several who were – in them but not, he supposed, in their conversation. He lowered his voice.

'I said, "Who are you?"'

'My name makes no difference to you. I work at the Plaza. I'm a porter. Listen, those people you was asking after – if you know what's good for you, you stay away from them. They have too much to lose. You can get what you want without going near them. Look, I'm risking a lot talking to you like this. They don't know I know anything about what goes on, but I listen at doors. I have to protect my interests, know what I mean? I don't know what you're after. I'm not queer, but you seem like a nice guy and –' here he put his hand on top of Hanson's '– I think we understand each other. Know what I mean? It'll cost you next to nothing and I can keep my trap shut.'

Hanson thought him nice enough for a quick grope, but he wasn't interested in paying for him. For once, he thought, he would not mix business with pleasure. He told the guy he had no cash on him to speak of. That was his first mistake. The porter's eyes narrowed and he looked a lot less friendly.

Hanson was about to produce Stein's photograph again. In order to do it, he tried gently removing the man's hand. That was his second mistake.

'Fuck you then!' the porter snapped. 'Just don't blame me when you end up with a knife in your back.'

He got up to go.

'Who is it I should be afraid of?' Hanson asked. 'Is it the mob?'

The porter scoffed. 'They *act* like they was the mob. No, it's not the mob you should be scared of. I'm not saying nothing more.'

He appeared to change his mind about something. In an overloud voice, as if he were speaking for someone else to hear, he said, 'Pity. You have a nice face. Maybe next time?'

Meanwhile, he had written something on a beer mat and

secretly shoved it across the table. Hanson, realising what he was supposed to do, quietly put it into his pocket. If the guy wanted to give him his telephone number that was OK. Maybe one lonely evening when he was desperate, he might even call it.

The porter left the bar. At the door he turned round again. Hanson was busy wondering how the Plaza Hotel fitted into the great scheme of things when the door opened and a Puerto Rican youth walked in. He glanced around the bar and walked confidently over to Hanson's table.

'Chico,' he said. 'I guess you're my date.'

They ordered beers and sat for some time just drinking and weighing each other up. When the conversation started it was stilted. They were still not sure of each other.

Hanson was wrestling with two opposing feelings. He wanted to assert his authority and he wanted to get on the right side of this very presentable renter. He doubted his own motives, but he was trying not to worry about that just now. The cop in him scored the first goal: he asked Chico about Arnie.

'He's a bastard and I hate him, but he's kinda cute to look at. You say his name is Arnie? Well, I don't know about that. He and me, we got close one evening, know what I mean? Then I realise I'd hooked a fucking shark and he was all ready to eat me alive. What am I supposed to do? If I went to the cops – I don't mean to insult you here – if I went to the cops, they'd be more on his side than on mine. He's a nutcase, man. He seems to think I belong to him. If I'm not at the john when he calls round, he gets mad at me next time. One time he gave me this weird poem – it didn't make much sense but it kinda scared me.'

'Poem?' Hanson said. 'What poem?'

'Something about not being able to eat no fat or something. I don't know – it was a kid's poem. I tell you, it didn't make any sense.'

Hanson was thinking about the poem and making connections. He dipped his finger in the froth on his beer and licked it off. It was the sort of gesture Freud might have had something to say about. There was silence for a minute or two.

Hanson was thinking maybe Arnie was more than just a blackmailer but he needed more than 'some weird poem' to prove it. 'Do your customers often turn sour?' He asked.

'You get all kinds, some of them might be screwballs – how the fuck would I know? I take care of myself.'

It was worth a try: Hanson asked him, 'Have you ever been anywhere near West End Avenue? Perhaps there was some freaks' party going on and you were asked along?'

Chico was suspicious now. He lit a cigarette and leant back, studying Hanson's face for clues.

'That part of town is full of fags – rich fags,' he said. 'Why d'you think I would be asked over there?'

'Because you're nice-looking,' Hanson answered, trying not to make it sound as predatory as it felt.

'If I'm nice-looking, why don't you do it with me?'

His directness took Hanson by surprise. Friendship can blossom anywhere, but forced flowers die quickly. He wanted more time.

'I do everything. I know what you homos are into,' Chico went on.

Hanson's face remained blank. 'You're not a homo yourself then?'

Chico leant forward and placed his finger on Hanson's cheek. He traced a line with it, all the way around Hanson's jaw, as if it were covered in cream and he were going to lick it off.

'Mister,' he said. 'I am whatever you want me to be. It's my business and I'm good at it.'

It was not a nice thing to do, but Hanson had a hankering to make Chico jump through a few hoops. If he's good at his business, thought Hanson, let's see how good.

'Tell me about it. What sort of things do you do for guys?'

Chico bounded through the hoop without any effort at all.

'Mouth, ass, hand jobs – I've done everything. There was one guy, he liked me to fuck him, but he liked me to do other things too. He had me undress and then put on lady's underwear for him. So my cock was all there in the satin and lace. You like that? I got a real smooth body, just like a girl – I don't mind if you like that.'

Hanson said he didn't like that. It wasn't true and Chico must have known it.

'Or he had me over his knee. He got another hustler to wallop my butt with a paddle. He made me all red and sore. Jesus! I can feel it now. You can do it for me all by yourself, I'll bet. I'd kinda like to be put over your knee with you being so strong and nice-looking.'

Hanson's face was a picture. If this was the menu, he was tempted by every dish. He felt his hand being grabbed under the table and pressed to Chico's bulging crotch. It felt good to touch and it caused a reaction in Hanson's own pants.

He decided to try a small experiment. Something about Stein's diary had been bugging him and he wanted to test it out. He called this mixing business with pleasure and he was all for getting high on the cocktail.

'I want to hear what happens when you undress and put on the lady's underwear,' he said. 'I want to hear about you being spanked. Feel here.' He made Chico feel his throbbing cock. 'I'm telling you, I really get off on sexy stories.'

Chico sighed. 'Another fucking freak!' he said in a matter-of-fact voice which intended no offence. 'OK, mister. That's cool. If it's what gets you going, do you see me wanting to argue?'

Ten

————

First, let me tell you, I like girls [Chico began]. I guess it's just as well 'cos someday I plan to get married to one. Thing is — I like guys as well and I like them plenty. I like all types too: young, old, black or white. I do anything and I don't care. That's what makes me such a fucking good hustler.

Anyways, me liking girls is useful for my work — you might think that strange, but it's true. You see there's this rich bastard who likes to have me with him for show. He is, how you say, 'not attractive'? OK, I'll be honest with you, he's an ugly shit, but he pays plenty so what do I care?

He has this thing for women's clothes. He's not too keen on the girls that go inside them — he just likes the clothes. He gets real turned on to think of me walking beside him in my jeans and shirt, looking all dirty and young and, like I'm a real big-shot punk and all the time he knows I'm wearing pink, lacy panties next to my crotch.

(You are gonna pay me for telling you this, ain't ya? Good.)

Well, this guy, he says he thinks of my dick in there, all curled up, asleep in my pubes and all covered over with pink silk. He says it turns him on just to think of it because it makes me his special boy.

I think I know what he means. He wants me to look as though I own the block, but all the time he has this secret on me, you know? He knows that, underneath, I'm not so tough as I look because I'm wearing those girl's things and that's something shameful for most punks.

He once had me wearing a chastity belt and I guess that's the same sort of idea. He had my dick locked away in this heavy, leather contraption and he kept the key of it. I tell you, when he finally unlocked me, I was fucking exploding, wanting to jerk off. He – er – he . . .

Anyway, that's something else – you want to know about the parties, don't you?

I'm not the only young guy who goes, the hell I'm not. Neither am I the only normal-looking one. There are plenty of freaks there, but a lot of ordinary people too: ordinary people behaving like freaks I mean. I suppose they're freaks all along – inside at any rate.

So, there I am, with my silk panties on under my jeans and feeling like I'm in good company here 'cos everybody has some kind of secret.

There are guys there, I'm telling you, man. They don't care what's done to them. First time I went, I thought my old guy would have me joining in the fun, but, when I put my hand on another guy's ass, he gave me a real sharp look as if that wasn't allowed. I reckoned he was scared I'd get off on being sucked, or fucked up my butt by one of the other good-looking hustlers there and I'd leave him alone.

(How strong do you want this tale to get? You want me to go all the way?)

He's a bastard – and I call him that because he is one: he really is not a pleasant person. He's grinning at me the whole time, watching for how I react to everything. Then he comes up with a surprise for me: he says he'll pay as much as a twenty dollars extra if I get naked and let people do things to my body. I ask what sort of things and he takes me into this room where there's a guy . . . I didn't believe what was happening to him.

Well, I'm not so rich I can refuse this sort of offer but, and I don't regret this, I said 'no' when I saw what was happening to him.

Man, I don't have no hangups about the way people get their rocks off, you know? I don't think it's up to me to say this thing is disgusting or that thing is not moral. As long as no one is being forced into it, who cares? I used to say 'as long as no one is being hurt' but, I tell you, this person was getting hurt plenty and, from the way his cock was, I'd say he was enjoying every second of it.

He was strung up by his ankles from a meat hook. There were two other guys attending to him. They'd shaved all his hair off – I mean off his cock and balls and under his arms and everything. He had his hands cuffed together in front of him and then chained up to a belt they'd made him wear round his waist. They had this gag thing in his mouth and they were knocking seven bells out of his ass, the tops of his legs, his back – everywhere they could hit. They had these old-fashioned whip things – you know the sort with lots of long tails?

I could see it was for real because it was bringing up all sorts of marks on his skin. He was no older than me and it wasn't as if he had the kind of face he'd have to hide in a brown paper bag, if you know what I mean. That's how he got his kicks. It don't seem right.

My man didn't join in any of this. He was strictly a voyeur. He stood there watching what they were doing and watching me looking on at it.

I felt all this was kinda freaky at first. He's probably one of these very moral people who go to church and all that stuff. They're usually dribbling at the mouth when dicks are out, but they're scared shitless of getting into it themselves. They spend half their lives jerking off.

(Hey! I don't mean I think you was one too. I wouldn't think you was a church person just because you like dirty stories.)

The guy's hands were over my butt most of the time and he must have been feeling smug because he had a handsome kid next to him. Everybody must have known he was paying for me but he didn't seem to care. He liked it that so many people were admiring me. It was strange: I felt like I was property and I was, like proud, I was good-quality stuff.

We left that room. He wanted to watch me doing it to another guy but he was going to pick the guy I had to do it with. I was just a little drunk by the time he decided and I was ready to ball.

There was this pretty-looking blond guy, just a bit older than me and – can you get this? – he was in a cage. It was fucking incredible! He was stripped naked and his hands were in chains: those heavy, iron chains that you see in pirate movies.

He had beautiful eyes – I think they were blue – and he looked kinda lost. He was holding on to the bars of his cage like he was waiting for somebody to come and pay him attention. I was surprised nobody had. Then it came out that my boss had paid for him and he'd been reserved for me to fuck.

They got him out of the cage. There were some guys who'd come along with us; I suppose they knew there was going to be some kind of show. They made the guy from the cage lie down on the floor with his hands raised up above his head. The room was lit in unusual places with red so it threw shadows all over him. I said he was blond, and he must have been in the real light because his hair – on his head, under his arms and round his dick – it had taken the red light completely. It made him look – how d'you say it? – sinful. His chest was nice. I get horny when I see a man's chest.

The guy who was paying me gave me the nod and I knew what I had to do. I pulled my shirt up and it was good to see the guys were all looking in my direction all of a sudden. It was maybe stupid for them to do this when they had a naked prisoner lying there on the floor with his ass just waiting to be plugged by someone's dick, but do you see me complaining? I'm not bad in the physical department and I guess they wanted to see what was underneath.

I made a thing of taking my shirt off. I made sure I flexed my muscles to do it and gave them an eyeful of my arms and my pits. I think they like that. I could see the old man sneering. He was thinking they'd go ape when they saw what I was wearing under my jeans.

So I stripped and made sure they was all looking at me. I could see the guy I was gonna have to fuck was looking too. I hope he liked what he saw but he wasn't gonna be given a choice in the matter so what could I do? I knew one thing, and this might sound like boasting: if I had to have my ass fucked and I had no say in who was gonna do it to me, I would feel better for it being somebody who looks like me.

I did the same thing with my pants as I had with my shirt: I took it real slow so they'd get the full effect. I pulled them down inch by inch so they could gradually realise what I'd been made to wear: all dainty and useless against my hairy legs, trying to hide my big, fat cock. When I finally shook the pants off I noticed one guy groping another and one more jerking himself already. The old guy just stood there, some way back. I think he was smiling but it could have been he was looking hurt. If he was, my heart didn't exactly bleed for him.

I lay on top of the kid on the floor and he got his hips up so I could get my cock into him. He had nice, thick lips and I started kissing him, but one of the guys looking on gave me a crack across my butt with a belt to make me stop. I looked around at my old guy, but he just stared right on like I was in a film and he couldn't talk with me no more. I tried not to look at him again.

The kid on the floor put his head to the side of mine and I

138

felt him nibbling my ear a bit — not so's anyone could see. I tried to go into him smoothly because I didn't want him hurt. I mainly succeeded, but he gasped out a bit when I pushed through.

My cock was feeling like it was being squeezed by a closed fist. He was so fucking firm down there. I guess he wasn't used to being fucked because he was panting, very slow and careful — like they tell you to do when you're first getting used to the idea of having dick inside you.

I lay still for him, so he could relax his muscles round me but the belt came down across me again. I wasn't sure I was into that. I turned round to see who was doing it and it was this big guy who was maybe about forty. He had a patch over his eye and tattoos all over his arms. His body was solid as rock and he was kinda swarthy looking. I tried giving him a real mean glare but it was nothing to the one he gave me back. He tapped the belt against his leg like it was a live thing and he was holding it in check — but maybe not for very much longer if I didn't watch my step.

I knew what I was supposed to do and I did it. I fucked the butt of that blond guy and kept it going hard and fast even when I knew he was finding it hard to take. He was either a good sport, or they were paying him a fortune, or he was getting off on it — I don't know which.

His cock was stiff and poking into my stomach. I'd like to have got it inside my mouth but maybe I would have ended up being the next in that fucking cage if I'd tried doing what I hadn't been told to do.

I was scared — a bit. I know I can look after myself but there were some big guys in that room. Not just Mr Fucking Eyepatch, but his friends were pretty mean-looking bastards as well. My blond was about the only one who looked nice enough to walk down the street with. He was squirming about under me and his chains were making a racket. One of the guys came over and trod on them so his hands were pinned to the floor. He stuck to just moving his hips about after that.

I could tell he was trying to make it feel good for me and, man, he was succeeding. I come quick as a rule and this was one time when I really didn't want to. I stopped every so often so it wouldn't be all over before I knew it. Every time I did, the blond bucked his hips up and down to get me going again.

I really wanted to kiss him and I thought it was worth a few strokes of the belt, so I did it. Sure enough, the whacking started as soon as I got my lips over his. It was a warning at first. Then, when the guy knew I was gonna carry on necking with this kid no matter what he did, he laid into my ass and the back of my shoulders like he really meant business. Funny thing was, I didn't care. It hurt, sure it hurt – and real bad. But the hurt sort of melted into the kissing and the kissing was so sweet. My cock, all squeezed tight into the blond kid, and my tongue halfway down his throat, and my back stinging from this vicious bastard giving me a whipping: it was all one and the same thing.

I fucked him again, but only when I'd had my fill of kissing. He gave me a look like he thought me a real hero. Course, he hadn't been hit at all because of my body protecting him. I wondered if they would give him a whipping afterwards or just put him back into his cage for the next time he was gonna get fucked.

When I came it was like I'd never come before. I shot loads of it, right into him. The blond was smiling at me all the while, like he was pleased he'd been able to make me do that. I think he was the nicest guy I've ever fucked and I don't even know his name.

Eleven

It was some story – and all made up by a street kid at a moment's notice. Hanson's cock was pumping blood like it was going out of fashion.

'What say you we go back to my apartment and do the business?' he said. (It was clear it was what they both wanted.) 'You can call a friend and say where you are just in case I turn out to be screwball. I'll pay you whatever you like – as long as it's reasonable.'

Chico was on his feet almost before Hanson had finished speaking.

'And I get my cab fare?'

Hanson would have probably agreed to buying him the cab outright. It was just a shame he couldn't claim the whole thing on expenses.

'That was a pretty good story,' he said.

Chico smiled happily. 'You liked it. I can do you anything you want, mister. If you like I can even have it where I get fucked by spacemen – whatever you want.'

Hanson stopped. 'Is it difficult to tell stories like you just did?'

Chico shrugged. 'It's better than telling the truth, don't you think? The truth is boring. I use bits of what I know and I kind of put them all together. The blond kid is somebody who works in the drugstore at the end of my block. The old guy is just like my father's boss. The sex stuff is what I'd like to do and, if you like, you can do some of it to me.'

Hanson tried to look disapproving – just to see how the kid reacted. He reacted by becoming defensive.

'Hell, man! You asked for a story. You want the truth? The truth is guys get me up against a wall and then say they can't juice because they're too scared of someone coming by.'

'Is that how it is every time?' Hanson asked. Chico calmed down.

'Not every time. If you and me ball, maybe I put that in my story next time and you'll be able to say, "Hey! That handsome cop in the story is really me!" But most tricks are nothing but work. Let me tell you, stories about fairies are usually best when they're just fairy stories.'

Or nursery rhymes, Hanson thought.

Chico didn't pay the apartment any attention at all. He checked it over like a workman sizing up a job.

This done, he threw himself on the bed in much the same way as Flynn had. Hanson had to stop himself making too much of the reminder. Just because he was screwing every guy he came into contact with didn't mean his love for Flynn wasn't still pure.

Chico propped himself up on his elbows, he was chewing gum. He proceeded to size up his customer just like he'd sized up his place of work. Hanson wondered if he was thinking how long he was prepared to give this 'call-out'.

It was an unworthy thought and he put it away with his memories of Flynn. Chico was doing this for cash – that much he'd made plain, and what was wrong with that?

'You want me to undress?' Chico asked him. 'Or are you

going to be real neat and take everything off me bit by bit. I like that, it makes me feel special.'

'You're special all right,' Hanson said. He opened the windows to let some cool evening air into the apartment. It had been another hot day and the breeze was welcome. He felt hot and sticky and he wanted to get into the tub.

'I need to go and take a bath,' he told Chico. 'How about you wait for me?'

Chico said, 'It's not good to waste hot water. How about you and me take a bath together?' As far as Chico was concerned it was probably all part of the service but it was a sweet thought and a tempting proposition.

The tub had not been designed to take two people so they had to get very close: Chico in between Hanson's knees with Hanson's hard cock squeezing into the cleft between his buttocks.

Chico accepted Hanson's arms around him and even went so far as to hold them there, tenderly – as though he really were Hanson's boyfriend. He lay against Hanson's hard chest while Hanson relaxed into the gradually deepening water.

Chico, for all his wanting to be undressed in a special way, had stripped quickly and efficiently, just as anybody might in a locker room. Now, while the tub was still filling, Hanson took the opportunity to look at his nude body.

He was a little on the skinny side, with olive-coloured skin and slim, runner's legs. His body hair was not extensive but where it appeared – under his arms, below his navel and spreading down to his dick and balls – it was profuse. His nipples were small: raised out slightly from his slim chest. He had nicely developed muscles on his upper arms, his shoulders and his thighs. Muscles that would in time transform him into a godlike creature but at the moment merely suggested his recently found status as an adult.

He had a long, kissable neck, around which he wore a St

Christopher medallion on a thin gold chain. His athletic and masculine frame was belied by his long, girlish eyelashes and curly black hair.

His cock floated in the water. It was semihard and uncut. The foreskin cloaked the head in a hood of wrinkled skin. He was very unselfconscious about it. It was his tool, thought Hanson. He's probably real skilled when the time comes to use it.

Hanson enjoyed hugging him for a moment or two. He didn't want to rush things but he was determined he would sample all Chico had to offer. His own cock was full as could be and it would have been all too easy to jerk himself off looking at that handsome young body, but he had other plans.

He turned off the tap with his toes and gently disengaged himself from Chico, tweaking one of those delectable nipples as he did it. Chico craned his neck round and gave Hanson his lips and tongue. They suckled each other for as long as it took for Hanson to move Chico round to face him. He got hold of the soap and rubbed it over both of their chests. Giggling, they experimented with the slip-sliding feeling when they rubbed their fronts against each other.

Hanson had hold of the back of Chico's neck. His kisses wandered from Chico's lips to the rest of his face. It seemed to work: Chico's cock gained the extra stiffness it needed. Hanson raised himself out of the water and soaped his own backside. Chico caught on pretty quick and finished the job for him.

His soapy finger slid inside Hanson's hole and probed him like he meant it. His mouth was open and his tongue curled against the back of his teeth. He was fully with what he was doing.

Hanson was too: he even thought it possible that a few more bathtimes like this might cure him of his love for Flynn. He let his inner responses grow without trying to force them. The jabbing digit was nudging at his prostate and giving him fleeting starts of pleasure and a growing need to have something larger up him.

They were both kneeling in the water. Chico's soap-covered hand was encircling his own cock and Hanson's at the same time. He closed his fist around their two shafts and spread the soap up and down. Hanson helped him out by doing the same for their tight sacs down below. They kissed again and again, Chico leaving off every third go so he could also give Hanson's chest and nipples some attention.

'You want to fuck my ass?' Chico asked. 'Or you want me to fuck you? I don't mind which, but I sure as hell want it to be one or the other and fast.'

'You fuck me. That's what I want. Do it so I know about it.'

They stood up and soaped each other some more – all over. Chico's buttocks were the best bit for Hanson. They were absolutely perfect: round and plump with a firmness that begged to be tested with a belt or a strap. Hanson wondered what it might be like to kiss the hot little hole they concealed.

Chico's penis was pulsing in Hanson's hand. He had slicked it with soap so much it was difficult to get a hold of it. The stuff had gathered in white ridges where the foreskin had pushed it and it looked like spunk. No matter, the real stuff would be along any time now.

Hanson turned round and steadied himself against the wall with his hands and legs spread like a suspect waiting to be searched. He felt slippery hands at the sides of his torso, they came round and hurt his nipples making him yelp.

'I'm sorry, man,' Chico whispered.

'Don't be,' Hanson said. 'I like it.'

The hot, fat cock was pushing at his hole. He breathed in deep, expecting it to give him hell when it went inside him. It turned out to be surprisingly easy. The head of it prised his hole open and stayed there for thirty seconds or more, letting him get used to it. At the same time, Chico played with his nipples, making him squirm enough to admit a little more cock without even realising.

Soon, they were coupled absolutely and Hanson felt complete. He didn't want Chico to move just yet. It was good enough to feel himself stuffed and just let Chico's busy hands wander over the front of his naked, lathered body.

He enjoyed it especially when Chico's hands found his groin and pressed at the root of his dick. It made his knees go and so forced Chico's dick to slide out of him a little.

In this way the fucking started: a few accidental jolts followed by more controlled pushing – in and out, in and out, the soap making it easy for them. To stop them slipping, Hanson brought his hands round the back of both their bodies and was able to grab Chico's ass cheeks and pull them wide. He flung his head back against Chico's shoulder and gasped at a particularly determined thrust.

'Baby! What makes me think I'm not your first?'

Chico wasn't into talking on the job. He gave Hanson another full push and then rested for a second or two with his cock embedded in Hanson's backside. Hanson churned inside as soon as he stopped. He bucked back to force the fucking to start over. He got more than he'd bargained for in return.

Chico's hand clamped over his mouth. He carried on fucking and his movements, instead of being loving, were brutal. He hissed through his teeth and twice gave Hanson a sharp, painful bite on the neck. Hanson closed his eyes and entered, uncomplainingly, into heaven.

He knew Chico was near to coming and he wanted them to come together. He gyrated his hips against Chico's groin and was grateful to find Chico's hand tightening around his cock. He held his breath and concentrated on the enigmatic stir around his cock head, waiting for the feeling to broaden as he knew it would. For a while it evaded him. The sharp pushes into his asshole, showing that Chico was about to let go his own spunk, did it for Hanson. His body lost all its strength as the life juice shot out of his penis. At one and the same time, his gut was filled with Chico's spunk. Hanson almost cried.

They held close for a long time, recovering and enjoying each other. Then Chico withdrew his limp cock, making Hanson wish it could stay in there all night. He guided Chico down into the water and started to bathe him.

Later, Hanson cooked for them both. OK, so it was only some pasta and sauce, but it meant they could sit and make cow eyes at each other across the table. Chico even volunteered to fix his price right there and so spend some leisure time with Hanson. It may not have been the most romantic gesture in the world but was kind of nice.

Later still, Hanson walked with Chico to where he could hail a cab. He was on his way back home when he decided he'd like some candy. As he was searching through his pockets for dimes he found the beer mat the porter had given him in the Blue Parrot. He had assumed it was the guy's telephone number and he'd already decided not to bother with him. He glanced at the scrawled name written there and it gave him an unpleasant surprise.

He looked around the street and, though nobody was paying him much attention, he felt he was being watched. He struck a match. Only when the beer mat was safely burning in a trash can did he think he was safe. He hurried home.

Twelve

It was raining; it had been raining all that day. Hanson had had a sleepless night. The porter's note had really got to him.

He felt like he was being watched the whole time. He'd even gone round the apartment looking for bugging devices. Eventually, wearily, he had sat by his open window and watched the street below. People were scurrying about under umbrellas; or dashing across the sidewalk from their cars; or just sauntering along in shirtsleeves defying nature and challenging it to do its worst. Hanson was reading something suspicious into everyone that came by. He knew what 'paranoia' meant and it seemed a pretty useful word at the moment.

The world outside smelt strongly of wet and the sky rumbled with promised thunder. He had just about made up his mind to go walking in Washington Square Park just for the hell of it. Maybe he would take some bread and sit feeding it to damp squirrels while he got on with the business of contracting pneumonia. At least there he would be safe and as soon as he felt safe he could get on with being miserable. What special person was there in his life? Who even cared if he lived or died?

He'd already had one try at giving himself a talking to. He

tried again: fucking with Chico had erased all previous follies from his mind (he told himself). He was going to enjoy being free: free to flit from flower to flower and never, under any circumstances, stay for longer than it takes to grab the pollen.

In the ironic way these things happen, it was as he thought these words of wisdom that he had a caller. And wasn't it just his luck that the caller turned out to be none other than his discarded true love?

Flynn was soaked but Hanson somehow thought he'd done it on purpose so he could get sympathy. He stood there in the corridor with his saturated hat in his hand. His hair was plastered to his forehead; raindrops queued to jump off the end of his nose and his drenched mackintosh was wrapped tight around him.

'I only walked from the subway and already I'm soaked,' he said, making it sound like walking from that particular subway to this particular address was something he did every day of his life. Hanson wasn't sure what other thing he would rather Flynn had said but he decided to resent the friendly tone just in case doing other would make him a walkover.

'Come to report on what I'm wearing?' He hoped his sneer came across as devastatingly as it was intended.

Flynn did look a little ashamed of himself but not nearly enough that he deserved to be allowed in. Hanson was on his guard. He was already aware of the powerful magic Flynn was working on him. At one and the same time, Hanson managed to show his displeasure and imagine stripping Flynn of his wet clothes, rubbing him dry and then . . .

He coughed so he wouldn't betray these thoughts but his eyes had probably done all his betraying for him. Flynn's disarming blush was rising up his neck and across his face. Hanson's cold front almost thawed. Wouldn't it be so much nicer to say, 'Forget what you did; let me bury my face in the hair of your chest'?

'I want to level with you,' Flynn said. He looked like he was going to try the 'It's not how it seems' line but he probably guessed Hanson had seen that movie and wouldn't be impressed.

'Or maybe you didn't get what it was you were looking for the first time you were here and you've come back to look for it again,' Hanson sneered.

Flynn shook his head. 'You'll understand when I tell you. And, if you take my advice, you'll let me in. There are things you should know.'

Hanson moved aside to let him enter. Flynn stood in the middle of the room, very uncertain of his welcome.

'I guess you ought to get out of those wet things,' Hanson said grudgingly.

Flynn seemed to take this to be an armistice. He got out of his coat with an eagerness to put things back to normal that Hanson thought premature and not a little presumptuous. Underneath, Flynn was wearing a tight cotton T-shirt and jeans: he'd dressed for the occasion. Hanson thought this was a cheap trick and, as cheap tricks went, he kind of liked it. Flynn's bulky frame was just as good as he remembered it.

'Drink?' Hanson asked, knowing full well this was not the kind of offer a wronged man should make.

Flynn accepted. He would have asked for ice but Hanson's voice had all he'd ever want. The liquor was brought and drunk in silence for a moment or two. Then, after a deep breath, Flynn said, almost in a whisper, 'I am not a cop.'

'I know,' Hanson said grimly. This made Flynn sit up. From his surprise, it could be assumed he didn't credit Hanson with being very good at his job.

'Did you think I wouldn't have checked you out?' Hanson said. 'First I get "he doesn't exist". Then I get a call to tell me they've lost your records. The lady on the phone was not exactly in the Alger Hiss league when it comes to the lying game. When police departments start covering for a cop who is not a cop, there's usually a big cheese behind it all and he usually goes by the name of Hoover. You're FBI, aren't you?'

Flynn looked impressed, which was insulting. Insulted or not, Hanson decided to play it safe. He didn't yet know how far Flynn was involved in the big picture. He still hoped that answer was going to be 'not a whole lot'.

'Come on, it doesn't take Sherlock Holmes,' he said. 'I know I'm right. Now supposing you tell me why the hell I've managed to attract my own tame FBI agent. I take it it isn't because I cheated at cards. Nor is it what I thought – that maybe, just maybe, that tame FBI officer liked the look of me.'

Flynn was the colour of raw steak; his blushing was one heck of a drawback in the profession he'd chosen for himself. He drained his glass and Hanson refilled it for him.

'It was your boss – Roach,' Flynn said at last.

Hanson had guessed this already.

Flynn lit a cigarette. 'I don't need to tell you,' he went on. 'He's one of those conservative types who think Eleanor Roosevelt is the daughter of Satan. He doesn't like you.'

This too, was hardly news. Roach didn't like anybody.

'He had his suspicions about you and he reported them,' Flynn went on. 'The Bureau has a policy of collecting information on public servants who might be a security risk. I guess Roach had his reasons for sucking up to them; most informants have. They always like people who play the game their way. It won't have exactly done his career a whole lot of harm.'

'His reasons were that he's a worm with shit for brains. What were your reasons? Did you find proof that I'm a fag? By that I mean, the kind of proof you can take back to your masters. I guess "sure, he's queer; I've just had my dick up his backside!" isn't *quite* what they want to hear. I hope you got what you needed, that's all!'

If it were possible, Flynn would have gone redder. Hanson felt better for his tirade. He poured himself more whisky and decided to get drunk. After three or four large measures, his cock would no longer function, then he'd be able to throw Flynn out and so retain his dignity. He'd feel lousy in the morning on both counts but if he stayed sober they'd end in bed. It was one way to deal with this kind of problem: Odysseus bound himself to the mast; Mark Hanson got blind drunk.

'I thought if you had to be investigated, maybe it's best you be investigated by me,' Flynn protested. 'That way only good things would go back and you'd be in the clear. I was trying to help you, dammit!'

It was tempting to believe this; Hanson wondered if he could. He decided he would give it a go, but keep his scepticism on a low light just in case. It was J Edgar Hoover who was really to blame for all this mess.

'Hoover himself is queer,' Hanson said. 'That's why he's so fucking paranoid about it all. Are you telling me he employs homosexuals specially to inform on other homosexuals? Nice work if you can get it.'

J Edgar's sex life was obviously protected information. Flynn was really not comfortable with its being mentioned. He looked about him as though he thought another agent would be there behind the curtains.

He eventually recovered enough to say, 'They don't know about me. I pretend I have a girlfriend. We're to be married soon.'

'Great. I'll come and throw rice.'

'Christ!' Flynn exclaimed suddenly. 'You were just a name on a file. I didn't know you! They told me to go get the dirt on you and I had to at least *look* like I was doing it. I'm sorry I misled you, but what else was I supposed to do? I really like you. I don't want you to think badly of me and I've made sure no dirt will stick to your career. I'm not exactly proud of the job I do – they never train you to deal with feeling like a snake. If it helps any, I'm gonna resign before they have me bugging my mother's phone to prove she's a Bolshevik. OK?'

During this, he paced the room, flailing his arms around and shouting lots. Hanson watched him, fighting his desire to kiss and make up.

'My heart bleeds,' he said. 'Now, suppose you tell me this: who was Stein and how come he ended up dead?'

Flynn sat down. 'Stein's a nobody,' he said. 'You should have done what Roach advised and filed the case away in the trash. He was a fag who died – fags who die are not investigated. Unless, of course, they happen to be dead fags who double as fine, upstanding American citizens. There's more than you'd imagine of them but not Stein – Stein wasn't one of them.'

'I don't suppose it's possible that a man can genuinely be both those things?'

Flynn shook his head. 'Not if you follow the rules. People think the Soviets are oppressed – Stalin was a monster and Khrushchev is as bad. They talk about propaganda, filtering news broadcasts, tapping phones, relatives informing on relatives – all those nasty, commie things the FBI is keeping us safe from. Do you want to know how the FBI is doing this? It's doing it by propaganda, filtering news broadcasts, tapping phones and getting folks to inform on anybody and everybody. We're no different to Russia. It's just that they call it "communism" and we call it "democracy". Both systems run on exactly the same lines.'

Hanson would normally have argued against this like any decent American would. Now he stayed silent. It was not pleasant, but he didn't doubt it was true.

'I'm good at my work,' he said at last. 'I want to be better at it. Other men have achieved high positions with more skeletons in their closets than I've got.' He thought about this for a second or two and what came into his mind made him angry. 'Why the fuck can't they just leave us be!' he shouted. 'You want me to say what you did is OK because you didn't actually come up with anything? There isn't anything to come up *with*! I have never been blackmailed; I am not a security risk. I am a good cop who wants to get on with his job! Try telling that to Mr Hoover!'

'That information is exactly what I've given in my report. Your files contain nothing you need worry over.' Flynn sounded like a doctor giving, for the umpteenth time, a clean bill of health to a hypochondriac.

'So I'm still not sure how Stein — who was nobody important but who nevertheless is dead — fits into this case.'

Flynn shrugged. 'He was the filling of a blackmail sandwich. He had something on somebody and was using it to get cash to pay some other person who had something on *him*. No need to guess what the "something" was. We don't know the identity of either of the other people. It's possible the one who was fleecing him will turn up at some point. Blackmail goes on often enough and there's not much the law can do to stop it. I think Stein died of heart failure during sex. I don't suppose there's very much more to it than that.'

Maybe this was true, but Hanson wasn't so sure.

'What I really wanted to say,' Flynn ventured after a long pause, 'is I hope I tried to make things right with you and I hope to God I did it for the right reasons because . . . I really like you. I like you a lot.'

Hanson had worked this one out as well but he was not impressed by it.

'I can't believe you!' he cried. 'You are a homosexual, Flynn! And yet, before you knew me, you were prepared to ruin my career on account of my being homosexual too! Then, when you find out I'm no slouch in the bed department, you expect me to forget how you came by me and fall into your arms. "Falling into the arms of another man" being exactly the "crime" you're investigating me for in the first place! Call me old-fashioned, but I think the whole thing is crazy and it stinks.'

Hanson ended the prosecution's case and fell silent. He wasn't delivering a verdict just yet. His own position gave him pause.

His job involved defending a law he'd broken: he was not completely blameless of hypocrisy himself.

Perhaps Flynn thought he was a pushover. Perhaps he thought Hanson would say, 'No worries, man. We can still be friends. We can still be *lovers*!'

Perhaps they could.

The frustration of the last few weeks bubbled up and spilt over the edge. Hanson was bitter and he needed to get the shit out of his system. Floating above his anger were good thoughts, noble thoughts. He loved this man. He wanted to settle down with him. Noble is all well and good but it doesn't stand up to wounded pride. Wounded pride fought dirty and left Hanson's better self bleeding.

Oh sure, he thought sarcastically. Settling down wouldn't be too difficult. There might be the odd time in the future when I get myself a bit hot under the collar because my boyfriend has to go off to the office to trade secrets about our sex life to the FBI. There might be the odd unkind word said over breakfast when Flynn has to sign a paper or two to say he isn't queer himself but his boyfriend is! In time, when my career is totally destroyed and I don't miss it too much any more, then perhaps I might just accept Flynn as a double-crossing shitface who set me up so he could ass-lick his masters in Washington.

'It's a corny thing to say . . .' Flynn began.

'Then don't say it!' Hanson snapped back.

He faced the wall and deliberately brought his head back, threatening – and intending – to smash his skull against the plaster. Flynn shot up from his chair and put himself in the way. He grasped Hanson by the shoulders and tried to look directly into his eyes to show how sincere he was being. It didn't work. In fact it made him look even more shifty. Hanson thought nastily that maybe Flynn was everything you'd want in an FBI agent.

'I HAVE NOT SAID ANYTHING ABOUT YOU.'

Flynn said this in capital letters with underline but it still didn't wash. Hanson turned his face away. Part of him was still being objective and he was aware he was really playing his part to the hilt. He was being the wronged woman, the put-upon wife, the deceived husband. He had every right to feel injured but maybe there wasn't any call to put himself on the critical list.

Flynn was still trying to make amends. Hanson forced himself to concentrate on what was being said to him.

'In fact they have the opposite impression. Don't you think it's better you've been investigated and found to be clean? They even won't bother keeping your file. You're above reproach – I've seen to it.'

'Clean', 'above reproach' – the very words sounded tarnished now. Hanson thought of all those upstanding guys in the police department, the Bureau, the government, and he wondered how many of them were standing up for an ideal they knew could not possibly hold. How many of them were fucking who they shouldn't: whores, guys – reds even. How many of them were drunkards who pretended to be sober, wife-beaters who preached nonviolence, spies who demanded loyalty? It made Hanson sick to his stomach to think about it. Especially as he knew he was one of these people himself.

'So what's the deal?' he said bitterly. 'You carry on arresting men for touching each other's dicks, do you? And I give you mine up the butt whenever you want it just in case you get tempted to join with them? Is that it?'

'I never did that,' Flynn said. 'I had to have a cover to get you to talk to me. To tell you the truth, the only reason I know about the tearooms is I once tried to pick someone up in one. It was years ago. I haven't been near those places since.'

That blush again, the one that had attracted Hanson when they first met. Damn it! The guy could make Cardinal Richelieu feel sorry for him.

'Am I being bugged? Are they listening to us?'

Flynn shook his head. 'Do you think I'd be saying what I am if they were? No, I told you, you're clean.'

'Do I carry on with my investigation into Stein's death?'

Flynn shrugged. 'I told you – he probably died of natural causes.'

'It didn't look very natural from where I was standing.'

Hanson was wondering how much worse it was all going to get, but he wanted to know everything. Flynn was looking decidedly uncomfortable but he was on a nonstop train to the confessional.

'Stein's death was convenient to us. The Bureau needed to put you where you might be indiscreet and a queer killing seemed perfect. Roach let you have the case and I was supposed to monitor what you did with it. We expected you to start screwing the witnesses or something – I don't know. Our orders to trail you came from high up – very high up.'

Hanson sat down heavily. Flynn came up behind him and massaged his shoulders. A sensual massage was not what he wanted but he put up with it because it felt nice and his cock was waking up. Soon he was feeling just a little like being in love once again.

'I'm sorry,' Flynn said again. 'I wanted to tell you all along but I was so scared. You know what J Edgar's regime is like. They can hear you when you're having a shit if they want to – watch you, even. There's nowhere safe from it.'

'But why am I so goddamn important they should go to all this trouble?' Hanson said. He caught hold of Flynn's wrist and swung him round so they faced each other. 'Am I some kind of threat to national security? Have I been balling with Soviets or something? What is it?'

'The Bureau has a long memory. You gave evidence for a Sergei Shuvalov back in 1950.'

Hanson couldn't believe his ears. Shuvalov was a thick-set Ruskie with an open, peasant's face and the body of a super-hero. He had fallen foul of the authorities for no good reason and had been under threat of deportation. He had happened to be a neighbour of Hanson's – nothing suspicious, nothing to do with Hanson's work. Hanson had given a character reference, that was all. Shuvalov had lost the case and been packed off back to Moscow. Most people had said that this was a good thing too. Hanson had felt sorry for him but not for very long.

'Is the government so paranoid?'

Flynn went very quiet and buried his face in Hanson's lap. Hanson had not let go his wrist and soon they were holding hands, Hanson stroking Flynn's hair. He felt that he'd been tricked into doing this but he didn't know how and he didn't care.

He was aware Flynn's lips were only a few layers of cloth away from his erection. It would be cathartic for both of them to have violent sex right now. When they were done, Hanson might just decide to throw Flynn out on his ear. Or maybe he would forgive him and they would walk off into that sunset.

Was love worth all this? Hanson lifted Flynn's chin to see what expression there was on that perfect, symmetrical face of his. He couldn't tell whether Flynn was on the verge of tears or if he'd just had a rush of blood from having his head in a strange position. It was difficult to say.

Flynn buried his face again and mumbled something that only Hanson's dick could possibly have heard. Hanson lifted him once more so he had to say it loud and clear.

'I asked for this case because I saw your picture and I had the hots for you,' Flynn said. 'I figured, if I had to spend time working on somebody, it might as well be somebody I liked the look of and . . . well, they were accusing you of being a homo, so I knew there was a chance of something working out.'

Hanson was disgusted all over again. He pushed Flynn away from him and got up. Flynn, sensing his anger, rose also and backed towards the door.

'I'll let you think about what you want to do,' he said. He

spoke so quietly: as though Hanson's fury were something to be respected.

'No you won't, fucker! You'll stay here and we'll damn well have this out! I want to know every dirty little detail. I want to know just how much you've said about me and what it is. I want to know if I can ever trust you again!'

Tears threatened to sweep over Hanson's emotions. Boys don't cry, he remembered. Well, maybe this one did and maybe he just didn't give a damn.

All at once he felt weak at the knees and had a strong urge to curl into a little ball and sob. He followed that urge and soon found Flynn curled over him, rocking with him like a nurse-maid would with a child who'd taken a tumble. Flynn was saying he was sorry over and over. After a while of this, Hanson began to sort of believe it.

He put his arms around Flynn's neck in the way pet monkeys do. Flynn scooped him up and carried him like that to the bed. It was a touching and romantic gesture which showed Flynn's strength and let Hanson know that everything was all right now.

Hanson lay on his back and closed his eyes. Flynn was now standing above him, stripping off his T-shirt. Hanson looked at him through half-open lids and tried to smile.

'I guess we've fucked up,' he said. 'And there was me thinking you were everything I'd ever wanted.'

He knew he was sounding morose and he didn't care. Flynn came and sat on the edge of the mattress. He stroked Hanson's hair. Hanson, in an unconscious imitation of what Pearl might do, petulantly jerked his head in the opposite direction. Flynn bent over him and kissed his cheek.

'Nothing's changed,' he said in a voice that he intended to sound truthful. 'I can protect you.'

There was real peace between them for the first time in ages. Hanson sat up. He held Flynn's hand again.

'*That's* changed,' he said. 'I was your superior officer before.

159

Leastways, I thought I was. How do you think I feel suddenly finding out it's been you who's been looking out for me all this time?'

Flynn sounded just a little annoyed. 'Is that why you're so hurt? Because I've stopped being your subordinate?' Then he thought about it and relaxed his tone. 'Yeah, I guess I would be mad about that if it were the other way around.'

'So what we gonna do?' Hanson asked. He was now taking more notice of the naked chest in front of him. He was thinking how Flynn's nipples looked so large sometimes and at other times – like now – they could shrink to being small buds of wine-coloured flesh, sticking out so it was tempting to bite them.

Also tempting was the lovely hair on Flynn's front. Hanson said this and Flynn said he'd never been particularly keen on hairy chests.

'You're kidding!' Hanson said. 'It's *beautiful*!' He reached out for it and threatened to pull just one hair out by the root. Flynn stayed where he was, willing to let him do it.

Hanson let go and gave Flynn a playful punch which seemed somehow ridiculous after all their intimacy. They both found the action funny and it at least broke the tension between them. Then Hanson got serious again, but this time he was serious because his dick was fully charged. Flynn recognised the signs and waited to hear what Hanson had planned.

'You gonna give me back my self-respect?' Hanson said, although it wasn't exactly his own voice any more: it was a shade deeper than normal and devoid of expression. It meant his words were part of the sex game he'd embarked upon.

Flynn got off the bed and knelt on the floor. He put his hands on top of his head and lowered his eyes to the ground. He looked good: his belt was undone – and his top buttons. He was all ready for taking.

Thirteen

'Get yourself down to your shorts,' Hanson said. His voice sounded strange to him, as if he'd not wholly recovered from laryngitis. He leant up on his elbow, slowly unbuttoned his shirt and pulled his braces off his shoulders – but that was all. There was plenty of time and he thought it may be kind of nice to have Flynn without a stitch while staying fully clothed himself. It would show Flynn how things ought to be. He may even keep him naked for quite a while, have him do jobs around the apartment bare-assed. He wouldn't be so quick to act the big FBI agent then.

Flynn was easing his trousers down. Did he always do it this way – like he was Gypsy Rose Lee or somebody? Maybe he was a little too sure of his own attractiveness. Hanson told him to get them off and stop fucking around.

Flynn obeyed readily and Hanson was able to gauge how well this approach was going for him by the stiff rod that was now poking out of his undershorts. It must have been pointing down his leg before it had grown hard. Now it was caught: erect and tempting, tight against Flynn's wonderful thigh.

Hanson knew he had as much hair on his own legs as Flynn

– OK, maybe not quite as much – but what a difference it made when hairs were jet black instead of light brown!

This was all his, he told himself. This hairy, sexy animal of a man was all his and he had been dumb enough to think maybe his own pride was a bit more important. Bullshit! He didn't care what Flynn had done – he might have compromised the President for all Hanson cared.

'Come here and let me have a feel of your cock,' he said. He still used no expression in his voice. He didn't need Flynn to know that the sight of that near-nude body was turning him to mush.

Flynn stood right up next to him. His cock twitched as much as it was able. Hanson flicked it with his finger and thumb – not hard, but it made Flynn wince.

'You complaining, boy?' he said.

'No, sir!' Flynn shouted this loud and clear like a freshman at a military academy. He was directing his eyes upward now, but keeping his hands on his head. He spread his legs, pulled his stomach in and filled his lungs with air. Hanson lay back again and, for a moment or two, just enjoyed watching him standing there like that. They had no need to rush. He stroked his own crotch with his hand. It was jumping about in his trousers, wanting to come out and play.

'I want to see you do twenty physical jerks,' Hanson said. 'Now!'

'Sir!'

Flynn got to it without a pause. Soon Hanson was able to see sweat forming on his back and forehead. He was fit and the task was nothing to him but it still demeaned him to have to do it like that – nearly naked – in front of somebody he knew.

'Do it again,' Hanson said when he'd finished. 'And this time, put some effort into it.'

While Flynn sweated and panted in a really satisfying way, Hanson was planning on what to do next with him. He had liked to be bossed around. Could it be taken further? Hanson remembered him bent over the desk, reading Stein's diary, his hand rammed down the front of his tight trousers. At the time, Hanson had seen that document as a piece of evidence; he should have seen that Flynn thought no more of it than the muscle mags he'd looked at later that evening. Hanson felt aggrieved but he still had a nagging feeling there was something more to all this – something they were all missing. Maybe it wasn't murder he should have been investigating – maybe it was blackmail.

Flynn had stopped exercising and was standing as he had been before, getting his breath and waiting for further orders. Hanson told him to turn round. He pulled down the elastic of Flynn's shorts and, leaning over, took a long, satisfying lick of Flynn's hairy buttocks. His skin tasted of sweat: salty and hot. Hanson went further and put his tongue into the valley between the muscular cheeks. He let his tongue go the whole sweep of that beautiful hot place. On the way, he was able to lick right over Flynn's hole. He felt his beautiful man shudder when he did it.

'Bend over and support yourself by holding on to your knees,' he ordered. Flynn did it.

Hanson amused himself for some minutes by poking first one, then two fingers into Flynn's bottom. He finger-fucked him and then enjoyed a slower, more probing exploration.

'I'm doing this to you to let you know who's in charge here,' he said as he did it. 'I think you have this idea that you're the top dog in this relationship. I can't have that. You have to learn your place.'

Flynn seemed to weaken his stance when this was said. The soldier disappeared and in his place there was a whimpering supplicant, totally ready to please in any way he could.

'I want to be yours,' he said rapidly. 'I want to do whatever pleases you. I want you to be hard with me so I don't feel bad about myself no more. I'd like you to whip my ass and my back, but only if you really want to – but I want you to.'

Hanson clamped his palm over Flynn's mouth.

'Shut the fuck up!' he said nastily. He was feeling mean now and was all ready to do exactly what Flynn had described, but he would rather do it unprompted. He was determined to be in charge here.

Flynn was all mussed up. His cock was holding his underwear in place at the front while the tuck of his buttocks held it down behind. Hanson straightened it for him. He told Flynn to take a position over the desk. He was to spread his hands wide and grasp both sides, keeping his legs apart so his thighs were unprotected.

'And keep your fucking head down against the desk. If you start to shout, you'll get twice as much beating. You get me?'

It was good to look at Flynn in that classic stance, ready and waiting for punishment. Hanson had once worried about the buzz he got from this kind of thing. Now he didn't care. He was going to let those same scary pleasures take him over.

He started straightaway with a stinging swipe across Flynn's ass cheeks just to let him know what was in store. Flynn's muscles tensed and his body went through a spasm like it was undergoing cardiac revival. Then it relaxed again. Hanson noticed Flynn was biting his lip and screwing his eyes tight shut.

Hanson passed his hand over Flynn's backside, smoothing, rubbing like a mother who wants to ease the pain. Flynn tensed up again, expecting this to be the precursor to more hurt. Damn right it was, but Hanson wasn't going to make it so predictable. He could feel the inflammation he'd caused radiating out from under the cotton. The cool material slid easily over the hot skin; Hanson increased the pressure of his touch and enjoyed how the material runkled between his fingers.

Hanson pulled the elastic and released it to snap back against the base of Flynn's spine. Then he pulled it away again and looked down inside at Flynn's hairy, hard buttocks. He had to admit, he couldn't get enough of them. Any way you cared to choose, they were a feast for the eyes. This view could fast become a favourite: a sneak behind his underwear, peeking at what was supposed to be private. Hanson stared at the tiny beads of perspiration, the hair, the mysterious darkness between the two firm hills. He put his hand down there and felt the roundness: comfortable and deceptively firm. His finger went up the crack of Flynn's ass once more and into his hole. It was just visiting: just letting Flynn know he could do what he wanted.

Hanson removed Flynn's belt from the discarded trousers and doubled it over. He leant his body over Flynn's and whispered in his ear.

'I'm going to tan your fucking hide with your own belt and you're going to let me do it. When I'm done you're going to suck my cock until I come into your mouth and then you're going to lie next to me in my bed without touching yourself at all. In the morning, I'll decide whether I can forgive you enough to let you jerk off. Is that clear, boy?'

Flynn nodded, just about remembering not to seem too keen on the idea.

Hanson made Flynn kiss the belt that was about to bruise his backside. Flynn did it reverentially and even tried to get his tongue out on to it. Hanson hadn't asked him to and made the point by grabbing a handful of Flynn's hair and yanking his head away.

All this preliminary work was almost as good as actually flogging him: Flynn standing there, the picture of young, masculine strength; his bottom covered in those flimsy shorts (they were going to be no protection at all); his thick, powerful legs braced; his torso heaving every so often as he took yet another deep breath to prepare himself. For Hanson, seeing him was like having a beautiful meal laid out on the table where to eat it and spoil the display would be a shame.

He started with a few light strokes of the belt, which Flynn would hardly have felt. Hanson was teasing Flynn and teasing himself. He felt his previous anger rise back up into his chest and give power to his arm. It surged out of him in one vicious crack which brought a murderous yell out of Flynn, who spun round, his hands rushing to protect his ass.

'Jesus! What the fuck do you think you're doing, man?'

Hanson was put off by this for no more than a second. He let the belt swing down by his side and spoke calmly, icily.

'I said I was going to give you a beating. Did you think it was just for play? You deserve a beating and that's what I'm gonna give you.'

Flynn glowered at him defiantly but Hanson stayed his ground. The two men were vying for top position now and, if Hanson let go his superiority, he would never have it back. Flynn was trying to outstare him but soon realised he could not. The impact of the belt must have died down a bit. Flynn twisted round and pulled his shorts open to look at the damage.

'Shit! You've almost broken the skin. I'm gonna have a bruise!'

'You're gonna have more than one bruise. That is, if you and me are gonna stay friends.'

Flynn tried another tack: 'Look, why don't we just sit down and talk? Please, Mark!'

He'd never called Hanson by his first name. He was really worried. Hanson considered trying something else – fucking him, maybe – but, no, this was important for the both of them.

'Get yourself back over that desk and take your beating,' he said quietly. 'It's either that or goodbye. Take it or leave it.'

'We can't have a friendship based on you whipping my ass every time you don't like what I do. That's not the way things go!'

'Then we can't have a friendship.'

Hanson stayed where he was. He never left off staring into Flynn's face and he was pleased to see how this had brought, in turns, fury, worry, puzzlement and now, finally, blushes. This last showed Flynn was getting an inkling of how much fun it would be to have the kind of relationship Hanson was offering him.

'All the time?' he asked. 'You're expecting me to let you whip my ass every single time you get pissed at me?'

'Every time.'

There was a long pause, which may have meant Flynn was considering the proposition. It could equally have meant he'd already made his decision and he just wanted to give it some effect.

Without speaking he slowly turned his body to face the desk and adopted the position. He even thrust his buttocks out a little so as to make the target easier to hit. Last of all, he laid his face on to the surface of the desk. His eyes and mouth were now open and he had a calm look on his face. His backside wiggled a little from left to right: he was readying himself. When the next blow came across the seat of his pants, a blow just as forceful as the one that had given him pause, he just took it. Perhaps he inhaled a little deeper, but he did not flinch at all. Hanson gave him four or five more like it and still Flynn didn't complain, or shout, or stray from that position.

Hanson liked it that Flynn was still in his underwear, but thought it was about time to have him naked. It would give Flynn one more humiliation to deal with, one more test of his loyalty.

He recalled Stein with the pillowcase over his head. The image was perfect: the victim was not able to take any pride in his nakedness because he couldn't see himself. His butt would be naked solely for the pleasure or convenience of the person who was whipping it.

He moved over to the bed and stripped a pillow. He was pleased to see Flynn had already caught on to what he was going to do. There was a whimper from him and an attempt at a struggle as it was forced over his head, but he eventually accepted it and lay still again. He let Hanson yank his shorts down to his ankles and he stepped out of them obediently enough. As an added humiliation, Hanson stuffed the sweaty underwear into Flynn's mouth. There were a few muffled cries from under the pillowcase, but Flynn did not struggle.

His buttocks were deep red with crisscross marks where the belt had hit him. There were more than a few welts rising. Hanson felt along them and marvelled at the heat coming off. It was time to sooth him again.

He spat on his palm and rubbed as he had before. Flynn gave a low, almost imperceptible moan. It could have been a moan of pleasure. He shifted his stance slightly and Hanson squeezed the inflamed cheek as a warning. Flynn stayed as still as a statue after that. Hanson squatted down and kissed him all over his backside. This kissing wasn't for Flynn's benefit: it was so Hanson could taste the damage he'd done.

He eventually stood back and aimed his belt once again. Flynn bucked under its attack and Hanson thought he may have cried, but he did not try to escape it.

Hanson knew Flynn must have been finding his punishment pretty hard going by now because the flesh was raw as could be. He told him to kneel in front of the desk and put his arms wide so his back could be whipped as well. Flynn moved painfully but quickly into the new position while Hanson stripped himself half naked.

He smashed the leather against Flynn's broad shoulders, enjoying the patterns it made. Flynn, shrouded in his white hood, was totally shamed here. Hanson made fun of him as he whipped him. He called him names that he'd never used before for anybody.

His own sadistic impulses shocked and excited him. A resentful thought accompanied the belt every time it came down. Every time, Hanson's rage against the crummy system was leaving a fresh wound on Flynn's back. He knew he was getting out of control and yet he was unable to stop.

Flynn's torso began to collapse under the strain of it. He was still moaning but Hanson's voice and the cracks of the belt were drowning him out. To his amazement, as he shouted the insults, Hanson found himself to be crying. His anger had at last been sated and he was left with only a vague disappointment and his overriding love for Flynn.

Flynn looked like he was about to drop. Hanson let go the belt and rushed to help him. He held him tight: an exhausted naked body, still gagged and hooded.

They would have a rest and then Hanson would fuck him.

Fourteen

_____

I t was a week later.

Arnie Durant took off all his clothes and collapsed on to his bed. He was hot, he had a headache and he was frightened. Two men had tried to follow him home from his regular visit to the john on 33rd. He wanted to know who the fuck they were.

It was lucky for him that, deep down inside, he had some sort of self-preservation mechanism that told him within seconds if a guy was to be had or not. These guys were not.

He'd come home, gone straight upstairs and banged the door shut. His wife was worried. Let her worry: he couldn't help that. She would be pacing about below, wondering if it was a good idea to bring him in a drink. He didn't exactly know the answer to this one himself. Maybe he could do with a drink.

He had taken off his clothes. When she eventually entered the room to ask him what was the matter, his nakedness should be enough to tell her. Of course, when she finally got up the courage to approach him, if he didn't want to fuck her she would probably get his shoe thrown square at her face.

She was pretty enough and, when Arnie was in his 'normal'

mood, his cock would only have to smell her approaching before it woke up. Lately he'd been in his 'perverted' mood and it was men he wanted to satisfy his craving. Tonight he was all at sixes and sevens and he wasn't quite so sure. Rosemary was not, however, going to be allowed to use this as an excuse for not knowing what he wanted.

Her lighter-than-light footfall approached the door and Arnie felt himself cringe. He said nothing and he knew he was being unfair: how was the poor woman to know how to behave? Still, their relationship seemed to thrive on Arnie's unreasonable tempers and Rosemary's apologetic compliance in all he desired. He told himself she enjoyed it and she never gave him any reason to suspect he was wrong. Where else would she find a Montgomery Clift lookalike to grace her arm? She ought to consider herself damn lucky.

The tap on the door came; it went unanswered. Then came the slow turning of the handle. Arnie knew damn well she was trying not to wake him, but he was watching her efforts with a building irritation. By the time Rosemary poked her head around the door, she had worked him up so much he couldn't stand the sight of her at any price.

She saw he was awake and tried to smile. 'I thought you might want something, dear,' she said in her annoyingly small voice. 'What do you say I fix you a drink?'

Arnie's cock was engorged. It was not so because of Rosemary: it just was. He waggled it and sneered.

'Do I look like I want a drink? Gedoudahere!'

She scuttled away like a frightened bunny and Arnie was left with a feeling that he should maybe have been a bit nicer. When she was with him, he wanted to hit her; when she wasn't there he wanted to talk to her and tell her his troubles. He had told himself often enough that marriage takes time and in two, or three, or four years, maybe they would have settled down and she would have stopped being so damned annoying. Maybe by that time he would have stopped feeling urges towards men.

He wasn't a fairy or nothing: he was fit and healthy and he was as strong as the best of them.

Also, it had to be said, he was by no means the only normal guy to have become contaminated by these strange impulses. His forays into the exciting world of the pick-up joints and the tearooms had shown him there were quite a few. Since he'd befriended 'the boys' (a convenient way of describing them both to himself and his wife), he had been able to get his rocks off in all sorts of crazy places and he'd just begun to acquire a promising source of extra income which he had every intention of exploiting to the full.

Under his bed was a dirty magazine. It was hard-core, very difficult to get hold of. It had been printed in some guy's back bedroom and illustrated with lurid drawings. The cover had a drawing on the back and the title on the front: *Boy Blue*.

Arnie flicked through the pages. He had taken this copy from the apartment of one of its contributors in Greenwich Village. The guy had tried to squeeze him for money. He'd even put Arnie into one of the dirty stories as a kind of warning; he'd called him 'Billy' but it was obvious who it was. Arnie was supposed to wet himself thinking his wife or his boss would be sent a copy. Once, Rosemary had received a nursery rhyme in the mail. She'd asked him who he supposed could have sent her that? He pretended he didn't know but it was quite clear: 'Little Boy Blue come blow your horn'.

Arnie had sure got one over on that guy. He needed money to pay him – fine! He simply blackmailed him right back and the cash went round in one big circle without the guy ever knowing it. Arnie came off best with that game.

The writer guy had stopped the demands now. He'd also stopped paying Arnie, which was fine: there were others who needed their sex lives kept secret. Arnie had taken a tip from his teacher in that he often used nursery rhymes. They meant zilch, but the suckers read all kinds of things into them. It was amusing and what was wrong with that? Arnie was clever — there could be no mistaking it.

Arnie was not a queer — at least not in his own mind. The main difference between him and a real homo was that he was aware of the reasons why he needed to fuck with men. It was, of course, because of the dreadful things that had happened to him in the past. It was the same with others he knew: Charlie had been interfered with when he was a kid (well seventeen at any rate), Fred had been subjected to a freethinking teacher at school who had left the boys unsupervised to experiment with each other at nights. George had suffered from an overprotective mother and a domineering father.

Arnie himself had been brought up with a religion that had made impossible demands on him. At least, this was the only reason he could come up with — and there had to be a reason.

Right now he didn't care. For the next few moments all he wanted to do was get rid of that damned hard-on and forget that he'd acted like a louse with his Rosemary.

He wanted somebody stronger than himself; he wanted somebody who smelt of honest sweat; he wanted somebody who would be his pal. Every time he picked up a man, they turned out to be whimpering freaks who lived for nights at the opera and didn't want their bow ties to get rucked. They deserved to be drained of their fucking cash.

His latest 'client' was like that. He was too timid for really good sex so it was a good thing Arnie had managed to get some money out of him instead. If Arnie wanted really good sex, he let it happen inside his mind. In his mind he could have any guy he wanted and it didn't matter that the guy wasn't really available. He thought of the people who had followed him home and allowed himself to drift. He could see the face of one he'd fancied and he savoured it.

Square features — all regular and chiselled. The guy also had really nice, shiny hair which was flat back on his perfect round head. There was a shading over his chin and on his neck which added to his manly appeal. The guy was dressed in a sloppy suit which was the same style as his companions' garb but, whereas they were slick types, he looked as though he'd been required to be formally dressed against his will.

The fear he'd associated with these people was put aside for now and Arnie's mind allowed Square Face to come and stand by his bed. Arnie watched as his imaginary visitor took off his garments one by one.

As was the way with imaginings, the vision didn't have to remove his shoes or socks and seemed to get down to his underwear in a second. He was pale-skinned and nicely packed. He had tree-trunk legs and they were good and hairy. Arnie liked hairy legs, it was one of his things. Those legs were climbing over him now. The guy's crotch was close to Arnie's face. Arnie started to pull on his cock, desperate to keep the image there in front of him when the time came to shoot his load.

He heard Rosemary putting the radio on in the kitchen. The inane tunes, which would most times have been barely audible to him in here, seemed to swamp everything and kill his desire. He leapt up and shouted out the door, 'Do you have to have that goddamn thing on when I'm trying to sleep?'

It was turned off immediately and he heard Rosemary suppress a sniff. When he eventually went down to her she would be crying and he would have to say how sorry he was and what a bad-tempered hubby he'd been. He knew he was in the wrong but what could he do?

The weeping started from down below.

'So sue me,' he muttered to himself. He shut the door on it and went back to working his cock up to full erection.

Square Face had now got his shorts down and was giving Arnie a lovely view of a long, fat, uncut dick. Arnie opened his mouth to receive it. He felt a little self-conscious doing this but who was to see him? He craned his neck and tried to gag on the imaginary penis. He pinched his own nipples and made believe the man of his dreams was doing it for him. He stroked his balls and pummelled his cock. He was almost there when he heard the doorbell go downstairs. His dick collapsed immediately. 'Shit!'

He listened as Rosemary got herself together to answer the call. She would be fixing her face so their visitor would not be able to see she'd been crying. It was probably her friend from the Republican Wives' Club. If it was, Arnie would be able to finish jerking off in peace. He heard Rosemary go to the door. He heard a deep voice and it sounded suspiciously like it spoke his name.

Arnie panicked. He knew he'd been followed home. He quickly pulled on his pants as he heard Rosemary's footsteps coming up the stairs again. He was cussing away to himself as he hopped around trying to get his shoe on and looking for his missing sock. His shirt and vest were screwed up under the bed. He bent down to get them as the door opened.

'Arnold, dear, there's some gentlemen here to see –'

He would have sprung round and told her to damn well leave him in peace, but the 'gentlemen' she was announcing pushed her aside and entered the bedroom. Rosemary gave a little scream and stood rooted to the spot while the two guys – one of whom was Square Face – pinioned Arnie's hands behind his back. He felt cold metal snap around his wrists.

'What's he done?' Rosemary was saying over and over. 'Arnold, what have you done?'

They frogmarched him down the stairs. Rosemary was running after them, trying to put a coat over his shoulders to cover his nakedness. One of the men at least consented to take care of his shirt, his shoe and his sock. This was Square Face. His companion was not so accommodating.

'Fairies like to go about without too much on. Didn't you know that? They like to have their little feet feeling the dew on the grass.'

Rosemary surprised everybody, not least her husband, by slapping the man hard across his face.

'Take that back!' she shouted. 'You can't come in here and accuse my husband of such things. It just is not right! You take it back!'

The man rubbed his stinging cheek.

'I never hit a woman, for which you can think yourself lucky. Jeez! I can't believe you just did that!' He turned to Arnie. 'Are you sure she's female? Not one of your boyfriends?'

Arnie was trying to stay calm and failing miserably. He had a suspicion that Jim, the latest client, was behind this. He had looked like an ordinary man about town but he was a complainer: the type who wrote to the papers every time some dog crapped in the street.

'What's this all about guys?' Arnie said as they drove him away. 'I ain't done nothing. Hey! Is it that fag who tried to pick me up that time? Shit! It's so long ago I'd almost forgotten him! He said he'd get his own back when I told him I was normal, but I didn't think he'd go this far! What's he accusing me of? You don't actually believe him, do you? Or is it that bastard dago who tried it on with me in the john? Not that pervert! Now there you have a man who *is* a queer and I can prove it!'

They'd stopped suddenly and then reversed off the main street. Arnie started to panic even more. He suddenly realised they hadn't actually shown him any ID.

'Where are we going? Where the fuck are we going? Help!'

He screamed out of the window and one of the men gave him a whack across the face for doing it. Square Face grinned and it reminded Arnie of a crocodile who's spotted dinner. This was not the way cops usually behaved.

'There's this gent just happens to have hired our services,' Square Face said. 'Now listen up: I believe you made a certain proposition to this gent. We are here to do you a favour: we think we can persuade you he won't want to be bothered with it no more.'

He turned to his companion.
'How about we start persuading?'

Roach stood over Hanson's desk with a half-chewed cigar hanging out of his mouth and a racing paper under his arm. There had been a slight improvement in his manner since Flynn's 'enquiries' had exonerated Hanson from the charge of buggering on behalf of the Soviets. 'Slight' was the operative word, however. He jerked his thumb in the direction of the front desk.

'There's some dame says her hubby was arrested by two cops who weren't cops. They accused him of being a pansy and he got beat up. Now he don't want us to do nothing about it. He's claiming he slipped on the sidewalk and beat himself up. She wants us to solve the mystery. Queers are your province. Personally, I'm with the two men who did us the favour.'

He was already picking out a winner for the 4.30 at Saratoga. Hanson went to see the distressed wife.

In the lobby a petite woman was sitting, dabbing her eyes and trembling whenever she shifted in her seat. She looked up expectantly as he came in.

'Are you the lady whose husband has been having trouble?' Hanson said.

She swallowed a 'yes' and extended her hand.

'I'm Mrs Durant,' she began. 'My husband ... I thought those horrible men were after him for a gambling debt or something. He doesn't really gamble but –'

Hanson held up his hand. The last thing he wanted was a weeping female to have to calm.

'It's OK,' he said. 'Suppose you take your time.'

The ward was long and, as hospitals often do, smelt vile. Mrs Durant was a mousy little thing and kept on bursting into tears. Hanson asked her to wait outside while he had a word with her

177

husband alone. He already had a sneaking suspicion that he and Mr Arnold Durant may turn out to have an acquaintance in common. If this turned out to be true, Mrs Durant had every cause to be in floods.

The sister had privately confided that Arnie Durant wasn't too badly hurt but he was a cowardly sort and had made enough fuss over his pain to get him a bed for a night or two. She thought him a big cry-baby: there was nothing the matter but a black eye, a bust lip and a couple of cracked ribs.

'He won't be playing ball games for a while but I doubt there's anything we can do for him. I suppose he's only got himself to thank for it. I always tell these boys to stay away from trouble, but the Lord knows, they find trouble anyway. I don't understand the wickedness in the world today, but it's like they say . . .'

She was the type who would start talking Jesus if Hanson let her carry on. He thanked her and escaped.

He found the right bed and sat down on the edge of it. His first surprise was that Mr D was clear-skinned, sandy-haired and faintly freckled. His handsome features had been damaged, but not so much they couldn't be appreciated. His pyjama jacket was open showing a nice expanse of chest. He looked every inch the honest, trustworthy young man who would help old ladies across the street. Hanson had to remind himself he was on duty.

'Now suppose you tell me what this is all about,' he said.

Arnie shrugged and pretended to look exhausted. Hanson waited patiently. Just as he was about to speak, something in the corridor caught Arnie's eye. He tensed visibly.

Hanson swung his head round just in time to see a shadow disappearing. Arnie was looking worried now and he was trying to cover up his reaction to whatever it was he'd seen.

'Don't take no notice of my dumb wife!' he was saying. 'She worries all the time about just everything! I fell over because I'd had one glass too many. Is that any big deal? I'm sorry to have wasted your time but . . .'

Hanson wasn't listening to him. He rose and went over to the door. There was nobody in the corridor who shouldn't have been. He checked back on Arnie and saw he was still looking very anxious. Hanson nodded across to him.

'I'll be back in just a minute.'

Mrs Durant was waiting obediently on a bench at the end of the corridor. She was trying to be brave. Hanson was thinking it was a pity that her husband hadn't been hurt maybe a little more than he had been. She got to her feet expectantly as soon as she saw Hanson coming towards her.

As no doubt was the story of her life, Hanson had to brush her anxiety aside in favour of more important matters.

'There was a man who was about to go into your husband's ward. Did you see him? He must have passed this way.'

'Why yes,' she said. Surprise supplanted the anxious look for a second or two. 'He went through there – toward the main lobby.'

Hanson grabbed her hand and walked briskly in the direction she had indicated. She made no complaint, but obediently attempted to keep up with his strides. Twice, she went over on her heel and nearly fell but she recovered herself without a murmur and caught up.

They reached the lobby before their quarry would have had time to get out of it. There were a good many people there but not so big a crowd the man could have hidden.

'Do you see him?' Hanson asked.

Rosemary peered around and shook her head mournfully.

'I don't –' She stopped, suddenly delighted to be able to be of help. 'No, wait! There he is, by the newspaper stand. I recognise his coat.'

Hanson walked straight over to the man, who had his back

to them. He was about to tap him on the shoulder when the stranger turned round and it wasn't a stranger at all.

It was Jim.

It was the next day. Hanson and Arnie Durant were alone in an interview room at the precinct headquarters.

Arnie was shaking even though he was hefty enough to give a good account of himself if Hanson got to using his fists. Hanson almost felt sorry for him. It was strange how bastards, once stripped of their power, could turn on the lost look. Hanson had never beaten a prisoner in his life. Maybe it would be therapeutic to make an exception here. Instead he sat down and terrified Arnie some more by holding him in a long, steady, piercing gaze. Arnie tried to meet it but soon gave up and stared at the floor instead.

'They're just fairies,' he said. 'I think what they do is disgusting, don't you, sir? I mean it makes me feel sick to my stomach. They deserve all they get.'

'I would not recommend that as a line of defence,' Hanson said. 'Blackmail makes *me* feel sick to my stomach and I think it's you who's going to get what you deserve. That is, if blackmail is all. Maybe we should talk a bit about one of your "fairies". Tell me what you know about a man called Gregory Stein.'

Arnie shot him a look. Hanson smelt blood. He was on the right track here.

'Come on,' he said. 'Don't tell me you never heard of him because his name's in your book. You received large sums of cash from him, didn't you?'

Arnie admitted it. He shuffled about in his seat. He wanted to make a clean breast of things but couldn't make the first move. Hanson made it easy for him.

'You're one of these people yourself, aren't you, Arnie? You're a fairy, just like Gregory Stein and all the rest of them. Isn't that how you find your victims — by having sexual intercourse with them? You fucked their asses and then you fucked their minds – am I right?'

Arnie knew when he was beat. He was sweating now and he undid his shirt all the way down, pulling it loose from his trousers. Hanson knew he wasn't doing it to provoke – Arnie thought he was with someone who would have no interest in the curves and hollows of his fine, young-man's chest. Arnie was wrong.

Hanson allowed himself the briefest of glances and kicked himself for doing it. His dominating aura had slipped for a split second. Arnie had seen it go and he guessed the reason for it. It takes one to know one.

Arnie now knew exactly how he was going to handle this one. He pulled his shirt right out and undid the last two remaining buttons. He pulled his stomach in tight and thrust out his chest like he was about to lift a heavy weight. Hanson tried his best not to be interested but, like others before him, he couldn't help responding to Arnie's looks. He felt his cock grow hard inside his pants and knew he couldn't hide the fact.

Arnie was still careful of him. He was no fool and he didn't show his hand in any way. Perhaps he was a little more relaxed than he had been, but that was all. He sat back, letting his shirt fall away from his body and, with this to look at, Hanson listened to his story.

Fifteen

I go to bars in the village and hang around [Arnie began].
Usually there's someone gives me the eye. Get this – I always
check out their shoes! You see, usually, if the guy has money,
his shoes will be expensive. You can't always tell with the other
things the guy's wearing because rich bastards can go around
looking like fucking tramps.

This time I checked out his shoes and, as it happens, I was
wrong about him. Maybe he was wearing a pair some friend of
his had given him because he was too poor to buy his own
footwear.

I said hello and he told me he was some big-shot writer,
which I was not fool enough to believe. It was the 'big-shot'
bit I didn't think was the truth. Writers are all fags and they're
customers for me: they want to be famous and if folks knew
about their sex lives they'd never get there. They'll pay through
the fucking nose. Unless they're one of those experimental types
from the Village, that is. They don't give a shit.

This guy – he must have thought I was a hustler. That's
because I look like a man and not like a fag. He had a
lightweight voice and he was a bit sissy in his movements. He

had sort of pretty looks, if you know what I mean. If you stuck a wig on him and put him in a dress, he'd have passed for a girl. I didn't mind that.

I needed to fuck and I was thinking he would maybe do as he was told. I was feeling horny because I'd had a lot to drink and drink does that for me. Once my hard-on has gone down, I can get on with the day and think for myself again. Until then, I can't do anything other than find some way of getting the spunk out of my balls.

He was very brave at first. He just came right on up to me and asked me how much I charged and what I was willing to do to him. I'm no hustler but I thought I might as well take some money on account.

I thought he was rich. I thought he wouldn't miss a few dollars here and there.

I said I'd go the whole way for X number of dollars and he said he couldn't go anywhere near that price. I still didn't know he was broke – I thought he was being mean. It was no big deal: I'd get my dough in my own good time. I said I was feeling horny and being as it was my birthday I'd fuck his ass for nothing.

We decided to do it at his place because he was shit-scared of my wife interrupting us back at mine. She was away at the time, but he said he only lived a few blocks away and so what the hell!

As soon as I saw where he was living I knew he was no millionaire. It was over one of those fuck-for-nothing diners where you get grease on rye with dirt on the side.

He *was* a writer and what he really liked to do was write about faggot sex.

He was making up some sort of sex history, making it sound like it was real but filling in all the bits he wished had happened and never did. Fuck! It was good stuff, man! I got myself stiff as a poker just listening to it. By the time he'd finished just two or three pages he could have done what he wanted with me. I wanted to give him something to write about he didn't have to make up.

He said he didn't often have guys back because he was so scared and he hated himself for being a queer. There's lots like that – so what can I do? I reckoned I could give him a good time and he'd maybe feel a bit better about himself.

I knew a guy years ago who was like that. He liked me to play the hoodlum for him. I mean, I'm being honest with you, he actually wanted me to rough him up. When I did, he just spurted spunk all over me and asked me to do it again – couldn't get enough of it. I figured this guy might be the same sort. Look, sir, I really am levelling with you now. This is what happened.

I took off my shirt. I could see his eyes were all over my chest. He wanted to start feeling me up but when he made a move forward I took one step back. He stayed where he was – which was good. He had manners. He was letting me know I was in charge.

He thought it was just for his own pleasure that I was going to have him naked. He didn't know I was hot to see his body. He dressed himself like a real fag – he was even wearing a yellow bow tie. I guessed he would be much nicer when he was stripped.

He was stock-still, looking me up and down, maybe a bit – how d'you say? – 'apprehensive'. I took a step forward and he made as if to back off, just like I'd done with him. I said he was to stop right where he was and he did. He was just like my puppy dog from way back – obedient, would do anything he was told and wasn't about to complain when he got a box round the ear by way of thanks.

I told him to take his top off and he did it – trembling like a leaf now. He had to be ordered to take off each thing: tie, shirt, undershirt, shoes, socks, pants. I let him keep his shorts on for a little while. I liked him to be kept wondering when he was gonna have to go nude. I wanted him to be worried about having to show me his dick, see?

I told him I was gonna maybe fuck his ass but first he was gonna have to suck my dick. He was very willing. I didn't like him being so willing. I asked him why he thought I was being so kind as to soil myself with a shit like him.

He looked all confused because I'd started giving him the rough side of me and he hadn't bargained on it. He started to stammer something about did I really think he was a shit? I just came right on up to him, close, face to face, and I gave him a gob of spit, right in the eyes.

He went right down on to his fucking knees and balled — absolute boo-hoo tears. I hadn't hurt him at all, I swear to God! I got the idea it was something he'd been wanting to do for a long time and he'd just needed the excuse.

I got hold of his chin and made him look upward. My spit was running across his face and his eyes were shut tight. I spat on him again. This time I was real slow about it so there was a good mouthful of it that hit him. I got my hand and mixed the spit up with his tears. I rubbed it all round his mug. I must say it looked good to me. He had a real nice face, even when it was all covered in my spit and his tears.

I opened his mouth up with two of my fingers. I spat into his throat. He tried to swallow it, but I gave him a swipe and he gagged on it but he kept it in there. I told him he was to keep his mouth open like that so I could get my dick into it the moment I felt like it.

I think he was getting the general idea. He'd had his fill of crying by now. He stayed on his knees, which was fine by me. He was still shivering, but that could have been because his apartment was cold and he wasn't wearing nothing but his shorts. I could see his prick was ready for action and, I must say, I was just about ready to give it some.

He kept putting his hands over it. Protecting himself I

suppose. Maybe he was embarrassed at having to kneel in the middle of his own room with another man looking on.

His eyes were still shut and I told him to open them. This time he was able to see the spit coming for him. I told him if he closed his eyes before it hit him, his ass would pay the price later. He was real scared, but he managed to keep his eyes wide open, even when it hit him. He blinked a bit. That just made the spit go right inside his eyes. I liked that.

After, he hung his head as though he was ashamed of letting me do this to him but I could tell he was enjoying it. Even the shame of it was turning him on. They're like that, these freaks – you can do what you like to them and their pricks stand up all the way through it.

I was thinking what else to do with him. Maybe it would be good to have him tied up before I fucked his face. I get this from a book I had when I was just a teenager. It was a book about smugglers in some English town. There was a picture of the guy who the story was all about and he'd been captured and was going to be hanged. The picture was really beautiful – it showed this handsome young buck. His shirt was torn away and he had only a few pieces of rag to cover him down below. His hands and his legs were in irons: real heavy chains – and one round his neck too. He was fastened to the wall of his prison cell and he looked kinda noble. I kept looking at that picture and imagining what thoughts were going through his head while he waited for them to come for him. I was with him all the way to the gallows. I tell you, it was almost a let-down when he managed to escape. Ever since then I've had this thing for guys being chained: most times that's impossible because there aren't any irons to fasten them up with. I make do with rope and that's almost as nice to see.

This Stein was no hero at all but he was kind of soft and gentle, which was just as good. He made me want to be so goddamn hard on him. I wanted him to break down com-pletely. When I'd made him into a snivelling wreck and he was pleading with me for mercy, then maybe I would switch to being the nice guy.

Yeah, 'being the nice guy' – that means I hold him and stroke him and tell him not to ever worry his head again because I'm gonna be his big brother and look after him for ever. It's the change of attitude makes the loving so sweet, don't you see? Just loving him without the other shit wouldn't be nearly enough to satisfy. He was gonna have to have the whole thing thrown at him first.

I looked through a couple of drawers. He stayed put during all this. He didn't seem to mind I was going through his things and maybe I was gonna rob him. Perhaps he had nothing worth taking.

When I came back with a couple of neckties, he looked fit to bust with excitement. I stayed real calm: just told him to put his hands behind his back because I was going to bind his wrists.

I did it tight enough to stop him struggling to get free. When I'd done I could see he tried to test the knots. He was maybe worried I was some kind of nutcase he'd got himself involved with. Anyway, it was too late now because he was going nowhere until I said so.

I told him to stand up and keep his legs apart. He had a bit of a struggle doing that without using his hands at all, but he managed it in the end. I brought a chair and sat opposite him and just spent some time taking in the sight and smiling to myself. He wasn't meeting my eye so I ordered him to do it.

Sir, I think that's one of the most beautiful sights in the world – a good-looking guy with nothing on but his underwear and his hands tied behind him. He's looking you straight in the eye, not because he wants to, but because you've told him to do it; his prick's so big inside his pants and his face is only just drying out from where you've been spitting all over it.

Beautiful – but not the best. I went over to him and pulled his shorts down. His fat, pink dick was all there for me to look at and I thought it was just the tops.

He wasn't a man now, he was a prisoner — or an animal even. I mean, animals go about with their cocks bobbing about between their legs, don't they? Men are supposed to keep them covered. This guy was an animal and he was all ready to be serviced.

I made him step out of his shorts and I pressed them over his nostrils so he could smell the sweat, piss and shit from his own body. I was telling him to breath it in real deep.

Remember, I was still wearing my jeans at this point and I could tell he was just longing to see what sort of meat was about to go into his gut.

I got my belt off and cracked him across the ass. He moaned nicely and so I gave him another and then another. I just lost it, sir. To be honest, I think he wanted every bit of the beating I gave him. I kept checking his prick and it stayed hard. It was even drooling at the end so I guess he couldn't have been so against what I was putting him through.

When I'd beaten him down to his knees again, I moved along behind him, undid my buttons and filled his butt full of my cock. It felt real nice in there and I was paying no heed to him gasping at how big it was. He was gonna have to take this one, no matter what. I pumped myself inside him and he was soon groaning away just like they always do. I felt round to his front and his lovely prick was still hot and hard.

What was funny was I was thinking all the time of how he was gonna write about this in his story.

I didn't let myself shoot because I wanted to do that into his mouth. His ass was gripping my dick all around, squeezing it — God! I love that feeling! I nearly didn't pull myself out of him in time.

My dick was clean enough but I suppose it must have smelt and tasted of the insides of him. I made him wash it with his tongue. He licked around it first of all, lapping it up. Then I shoved the whole length of me into his open mouth. I made him suck me hard. I was hitting him across the face — not so it was gonna hurt him, just to keep him in his place. He was sucking my dick and doing what he was fucking told. I liked that. I liked it a lot.

Before I knew it I'd spurted jism into his mouth. He was gulping it down his throat. I told him he was a pathetic fuck-up and only freaks like him want to swallow another man's spunk like that. He was nodding hard – he was wanting to tell me he agreed with every word I said.

I made him jerk himself off in front of me. I sat down in the chair and made him stand right, square facing me. I told him to keep his legs wide apart and play with himself until he shot his load. He was real shy but he did it. I could see when the spunk was gonna come out when his legs went like they was made of rubber. I told him that if he dared to fall on to his knees he would get my belt across his back again. He just about managed to stay standing. His fist overflowed with lovely creamy white juice. I told him he had to drink it all. He put his hands to his lips and swallowed it down. He licked his hands after and, you know what? He was looking at me the whole time and he was smiling.

Sixteen

'So, what are you saying? Durant killed Stein – some kind of accident maybe? The sex games went too far? I don't believe it.'

Flynn was lying on Hanson's bed. They were likely to make love any second. Hanson turned on to his side and began to unbutton Flynn's shirt. Flynn jokingly slapped his hand.

'Cut that out! OK, you've made me admit what I do not wish to admit: I'm in the dark. I have no idea what happened here. As an investigator, I'm a complete washout. Suppose you enlighten me, Mr Detective.'

Hanson thought for a moment. Of course Flynn wanted to know what had happened, but he didn't have to have it handed to him on a plate. Hanson wanted to see if he could work things out all for himself. Then he changed his mind. As if it mattered anyway. Nobody was going to be prosecuted in connection with the Gregory Stein case. The whole thing stank and there was no getting away from the fact.

'I have an idea,' he said at last. 'I'll take you through the whole thing, step by step. Every time we reach a point where you have enough information, I will challenge you to reach an answer, just like I did. If you get it wrong, you take off an item of your clothing. If you get it right, I will take off an item of my clothing. If you are bare-assed before you have all the answers, I get to fuck you. If either you find all the answers, or I am naked before you, then you get to fuck me. How about it?'

Flynn laughed long and loud. 'You're nothing but a fucking pervert!' he cried.

There followed a silence which slowly became heavy as Flynn caught a bad dose of Hanson's lust. It wasn't long before it became clear they were going to fuck anyway. Flynn must have decided he might as well try to salvage some professional dignity out of the thing.

'I agree to your challenge. If you have me naked before you are, or before I know who killed Stein, you have the use of my asshole for the next hour. What the hell! You have the use of my asshole for the next ten years!'

'OK,' Hanson said. 'Let's start. We know Stein was black-mailing somebody and also he was being blackmailed himself. What's the connection between these two statements?'

'Is this your first question?' Flynn asked. He was confident he knew the answer because he made no move to take off his shoes (always the best thing to start with if you want to win at strip poker). Hanson gave him this easy one as a present.

'Yes. That can be the first question.'

'Right. Stein was being blackmailed and, in order to pay the blackmailer, he put the screws on somebody else. "The filling of a blackmail sandwich" – it's what I said, remember? You lose. Take something off.'

Hanson unlaced his shoe. He removed it and tossed it aside. He would decide later whether he wanted Flynn inside him or vice versa. He was sure he could steer this game either way: the decision would be up to him.

'Right. There's a surprise in store every step of the way with this case. Here's the first one. It was an open sandwich: Stein was blackmailing the *same* person who was blackmailing him.'

Flynn sat up, losing his 'I'm so smart' attitude – for the moment at least.

'Stein was blackmailing Arnie Durant and Arnie Durant was blackmailing Stein? Tell me how you work that one out.'

Hanson had to be honest. There were other times when he would be able to boast. 'I didn't work it out,' he said. 'Durant told me. He had sex with Stein; Stein threatened him with cryptic nursery rhymes. Arnie threatened right back but he did it anonymously. Stein was terrified of going to jail. He paid up like a baby without ever knowing that the person he was draining was the same person who was draining him.'

'Which was Arnie Durant,' Flynn said, just to prove he was a good listener.

Hanson loosened his tie and got himself comfortable. 'That's right,' he said. 'He paid Stein his own money back and then collected it from him again. It amused him, so he said.'

Flynn was waiting for another question. It was clear he was absolutely divided between wanting to know what had happened and wanting to get one of them naked. Hanson thought it wouldn't do Flynn any harm at all to get himself all hot and bothered. He took his time to reach over for his cigarettes, light one and enjoy a good half of it before he went on.

'Stein wanted to be a writer but he was worse than shit at it. He contributed to a magazine for grown-ups. It was a shame – he had a talent for that but it made him zilch money. Stein was writing beautiful prose describing what the great American public would call "sick fantasies". He wrote the stories as a diary, as though they'd really happened – and parts of them actually had. If any of his boyfriends didn't pay his hush money he'd threaten them with the magazine. Mr Clean-Living America does not want to be represented in pornographic prose. Now, there were things that told me it couldn't be a real diary.

Want to know what they were? You lose your shoes when you get it wrong.'

Flynn considered a bit and then tried a guess. 'It's obvious. It was just a notebook.'

'A lot of people use ordinary notebooks for their everyday thoughts and observations,' Hanson said. 'You lose. Ditch your shoe.'

'So? Tell me.'

'Stein's mother said he always attended synagogue on Saturday.'

Flynn looked puzzled. It was how he was supposed to look. Hanson was enjoying himself.

'Stein begins his writing by saying he should have been at synagogue on the day he met a person called Billy. Billy is probably a mixture of Arnie Durant and some fantasy guy, but the important thing is it was *New Year's Day*.'

Flynn saw the light. 'Jews don't go to synagogue on New Year's Day unless it also happens to be a Saturday. When was the last New Year's Day on a Saturday . . .'

'Five years ago,' Hanson said. 'I checked. At first I thought he might have been talking about Jewish New Year but that's in the fall and Stein heads his entry "January". So, it's either a very old diary or it's all made up.'

He looked across at Flynn, who wasn't playing fair.

'Come on,' Hanson said. 'You have to get rid of your shoe – and, being as you've hung around so long, how about you ditch your other shoe and your socks as well?'

Flynn grinned his amiable, hobo's grin. He was quite happy to lose this game. He took off his shoes and socks and lay with his good, solid feet near Hanson's mouth. He went along the line of Hanson's jaw with his toe. Inevitably, the toe found its way into Hanson's mouth and Hanson took a pleasant break from playing Sherlock to suck on it.

He kept Flynn's foot held against his cheek as he went on. 'There were other things too: he'd written a note in the margin about an older fat man in drag. It doesn't seem to enhance the story and at first it does look like the sort of thing you tell your diary: ". . . If he reads this he'll know he'd better watch his back." It was in fact a direct challenge: the man in drag turns out to be a big surprise but Stein got the biggest surprise of all – he got murdered because of him.'

Flynn smiled. 'Shouldn't this sort of thing happen in the library of an English country house?'

Hanson was enjoying his part and wasn't about to be upstaged by flippancy. 'I think maybe you'll be less jokey about it when you know the whole story,' he said.

'Maybe you'd better correct my behaviour.' Flynn slid his belt off his trousers and laid it beside him on the bed. Hanson took it and laid it aside.

'You are going to get a nice, gentle fucking up your ass,' he said. 'There'll be time enough for all the rough stuff in the years to come.'

He'd got Flynn's attention back. He went on: 'So tell me: what sort of *sicko* goes to parties in lady's frocks?'

He might have been joking but he gave the word 'sicko' all he had. Flynn looked up, surprised.

'OK,' Hanson said. 'I didn't mean that. There's nothing sick about female clothing but there's something plenty sick about this particular transvestite charmer. You lose your shirt if you can't get his name.'

Flynn sat up and unbuttoned his shirt. Hanson stopped him. 'You can't just give in like that: you've got to try! It won't be the same if I win without an effort.'

'Clark Gable? Mickey Mouse?'

Hanson took a piece of paper from his desk and wrote a name on it. He held it between his finger and thumb and waved it like it was the card Flynn needed to win the game.

'OK,' he said. 'Your shirt comes off if you can't tell me what name is written here. If you get it right, you'll have the answer to what happened with Gregory Stein and you'll also have my balls on a plate.'

'You're that confident, huh?' Flynn was craning his neck, trying to see if he could read the name but Hanson held it close to his chest. He was wondering if it would be a bad idea to disclose what he knew before they made love. The revelation might just put Flynn off his stride.

Flynn tried some more wild guesses. Was it Arnie Durant? It couldn't be, Hanson told him. Durant might be the world's worst person to have your dick inside, but he was good-looking and young and he wasn't into drag. Flynn thought for a bit. Was it Roach? This one made Hanson laugh a lot. The idea of finding Roach in a dress at some homo orgy would be very satisfying if you had a spiteful mind and a camera handy.

'No,' he said. 'It most certainly was not Roach.'

Flynn wanted to get naked. His suggestions became more and more unlikely. Hanson thought at one point he was going to hit on the right answer by accident but he didn't. Eventually, he admitted defeat and obediently took his shirt off. The close, fine hairs of his chest were glistening with sweat. His chest filled out, causing his nipples to harden into two small peaks under his undershirt and his stomach tightened. He knew how good he looked and he knew Hanson knew it too.

'Seems a shame,' Hanson said. 'This is the last question and neither of us is stripped all the way. I suppose I didn't plan this game out properly.'

'Tell me who it was,' said Flynn. 'Who was the fat man in drag?'

He was like a kid at Christmas. Hanson wasn't going to spoil him by giving in to his demands.

Outside it was starting to rain. Hanson got up again and went to close the window.

'You came back to me on a rainy evening,' he said. 'I like it when it pours.'

Flynn rolled on to his stomach and, burying his face in the

pillow, thumped it with both hands. He let out a yell of frustration. Hanson sat beside him and slid his hand along Flynn's back under his vest. Flynn's body went loose again. Pretty soon his vest was on the floor and Hanson was lying on top of him.

'Who was the drag queen?' Flynn tried again, but this time he didn't sound so desperate for an answer.

'Wouldn't you like to know?' Hanson said. 'Tell you later. First, let's get you out of these damn clothes.'

Flynn stood up and allowed himself to be stripped. When he was naked he lay down again, expecting Hanson to do the same. Hanson looked troubled.

'I can't think what to do for the best,' Hanson said.

He lay down and protectively put his arms around Flynn's broad body. Flynn looked into his face, enquiring and just a little worried by Hanson's sudden seriousness.

'We've been talking blackmail,' Hanson went on. 'It's a filthy thing and it's been all around this case. There's something I found out from a porter at the Plaza Hotel. The party scenes in Stein's diary are not that dissimilar to some wild nights that did actually happen. Stein tried to get money out of someone very powerful. Someone with the power to disguise a murder scene as a sex game that went wrong. Someone who could absolutely cover their tracks.'

He said this with a smile but Flynn was looking very bothered indeed now.

'There's always been rumours about J Edgar Hoover and his relationship with Clyde Tolson,' Hanson said. 'It beats me how they've got away with being at the head of the FBI for so long and being such obvious homosexuals . . .'

Flynn tried to hush him but Hanson was scornful all of a sudden.

'Jesus! *That's* exactly how they do it, isn't it? Everybody's so shit-scared to mention anything about them in case they've got a bug in the room or a wire-tap on the phone! I tell you, if I could arrest anybody for this murder, it would be him. Yeah, I'd arrest J Edgar Hoover!'

Flynn was not happy now. Hanson had stood again and was pacing the room and talking in a voice rather louder than even he thought was wise. Flynn rushed over to him and clamped his hand over Hanson's mouth.

'Are you crazy? Do you want to get yourself arrested or – or . . .'

Hanson removed Flynn's hand and held him close.

'. . . or killed? That's what you were going to say, wasn't it? It's what happened to Stein all right. Let me spell it out: those parties at the Plaza have happened three or four times, always in secret, and always they're organised by Hoover's buddy, Roy Cohn. Hoover likes to put on frocks, doesn't he?'

Flynn said he had no idea; he said Hanson was crazy to say this; he said they shouldn't even think such things, let alone voice them.

'Hoover is the most powerful man in the country, next to the President,' he continued after a pause. 'Some say the most powerful man, period. His whole remit is the defence of liberty and freedom. How can you say he'd have someone killed to cover up his sexual deviancy? It just can't be true!'

Hanson was grim-faced now. 'So his thing is the defence of liberty, is it? Phooey! He blackmails people – everybody. He has tapes, he has photographs, he has an army of fucking people like you who he pays to dig up the dirt on anybody and everybody. You know I'm right. He tried to get you to do it to me!'

Flynn blushed, right on cue. 'Not that again,' he said. 'We've sorted that one!'

Hanson grabbed him and almost shook him. He had to make Flynn see how the whole thing was designed to trap them.

'He absolutely bargains on people having no integrity. He thinks men will do anything to save their own skin. He's got this country right where he wants it and it stinks! Yes, I believe he had Stein killed. I don't know how. I expect he sent round one of his boys to do the job. He probably had sex with him first. Stein probably thought it was his lucky day, poor jerk.'

Flynn sat on the bed and hung his head. He was trying to assess what he had been told but he couldn't take it in. Eventually he went back to Hanson for advice: 'I'll do whatever you want me to. I just want to stay with you. I don't care about anything else any more.'

Hanson kissed him. It was a kiss to show how proud he was of Flynn. It was meant to put heart back into him.

Flynn laid his head against Hanson's chest. 'I'm going to give them my resignation,' he said. 'I'll find some other job to do.'

Hanson squeezed him tight. 'Ataboy!' he said. 'And, while we're talking of retirement, I guess that goes for me as well. I don't think I can work in law enforcement when I know what I know. Do you think there are many places who would employ a couple of queer ex-cops?'

Flynn smiled. 'I guess we could always write the story into a book,' he said. 'We might get a few dollars for it.'

The rain had stopped. The dying sun was having a stab at getting back in control but, mercifully, the air had at last cooled. Flynn was kneeling astride Hanson, who was lying on his back. Both men were now naked. The breeze was kissing around their bodies, making them shiver slightly, but it was pleasant even so. Neither of them had moved for several seconds; they were enjoying each other's nakedness, enjoying being lovers again, enjoying time in slow motion.

From his worm's-eye view down near Flynn's thighs, Hanson watched the evening light shine through the hairs on his lover's chest. Each one was defined by its own shadow, like blades of grass at the end of a day's picnic. He had a mind to touch those hairs but he didn't bother. To raise his hand would break this freeze and he wanted it to go on at least for a little while.

Flynn gave a brief, inward laugh as though he had read

Hanson's thoughts and was in agreement with them. *He* wasn't going to move until he had to either.

He was looking down at Hanson, admiringly. He'd got the worse deal with this clinch because, from the position he was in, he couldn't get a view of Hanson's cock. His own was right there for Hanson to appreciate, all ready for action but, like life itself, action would just have to wait.

It was the sort of moment when the words 'I love you' would have come easily. They wouldn't have appeared coy or dumb. If Flynn had spoken them, Hanson would have probably responded in kind.

Maybe both men knew this and also knew, when this moment together was over, they would regret what they'd said and make stupid excuses for it: 'Gee, I hope you didn't think I was suggesting we get together and do anything permanent . . .'

No two men ever did anything permanent – it just didn't happen, it couldn't.

So, instead of speaking, Hanson pursed his lips and blew a shadow of a kiss in Flynn's direction. Flynn did the same back and they both smiled. It wasn't much but it was enough to get them moving again.

Hanson did what he'd been planning on for ten minutes or more. His hand came into contact with the lawn of hair before him and he spread his fingers wide inside it. It tangled around them and he pressed hard into the chest it covered. Still smoothly, still slowly, he raised himself up and brought his face into Flynn's chest. He went down into it and breathed deeply; he could hear Flynn's heartbeat. He laid his cheek against it and felt Flynn's arms coming around his head to cradle him. He responded, his arms going around Flynn's back so they were united as closely as it was possible to be without penetration.

The two men rocked each other sublimely. Flynn's chin, then his lips, came down to Hanson's scalp. Hanson felt a kiss on top of his head and turned back into Flynn's chest to return it. Love tunes kept rising up in his mind to provide a soundtrack to this scene. He would normally have thought them corny — now they were speaking to him as if for the first time and they were profound.

Flynn's cock was squashed in there between them. Hanson could feel the lump of it pressing into his belly. He extricated himself carefully from the embrace, noting how Flynn waited obediently to see what he wanted to do.

He grinned and stroked his index finger along the ridge of Flynn's shaft. Flynn shrugged to let him know it was OK with him. Hanson had to pull himself up the bed to be free of Flynn's body, though he didn't want to be free of it for long. He curled in front and pushed his face into Flynn's waiting groin.

The smell was heady. Hanson remembered it from the last time they had been this intimate: it was the smell God had designed so man could signal his readiness for sex. Hanson took a luxurious lungful of it before brushing his lips against the tight sac of skin that had produced it. Flynn's shaft was lying against his face; it filled Hanson's vision in an unfocused blur.

He brought his hand into play to keep Flynn's penis where he wanted it while he mouthed along it, taking care not to allow it too much pleasure too soon. Flynn thrust his head back and pressed the heels of his hands into Hanson's shoulder blades. His body had stiffened — like his cock, it was building up to release.

Hanson lapped the top of Flynn's dick with the tip of his tongue. He heard Flynn hiss back through his teeth because of it. Hanson then cupped Flynn's balls in his hand and pulled them downward — just a little at first and then, when Flynn had got used to that, more so until Hanson was pulling enough for it to hurt.

Flynn's cock inevitably slid fully into Hanson's mouth and he sucked it hard. Flynn's hands went down his back. Soon they were curled over one another and it didn't take any effort to manoeuvre round until they were both able to suck cock.

Hanson had heard of 69 before but he'd never done it and it was to him as though they'd discovered something new that was quite the best thing two naked men could do to each other – at least for the moment.

The slick massaging of his cock was not enough to bring his orgasm out of him. This orgasm was going to be special: it was meant to last, like a long, exotic drink. It was a sensation he had to concentrate on to appreciate it fully. If he let his mind wander – back to those corny songs for instance – he lost it and when he came back, he felt he'd wasted time. This refined and acquired pleasure was surely better than filling his head with a bit of ropey old Cole Porter.

All the while he took a care to give as much as he received. He noted the movements of Flynn's sexual arousal and tried to stimulate them. He saw how this led on to their reflecting each other's desire. It wasn't clear who was leading the dance and perhaps they both were. Then Flynn started to thrust himself hard into Hanson's mouth and Hanson could hear him grunt and splutter. He was going to come.

Hanson tried to rock his own hips in the same way. He would have liked it if they both could have come together – coming together meant they were in love and signified their sex had been special. It didn't work because Hanson was nowhere near and Flynn couldn't contain his spunk at any price.

Hanson wasn't sure Flynn had come until he tasted a prickling burn right at the back of his throat. He moved his tongue around and found it was stirring milky, thick fluid. Flynn removed his softening shaft and Hanson tried to savour the taste of come. It was elusive – the thought of its being there was seventy-five per cent of the experience. He gulped and swallowed.

Flynn shifted himself so they were both the same way up. He kissed Hanson, holding his lover's head in both hands to demonstrate how precious to him was every hair of it.

Hanson felt just a little disappointed – he had wanted to come and perhaps now Flynn would consider their activity to be finished. He allowed himself to be kissed but his brief sulk had been detected.

'What?' Flynn asked, concerned.

'Sorry,' Hanson said. 'I guess I'm not as virile as you.'

'Damn right you are,' Flynn replied.

He turned his back on Hanson and, reaching behind himself, grabbed hold of Hanson's cock. He rubbed the head of it with his thumb to bring it back to full hardness. He used his own spit to lubricate the hole where it was to go. He pulled his buttocks wide and pushed back to let Hanson in there.

Hanson sank his cock into that welcoming tightness and realised that the wetness of Flynn's mouth had been as an overture for this. Perhaps he wasn't as sensitive as other men; perhaps he needed this furious, hot grip around his cock before he could build sufficient feeling to spill his spunk.

He bit Flynn's shoulder, not to break the skin but to concentrate his passion. He slid forcibly up and down the younger man's anal passage and loved the gasps this produced beneath him.

Hanson was utterly consumed by the increasing thrill at the end of his penis. He heard himself uttering various guttural sounds in unison with Flynn's. He was dimly aware that Flynn had taken hold of his own cock and was jerking himself off. Had he thought for a moment, Hanson would have been jealous of his being able to do this so soon after coming.

He did not think: the intensity of that smooth tingle in his cockhead was becoming such that he couldn't hold on to it any longer. His teeth sank into Flynn's shoulder – a yelp from the other man showed he'd felt it. He gripped Flynn's body as hard as could be and gratefully let go. His spunk gushed out of him and filled Flynn's anus. At the same time Flynn let out another small cry and gradually allowed his body to relax.

★

They stayed like that all night. It was three o'clock in the morning when Hanson woke. His cock had slipped out of Flynn's backside but his arms were still tightly around the younger man, who was holding him by the wrists to make certain he wasn't going anywhere. Hanson squeezed and the sleeping Flynn responded to it.

It mattered nothing to Hanson that he wouldn't be a cop now. If the law was there to defend anything, it was to defend truth. If it had to do that by lying, then there was no point at all.

Then he thought of Pearl and Pearl seemed the bravest, most together person he had ever encountered. He hated that he'd once thought of her as a freak. Maybe he would go to her place tomorrow and just be up-front about what he was there for: 'Hi, my cock feels like it's grown to ten feet and it could use your lips on it.'

But, wonderful though Pearl seemed to him, she was too fey. Hanson had always assumed that men who liked men would fuck anything with a dick. He now knew that wasn't so: there were just as many shades of desire as with 'normal' guys. Pearl wanted a man who was turned on by her androgyny, somebody who had the hots for lace and satin maybe. Hanson preferred hair and sweat and stubble on the chin. Hanson preferred Flynn.

The metaphorical coin had been up in the air for long enough. It rang down on the floor telling him in no uncertain terms what he'd known all along. He stopped thinking now because his whole body had gone on to red alert. His cock was throbbing, his brain was shouting things to itself, his heart was a drum. This was some feeling! As he forced himself to accept the rush round his body without fighting it, it ebbed away, leaving behind it a wonderful calm.

IDOL NEW BOOKS

SUREFORCE
Published in November Phil Votel

Not knowing what to do with his life once he's been thrown out of the army, Matt takes a job with the security firm Sureforce. Little does he know that the job is the ultimate mix of business and pleasure, and it's not long before Matt's hanging with the beefiest, meanest, hardest lads in town.

£7.99/$10.95 ISBN 0 352 33444 4

THE FAIR COP
Published in December Philip Markham

The second world war is over and America is getting back to business as usual. In 1950s New York, that means dirty business. Hanson's a detective who's been dealt a lousy hand, but the Sullivan case is his big chance. How many junior detectives get handed blackmail, murder and perverted sex all in one day?

£7.99/$10.95 ISBN 0 352 33445 2

HOT ON THE TRAIL
Published in January Lukas Scott

The Midwest, 1849. *Hot on the Trail* is the story of the original American dream, where freedom is driven by wild passion. And when farmboy Brett skips town and encounters dangerous outlaw Luke Mitchell, sparks are bound to fly in this raunchy tale of hard cowboys, butch outlaws, dirty adventure and true grit.

£7.99/$10.95 ISBN 0 352 33461 4

Also published:

CHAINS OF DECEIT
Paul C. Alexander

Journalist Nathan Dexter's life is turned around when he meets a young student called Scott – someone who offers him the relationship for which he's been searching. Then Nathan's best friend goes missing, and Nathan uncovers evidence that he has become the victim of a slavery ring which is rumoured to be operating out of London's leather scene.

£6.99/$9.95 ISBN 0 352 33206 9

DARK RIDER
Jack Gordon

While the rulers of a remote Scottish island play bizarre games of sexual dominance with the Argentinian Angelo, his friend Robert – consumed with jealous longing for his coffee-skinned companion – assuages his desires with the willing locals.

£6.99/$9.95 ISBN 0 352 33243 3

CONQUISTADOR
Jeff Hunter

It is the dying days of the Aztec empire. Axaten and Quetzel are members of the Stable, servants of the Sun Prince chosen for their bravery and beauty. But it is not just an honour and a duty to join this society, it is also the ultimate sexual achievement. Until the arrival of Juan, a young Spanish conquistador, sets the men of the Stable on an adventure of bondage, lust and deception.

£6.99/$9.95

ISBN 0 352 33244 1

TO SERVE TWO MASTERS
Gordon Neale

In the isolated land of Ilyria men are bought and sold as slaves. Rock, brought up to expect to be treated as mere 'livestock', yearns to be sold to the beautiful youth Dorian. But Dorian's brother is as cruel as he is handsome, and if Rock is bought by one brother he will be owned by both.

£6.99/$9.95

ISBN 0 352 33245 X

CUSTOMS OF THE COUNTRY
Rupert Thomas

James Cardell has left school and is looking forward to going to Oxford. That summer of 1924, however, he will spend with his cousins in a tiny village in rural Kent. There he finds he can pursue his love of painting – and begin to explore his obsession with the male physique.

£6.99/$9.95

ISBN 0 352 33246 8

DOCTOR REYNARD'S EXPERIMENT
Robert Black

A dark world of secret brothels, dungeons and sexual cabarets exists behind the respectable facade of Victorian London. The degenerate Lord Spearman introduces Dr Richard Reynard, dashing bachelor, to this hidden world.

£6.99/$9.95

ISBN 0 352 33252 2

CODE OF SUBMISSION
Paul C. Alexander

Having uncovered and defeated a slave ring operating in London's leather scene, journalist Nathan Dexter had hoped to enjoy a peaceful life with his boyfriend Scott. But when it becomes clear that the perverted slave trade has started again, Nathan has no choice but to travel across Europe and America in his bid to stop it. Second in the trilogy.

£6.99/$9.95

ISBN 0 352 33272 7

SLAVES OF TARNE
Gordon Neale

Pascal willingly follows the mysterious and alluring Casper to Tarne, a community of men enslaved to men. Tarne is everything that Pascal has ever fantasised about, but he begins to sense a sinister aspect to Casper's magnetism. Pascal has to choose between the pleasures of submission and acting to save the people he loves.

£6.99/$9.95

ISBN 0 352 33273 5

ROUGH WITH THE SMOOTH
Dominic Arrow

Amid the crime, violence and unemployment of North London, the young men who attend Jonathan Carey's drop-in centre have few choices. One of the young men, Stewart, finds himself torn between the increasingly intimate horseplay of his fellows and the perverse allure of the criminal underworld. Can Jonathan save Stewart from the bullies on the streets and behind bars?

£6.99/$9.95 ISBN 0 352 33292 1

CONVICT CHAINS
Philip Markham

Peter Warren, printer's apprentice in the London of the 1830s, discovers his sexuality and taste for submission at the hands of Richard Barkworth. Thus begins a downward spiral of degradation, of which transportation to the Australian colonies is only the beginning.

£6.99/$9.95 ISBN 0 352 33300 6

SHAME
Raydon Pelham

On holiday in West Hollywood, Briton Martyn Townsend meets and falls in love with the daredevil Scott. When Scott is murdered, Martyn's hunt for the truth and for the mysterious Peter, Scott's ex-lover, leads him to the clubs of London and Ibiza.

£6.99/$9.95 ISBN 0 352 33302 2

HMS SUBMISSION
Jack Gordon

Under the command of Josiah Rock, a man of cruel passions, HMS *Impregnable* sails to the colonies. Christopher, Viscount Fitzgibbons, is a reluctant officer; Mick Savage part of the wretched cargo. They are on a voyage to a shared destiny.

£6.99/$9.95 ISBN 0 352 33301 4

THE FINAL RESTRAINT
Paul C. Alexander

The trilogy that began with *Chains of Deceit* and continued in *Code of Submission* concludes in this powerfully erotic novel. From the dungeons and saunas of London to the deepest jungles of South America, Nathan Dexter is forced to play the ultimate chess game with evil Adrian Delancey – with people as sexual pawns.

£6.99/$9.95 ISBN 0 352 33303 0

HARD TIME
Robert Black

HMP Cairncrow prison is a corrupt and cruel institution, but also a sexual minefield. Three new inmates must find their niche in this brutish environment – as sexual victims or lovers, predators or protectors. This is the story of how they find love, sex and redemption behind prison walls.

£6.99/$9.95 ISBN 0 352 33304 9

BOOTY BOYS

Published in September   Jay Russell

Hard-bodied black British detective Alton Davies can't believe his eyes or his luck when he finds muscular African-American gangsta rapper Banji-B lounging in his office early one morning. Alton's disbelief – and his excitement – mounts as Banji-B asks him to track down a stolen videotape of a post-gig orgy.

£7.99/$10.95   ISBN 0 352 33446 0

EASY MONEY

Published in October   Bob Condron

One day an ad appears in the popular music press. Its aim: to enlist members for a new boyband. Young, working-class Mitch starts out as a raw recruit, but soon he becomes embroiled in the sexual tension that threatens to engulf the entire group. As the band soars meteorically to pop success, the atmosphere is quickly reaching fever pitch.

£7.99/$10.95   ISBN 0 352 33442 8

— — — — — — — — ✂ — — — — — — — — — — — — — — — — — —

Please send me the books I have ticked above.

Name   ....

Address   ....

             ....

             ....

             .... Post Code ....

Send to: **Cash Sales, Idol Books, Thames Wharf Studios, Rainville Road, London W6 9HA.**

US customers: for prices and details of how to order books for delivery by mail, call 1–800–805–1083.

Please enclose a cheque or postal order, made payable to **Virgin Publishing Ltd**, to the value of the books you have ordered plus postage and packing costs as follows:

UK and BFPO – £1.00 for the first book, 50p for each subsequent book.

Overseas (including Republic of Ireland) – £2.00 for the first book, £1.00 for each subsequent book.

We accept all major credit cards, including VISA, ACCESS/MASTER-CARD, DINERS CLUB, AMEX and SWITCH.

Please write your card number and expiry date here:

....

Please allow up to 28 days for delivery.

Signature ....

— — — — — — — — ✂ — — — — — — — — — — — — — — — — — —

WE NEED YOUR HELP . . .

to plan the future of Idol books —

Yours are the only opinions that matter. Idol is a new and exciting venture: the first British series of books devoted to homoerotic fiction for men.

We're going to do our best to provide the sexiest, best–written books you can buy. And we'd like you to help in these early stages. Tell us what you want to read. There's a freepost address for your filled-in questionnaires, so you won't even need to buy a stamp.

THE IDOL QUESTIONNAIRE

SECTION ONE: ABOUT YOU

1.1 Sex (*we presume you are male, but just in case*)
Are you?
Male ☐
Female ☐

1.2 Age

under 21 ☐	21–30 ☐
31–40 ☐	41–50 ☐
51–60 ☐	over 60 ☐

1.3 At what age did you leave full-time education?
still in education ☐   16 or younger ☐
17–19 ☐   20 or older ☐

1.4 Occupation _____

1.5 Annual household income _____

1.6 We are perfectly happy for you to remain anonymous; but if you would like us to send you a free booklist of Idol books, please insert your name and address

_____

_____

_____

_____

SECTION TWO: ABOUT BUYING IDOL BOOKS

2.1 Where did you get this copy of *The Fair Cop*?
Bought at chain book shop ☐
Bought at independent book shop ☐
Bought at supermarket ☐
Bought at book exchange or used book shop ☐
I borrowed it/found it ☐
My partner bought it ☐

2.2 How did you find out about Idol books?
I saw them in a shop ☐
I saw them advertised in a magazine ☐
I read about them in _____
Other _____

2.3 Please tick the following statements you agree with:
I would be less embarrassed about buying Idol
books if the cover pictures were less explicit ☐
I think that in general the pictures on Idol
books are about right ☐
I think Idol cover pictures should be as
explicit as possible ☐

2.4 Would you read an Idol book in a public place – on a train for instance?
Yes ☐   No ☐

SECTION THREE: ABOUT THIS IDOL BOOK

3.1 Do you think the sex content in this book is:
Too much ☐   About right ☐
Not enough ☐

3.2 Do you think the writing style in this book is:
        Too unreal/escapist ☐   About right ☐
        Too down to earth ☐

3.3 Do you think the story in this book is:
        Too complicated ☐   About right ☐
        Too boring/simple ☐

3.4 Do you think the cover of this book is:
        Too explicit ☐   About right ☐
        Not explicit enough ☐

Here's a space for any other comments:

SECTION FOUR: ABOUT OTHER IDOL BOOKS

4.1 How many Idol books have you read?

4.2 If more than one, which one did you prefer?

_____

4.3 Why?

SECTION FIVE: ABOUT YOUR IDEAL EROTIC NOVEL

We want to publish the books you want to read – so this is your chance to tell us exactly what your ideal erotic novel would be like.

5.1 Using a scale of 1 to 5 (1 = no interest at all, 5 = your ideal), please rate the following possible settings for an erotic novel:
        Roman / Ancient World   ☐
        Medieval / barbarian / sword 'n' sorcery   ☐
        Renaissance / Elizabethan / Restoration   ☐
        Victorian / Edwardian   ☐
        1920s & 1930s   ☐
        Present day   ☐
        Future / Science Fiction   ☐

5.2 Using the same scale of 1 to 5, please rate the following themes you may find in an erotic novel:

Bondage / fetishism ☐
Romantic love ☐
SM / corporal punishment ☐
Bisexuality ☐
Group sex ☐
Watersports ☐
Rent / sex for money ☐

5.3 Using the same scale of 1 to 5, please rate the following styles in which an erotic novel could be written:

Gritty realism, down to earth ☐
Set in real life but ignoring its more unpleasant aspects ☐
Escapist fantasy, but just about believable ☐
Complete escapism, totally unrealistic ☐

5.4 In a book that features power differentials or sexual initiation, would you prefer the writing to be from the viewpoint of the dominant / experienced or submissive / inexperienced characters?

Dominant / Experienced ☐
Submissive / Inexperienced ☐
Both ☐

5.5 We'd like to include characters close to your ideal lover. What characteristics would your ideal lover have? Tick as many as you want:

Dominant	☐	Caring	☐
Slim	☐	Rugged	☐
Extroverted	☐	Romantic	☐
Bisexual	☐	Old	☐
Working Class	☐	Intellectual	☐
Introverted	☐	Professional	☐
Submissive	☐	Pervy	☐
Cruel	☐	Ordinary	☐
Young	☐	Muscular	☐
Naïve	☐		

Anything else? _____

5.6 Is there one particular setting or subject matter that your ideal erotic novel would contain?

_____

5.7 As you'll have seen, we include safe-sex guidelines in every book. However, while our policy is always to show safe sex in stories with contemporary settings, we don't insist on safe-sex practices in stories with historical settings because it would be anachronistic. What, if anything, would you change about this policy?

_____

_____

SECTION SIX: LAST WORDS

6.1 What do you like best about Idol books?

_____

6.2 What do you most dislike about Idol books?

_____

6.3 In what way, if any, would you like to change Idol covers?

_____

6.4 Here's a space for any other comments:

_____

_____

_____

_____

Thanks for completing this questionnaire. Now either tear it out, or photocopy it, then put it in an envelope and send it to:

Idol
FREEPOST
London
W10 5BR

You don't need a stamp if you're in the UK, but you'll need one if you're posting from overseas.